BEGINNINGS

BEGINNINGS

SOMMERFELD TRILOGY Book 2

KIM VOGEL SAWYER

BARBOUR
PUBLISHING

© 2007 by Kim Vogel Sawyer

ISBN 978-1-59789-405-0

All scripture quotations, unless otherwise noted, are taken from the King James Version of the Bible.

This book is a work of fiction. Names, characters, places, and incidents are either products of the author's imagination or used fictitiously. Any similarity to actual people, organizations, and/or events is purely coincidental.

Cover design by Müllerhaus Publishing Group

Published by Barbour Publishing, Inc., P.O. Box 719, Uhrichsville, Ohio 44683

Our mission is to publish and distribute inspirational products offering exceptional value and biblical encouragement to the masses.

 Member of the
Evangelical Christian
Publishers Association

Printed in the United States of America.

DEDICATION

For Rylin,
the precious new addition to our family.
Your life is just beginning, sweet boy. . . .
May you seek the Lord's wisdom early and grow
in the knowledge of Him.

ACKNOWLEDGMENTS

To my family: *Don, Mom and Daddy, my girls, and my little boys.*
Thank you for walking this pathway with me. I love you all muchly.

To my critique partners: *Eileen, Margie, Darlene, Ramona, Crystal,
and Donna.* Thank you for your support, suggestions, prayers, and
encouragement.

To the "brainstormers": *Deb R., Judy, Pat, and Deb V.* You brought
Beginnings to life. Thank you!

To my prayer warriors: *Rose, Carla, Connie, Cynthia, Kathy, Don,
and Ann.* God bless you—you are so special to me.

To *Joyce Livingston,* my "stained-glass expert." Thank you for your
advice, but mostly for your friendship.

To *Patricia MacDonald,* my "neonatal expert." Thank you for reading
the scenes and getting the vernacular right. You made it *real.*

To *Becky and the staff at Barbour.* Thank you for the opportunity to
work with you. I'm grateful to be a part of the Barbour family.

And finally, most importantly, to *God.* You blessed me with a new
beginning, and You've been with me every step of the way. I am
nothing without You. May any praise or glory be reflected directly
to You.

The fear of the LORD is the beginning of wisdom:
and the knowledge of the holy is understanding.
PROVERBS 9:10

ONE

Sommerfeld, Kansas

A wash of melted colors splashed across the concrete floor of Quinn's Stained-Glass Art Studio, coloring the toes of Beth Quinn's white leather sneakers. She raised her gaze from the reflection on the floor to the windowsill, where a scene of a dogwood branch with a cardinal nestled among white blossoms perched. Backlit by the late-afternoon sun, each carefully cut piece of colored, leaded glass glowed like a jewel.

As always, Beth got a chill of pleasure from seeing one of her finished creations. "Ooh, yes." She hugged herself and gave a satisfied nod. "Perfect."

The back door to the studio burst open, bringing in a gust of chilly wind. Beth spun toward the door, her hand on her throat. She slumped with relief when she recognized Andrew Braun, her lone employee, stepping through.

Andrew held up both hands as if in surrender. "I'm sorry—the wind caught the door. I didn't mean to startle you."

Beth laughed, shaking her head. In mannerisms and appearance,

Andrew reminded her a lot of her stepfather, Henry, who was Andrew's uncle. He was tall, with short-cropped brown hair covered by a billed cap that shaded his dark, walnut-colored eyes. He was so shy it had taken weeks before he would say more than *Hi* to her in conversation. But over the past two months of working together in the studio, they had finally formed a friendship.

At least, it was only friendship from her angle. She sensed a need to tread carefully. Getting romantically involved with Andrew Braun would open a can of worms the likes of which Sommerfeld had never before seen. And she'd already opened plenty.

"No harm done. And look!" She pointed to the stained-glass piece.

He carefully latched the door and glanced at the window. His eyes widened in surprise. "You got that cardinal one done already? I was going to solder the reinforcement bars for you."

Beth smirked. "All done. I didn't need'ja." She laughed at his crestfallen expression. "But you know if this one goes over well, there will be plenty of other opportunities for you to put the soldering iron to work." Oh, she hoped her statement proved true! Skipping across the floor, she grabbed his elbow and tugged him over to the window. "Well, look at it, and tell me what you think."

Andrew stood before the scene, pinching his chin between his thumb and forefinger. Beth waited, hands clasped in front of her, while he took his time seeming to examine every inch of the finished piece. Even though he had witnessed the creation of this window from her first drawings, there was always an element of excitement when pieces were viewed away from the worktable.

Finally, he gave a nod. "Yes. It's a well-done piece. I like the little yellow bits between breaks in the branches, which make it look like the sun is shimmering through. You were right not to put the cardinal in the center. Even though it's the focus of the piece, its placement to the lower right gives a better balance to the scene overall."

Beth smiled, basking in the approval of another artist.

"But"—he leaned forward, tapping one dogwood blossom with a blunt finger—"should this petal have been placed lower to give the illusion of lapping over the cardinal's tail feathers a little more? It would have added more dimension, I think."

She sent him a brief scowl. "I think it's fine the way it is. I've built in dimension with the varying background sky colors and the deeper green on the undersides of the leaves, which creates shadows." Defensiveness increased the pitch of her voice as she pointed to the elements she mentioned. "And look at the cardinal itself—the way it's positioned at an angle on the tree branch. There's plenty of dimension."

He looked at her with one eyebrow raised. "Yes, there is. But you asked me what I thought, and I think if the flower right above the cardinal had been brought down some—maybe a quarter of an inch—it would have enhanced the dimension."

Beth set her jaw, wishing she could return to the days when all he said was *Hi*.

Nudging her with his elbow, he grinned. "I made you mad."

She jerked away. "I'm not mad!" But even she recognized the irritation in her voice. Taking a deep breath, she said through gritted teeth, "Thank you for your opinion. I'll take it under advisement if I choose to duplicate this piece. Now. . ." Tipping her head, she pushed her long ponytail over her shoulder. "What are you doing here again? I thought you went home."

He shrugged. "I came back to do that soldering. But I guess I don't need to."

She grinned, satisfaction filling her as she looked once more at the cardinal. "Nope. You don't." Much work went into the completion of a stained-glass project, but Beth enjoyed each step of the process, from drawing the design to adding the reinforcement bars that prevented buckling of the leaded-glass piece. Yes, whether creative or structural, she relished every facet of stained-glass art.

With the tip of her gloved finger, she traced the line of soldered zinc that bordered the cardinal's wing. She shook her head, chuckling to herself. Never would she have thought when she made the journey from Cheyenne, Wyoming, a little over a year ago that she would stay in Kansas. Her goal had been simple—sell off the unexpected inheritance from her great-aunt, collect as many antiques as possible from the Old Order Mennonite community citizens, and return to Cheyenne to open an antiques boutique.

But those three months in Sommerfeld had turned everything upside down.

Clamping her hands around the edges of the glass, she lifted the scene from its perch on the windowsill. She grunted with the effort. The piece was larger than any others she'd made so far and heavy from the metal that bordered each glass segment. Andrew reached for it, but she shook her head.

"I can do it." She shuffled across the floor to the display bench along the back wall of her small studio. Sweat broke out across her forehead and between her shoulder blades. Once the scene was secured behind the wood strip that kept the finished pieces from sliding, she wiped her forehead and sent Andrew a triumphant grin. "See?"

His frown let her know he wished she would let him handle the heavier tasks, but Beth was determined not to depend on Andrew too much. Beth was determined not to depend on *anyone* too much.

She offered a suggestion. "As long as you're here, you could put away the shipment of glass that came this morning."

Andrew shrugged and turned toward the crate in the corner. Beth removed her gloves and put them in the top drawer of her storage cabinet. *This cabinet is really too pretty to simply house supplies,* she thought as she ran her hand over the smooth pine top. Two of her mother's cousins had built the cabinet for her, varying the sizes of the drawers and inserting dividers to keep everything organized. A quick glance around the steel building that served as her studio brought a second rush of appreciation. Watching the building go up in one day, reminiscent of an old-fashioned barn raising, had been thrilling—and scary.

She still marveled at the support she'd received from the community after their initial mistrust. Yet she realized their willingness to help didn't indicate approval of her. Since she hadn't joined their meetinghouse, she was still an "outsider." But Mom had rejoined, so they offered their newly claimed member's wayward daughter a helping hand. And now that they'd all had a hand in getting her studio up and running, she felt a real obligation to make it a success.

Her gaze returned to the dogwood and cardinal scene, her heart pounding with hope. A gallery in Wichita had commissioned the piece—her first real commissioned work after nine months of selling smaller, copper-foil pieces at craft fairs. If the gallery owners were pleased, it could lead to more work, and eventually she would be able to establish herself as a bona fide stained-glass artist.

So far, the response to her work had been favorable—her unique blending of colors that created a three-dimensional effect was unique to the stained-glass community—and she credited God with giving her the special talent. She longed to glorify Him through this gift.

Heading for the corner to retrieve the broom, she couldn't help smiling at her thoughts. A year and a half ago, she wouldn't have considered including God in her conversation, let alone being concerned about pleasing Him. But so many things had changed for Beth, both inside and out, and God was the most important addition to her life.

Andrew paused in transferring glass squares to felt-lined shelves, his brows puckered. "I swept just before I left at noon. You're sweeping again?"

"Uh-huh."

"Did you run the cutter while I was gone?"

"Nope." She ignored his sour look and drew the broom's bristles across the floor, collecting tiny shavings of glass. No matter how many times they swept, they could never get it all. The carbide cutter sent out miniscule fragments, and they had a way of traveling to every square inch of floor rather than politely staying beneath the cutting table. The small pile of multicolored bits took on the appearance of sugar crystals, but eating them would be a huge mistake. She'd have to exercise caution when the babies her mother was carrying were big enough to come visit.

Beth paused in her sweeping, her heart skipping a beat with the thought of the twins who would arrive in another four months. That was a change to which she still hadn't adjusted. After twenty-one years of having her mother to herself, she now shared her with a stepfather, a host of relatives, and soon, a new brother and sister. Although it had once been Mom and her against the world, now Beth often felt as though it was Mom's world against her.

Pushing the thought aside, she whisked the glass bits into a dustpan and dropped the broom. She crossed the floor and held the dustpan out to Andrew. "See? Glass sugar. I could sweep again right now and find more. I think it comes up through the concrete."

Andrew chuckled—a deep, throaty sound that always made Beth feel like smiling. "Oh, I doubt that."

She shivered as she dumped the glass fragments into the trash bin right outside the back door, lifting her gaze briefly to the crystal blue sky. No clouds, which meant no more snow. At least for now. She had discovered the weather could change quickly here where the wind pushed unhindered across the open plains.

After clamping the bin's lid back in place, she scurried through the doorway and nearly collided with Andrew, who stood right inside the threshold. His nearness made her pulse race, and she took a sideways step as she slammed the door closed with her hip.

He reached into his pocket. "I almost forgot. I got you some horse-shoe nails like you wanted." Holding out a small, crumpled, brown bag, he added, "There's a dozen in there, but if you need more, I can get them."

Beth took the bag and unrolled the top to peek inside. "Thanks. I'll probably need more eventually, but this will get me started." She offered a smile. "This will work so much better for keeping the assembled pieces in place when I work with larger sections. The lead scraps are fine for holding my smaller works, but as I try to enlarge. . ."

Andrew nodded. "Just let me know when you want more." He started for the door, then paused and turned back, giving his forehead a bump with the heel of his hand. "Oh. Uncle Henry and Aunt Marie are coming to our house for supper tonight. My mom said to ask if you'd like to come, too."

Beth rolled the bag closed as she considered his question. While she appreciated the efforts made by her stepfather's family to include her, she always ended up feeling out of place with her worldly clothes and pierced ears. Andrew's father was one of the worst—his scowling disapproval made her want to disappear. Not once had the man smiled at her, even in her mother's presence, and Mom was his sister-in-law!

As she sought an answer, she felt a yawn build. She gave it free rein and then pushed her lips into a regretful pout.

"I'm sorry, Andrew. Tell your mom thanks for the invitation, but I've been putting in some long days finishing up the cardinal piece. I think I'll just head home, eat a sandwich, and turn in early."

Andrew shrugged. "Okay. Have a good evening then." He stepped out the door, leaving her alone.

Andrew pressed his fork through the flaky layer of crust topping the wedge of cherry pie in front of him and carried the bite to his mouth. His mother made the best pie of anyone in Sommerfeld, where every girl learned to bake as soon as she was old enough to wield a wooden spoon. If he could find a girl who cooked as good as his mother, he'd marry her in a heartbeat.

Heat filled his face at his bold thoughts, and he glanced around the table at the visiting adults. They seemed oblivious to his flaming cheeks, and he released a small sigh of relief before digging once more into the pie.

Lately his thoughts turned too frequently to matrimony. Part of it, of course, was his age. At twenty-three as of a month ago, he was old enough to assume responsibility for a wife. . .and children. He chewed rapidly, dislodging that thought. Part of it was being the only son still living at home, his brothers all having established homes of their own. And part of it was Beth.

His hand slowed on its way to his mouth as an image of Beth Quinn filled his mind. Her long, shining ponytail, her bright blue eyes, the delicate cleft in her sweet chin, the way her slender hands held a pencil as she sketched her designs onto butcher paper. . .

"Andrew?"

Mother's voice from across the table brought him out of his reverie.

She pointed at his fork, which he held beneath his chin. "Are you going to finish that pie or just hold it all evening?"

A light roll of laughter went around the table. Andrew quickly shoved the bite into his mouth, certain his cheeks were once again blazing. On his right, Uncle Henry gave him a light nudge with his elbow.

"If a man's not eating, he has something important on his mind. Want to share?"

If the two had been alone, Andrew probably would have asked his uncle's advice on how to cope with these odd feelings he harbored for Beth. After all, Uncle Henry had loved Beth's mother for years—even during the period when she wasn't a part of the fellowship of their meetinghouse. Surely he, of all people, would understand Andrew's dilemma.

But they had an audience—Henry's wife, Marie, and Andrew's parents. So rather than approach the topic that weighed heavily in his thoughts, he blurted out the first thing that came to mind.

"Beth got that commissioned cardinal scene finished, and it's a beauty."

Both Uncle Henry and Aunt Marie smiled, their pleasure apparent. Equally apparent was Mother's worry and Dad's disapproval.

Dad cleared his throat. "One picture doesn't make a career, son. Don't put too much stock in it."

The cherry pie lost its appeal. He pushed the plate aside. For as long as he could remember, his father had discouraged his interest in artistic endeavors. How many times had he been told in a thundering tone that a man couldn't make a living with pictures, that he needed to set aside such foolishness and choose something practical? More times than he could count. The only reason Dad tolerated his time at the studio now was because during the winter months he wasn't needed as much on the farm. Yet Andrew knew that even when spring arrived he'd want to be in the studio. Unlike his brothers, his heart wasn't in farming or hog raising.

Mother put her hand on Dad's arm. "Andrew's doing Beth a big favor by helping in her studio."

"I know that," Dad countered, his gaze fixed on Andrew. "And I'm not telling him he shouldn't help her out. It's a Christian thing to do. We've all offered Marie's girl assistance in that undertaking of hers. I'm glad she's enjoying it and doing well. But neither should he start thinking that one commissioned stained-glass art piece is going to lead to a career that could take care of a family, which is what Andrew needs to consider. I want him to *think*."

Mother's hand gave several pats before she pulled it away. She sent Andrew an apologetic look. Andrew gave her a slight nod to show his appreciation for her attempt at support, but he knew any further talk would only lead to an argument with his father. He'd endured enough of those in the past. Didn't need one now.

Pushing his hands against the edge of the table, he said, "May I be excused?"

Mother nodded, her expression sad. As Andrew headed for his bedroom, he admitted having his mother's sympathy was a small consolation for the constant disapproval he received from his father when it came to using his talent. His God-given talent. . .

Andrew paused in his bedroom doorway, absorbing the phrase *God-given talent*. Didn't the Bible say that God gave gifts? And didn't the Bible say man should not squander what God had given? Why couldn't his father see past the end of his sunburned nose and recognize his way wasn't the only way?

Too restless to turn in, Andrew reversed direction and returned to the dining room, where the four adults still sat sipping coffee and chatting. "I know Beth has plans for that February craft fair at the mall in Salina. Since she's spent so much time on the cardinal piece, she's behind on cutting glass for the cross suncatchers that sell so well. I'm going to head over to the studio and do some cutting—help her out."

Mother's lips pursed, no doubt a silent reprimand for him having interrupted the conversation. Dad's lips pinched, too. Andrew knew him well enough to read his mind. Dad didn't want Andrew involved in the world of art. And he didn't want Andrew entangled in Beth's world. But it was too late. Andrew's interests were fully entrenched in art. . .and in Beth.

Before Dad could form an angry blast, Andrew turned and headed for the door.

Two

Beth stretched out on the sawdust-stuffed sofa and crossed her ankles. Although she appreciated not having to purchase furnishings, she was considering replacing Great-Aunt Lisbeth's ancient sofa with something modern. And soft.

Picking up the television remote from the little wood table at the end of the sofa, she aimed it at the glass box across the room and clicked through the stations. Thanks to the satellite dish on the roof of the house, she had a variety of programs from which to choose, but nothing caught her interest. With a sigh, she turned off the television and leaned her head back, closing her eyes.

Her great-aunt Lisbeth probably wouldn't recognize her house anymore. In the year since Beth had assumed ownership, she'd made good use of the money from the sale of Lisbeth's Café to update the house according to her own preferences. Electricity, which made possible the use of a central heating and air-conditioning unit; carpet over the hardwood floors; two telephone lines—one of which was used for the Internet; the addition of a washer and dryer set up in the utility porch; and a modernized kitchen. Not that she did a lot of cooking. But the microwave worked great for frozen dinners and for reheating leftovers frequently delivered by Mom.

Mom had slipped—with few bumps in the road, it seemed—back into the simple Old Order way of life in which she'd been raised, but Beth couldn't imagine doing without the conveniences of modern life outside of this little community. She wouldn't be here were it not for her mother and her studio.

And needing to distance herself as much as possible from Mitch. Even now, the pain of his betrayal stung. She turned her attention elsewhere.

Her thoughts drifted to the studio, where her newly completed project awaited packaging and transporting to the gallery in Wichita. A rush of nervous excitement filled her as she wondered how the gallery owners would respond to the piece. *Oh, please, let them like it!* her thoughts begged.

Her mother had told her God wouldn't have opened the doors to her discovering her unique talent for stained-glass art if He didn't intend for her to use it. But Beth still harbored a touch of insecurity. Her relationship with God was still new enough that—even though it carried a great deal of importance to her—she hadn't quite found her niche. She wasn't 100 percent sure where God wanted her to be.

Everything had fallen so neatly into place for her establishing the studio and getting started with stained-glass art. Mom believed this meant it was God's will. Beth still worried it might simply be a series of coincidences. Things had seemed to fall neatly into place for her to start an antiques boutique, too, but that hadn't turned out so well, thanks to Mitch. How could she be so sure this new undertaking would be successful?

She longed for the peace and assurance her mother possessed. Perhaps, she reasoned, it would come when her relationship with God had time to mature. She certainly hoped so. One thing was certain:

She would not involve someone else in this business venture. Not as a partner. She wouldn't put that much trust in anyone else ever again.

Swinging her legs from the sofa, she headed to the kitchen and poured herself a cup of water. Sipping, she looked out the window at the soft Kansas evening. The velvet sky scattered with stars still amazed her with its beauty. The sky seemed so much bigger here on the plain than it had in the city. It was quiet, too, with only the occasional hum of distant traffic offering a gentle reminder of life outside this peaceful community. At times, Beth appreciated the solitude and simplicity, and at other times, this life felt stifling.

Like now.

She slammed the plastic tumbler onto the countertop and headed to the utility porch. She plucked her woolly coat from a hook on the wall and slipped it on, pulling the hood over her tangled ponytail. The President's Day Extravaganza at the Salina Mall was just a few weeks away, and she needed to add to her inventory of small pieces if she wanted to fill the booth she'd reserved.

Tomorrow she'd be transporting the cardinal piece to Wichita, which meant a shorter workday. She might as well take advantage of these evening hours and get the pieces cut for at least one suncatcher. It would put her a step ahead. And a walk through the frosty January evening, listening to her feet crunch through the remaining crust of snow and breathing in the crisp air, might help release the restiveness in her heart.

Bundled, she headed out the door.

Andrew removed his goggles and picked up the glass pliers. Pinching the length of blue glass below the score line, he gave a quick downward thrust, and the first side fell away. He turned the square of glass and repeated the process until he held a perfectly shaped wedge of blue flat on the palm of his gloved hand.

Grasping the narrow end of the wedge between his finger and thumb, he held it to the light for a moment. The color changed from the deep hue of a blue jay's wing to the soft shade of a periwinkle blossom, and he allowed a smile of pleasure to grow on his face. Others might scoff at the joy Andrew found in admiring something as simple as the color variation in a piece of leaded glass held to a fluorescent light, but right now, he was alone. He could enjoy himself.

Humming, he pulled open the small top drawer that housed the carborundum stones and removed one. He carried the glass piece and the stone to a little bench in the corner, sat down, and began to smooth the rough edges of the glass.

Tiny bits of glass sugar, as Beth called it, dusted the tops of his boots and the floor around his feet as he filed. Hunkered forward, he carefully filed just enough to smooth the glass but not grind so much that it changed the size of the piece. There was little margin for error when it came to making the pieces fit together properly. His tongue crept out between his lips as he slid his gloved finger along the edge to search for snags. Finding none, he gave a satisfied nod and turned the glass to file another side.

He was busily filing the fourth and final edge when the back door burst open, allowing in a gust of wind that swept the particles of glass off the toes of his boots. Startled, Andrew leaped to his feet, and the slice of glass fell from his hand. It landed on his boot and then bounced onto the floor, one corner breaking off when it plinked against the concrete.

Lifting his gaze from the ruined glass wedge, he found Beth glowering at him.

"What in the world are you doing in here?" Hands on hips, her nose bright red, she faced off with him in a battle stance that might have intimidated a lesser man. But Andrew had confronted a much tougher adversary—his own father—so he found Beth's attack more disheartening than frightening.

"I wanted to help you get started on some new pieces for the show in Salina." He shook his head, looking once more at the piece of blue glass at his feet. "That piece won't be usable, I'm afraid." He bent over and picked it up, and as he rose, Beth took two steps toward him.

"Well, it scared me half to death when I saw all the lights on in here. I thought someone had broken in or something."

That explained the way she had come barreling through the door. Andrew frowned, rubbing his thumb over the length of glass in his hand. "I'm sorry. I didn't mean to scare you. I really just wanted to. . . help."

She plucked the piece of glass from his hand. She examined it, scowling a bit when she encountered the chipped corner. But when she looked at him, he read a hint of remorse in her eyes. "You had this one ready to go, didn't you? And I scared it right out of your hand."

A grin tugged at his lips. "I guess we're even then, huh, for scaring each other."

Without answering, Beth walked over to the storage cabinet, pulled a ruler from one of the drawers, and measured the piece of glass. "Well, this won't work for one of the long rays anymore, but you might be able to trim right below the chipped spot and salvage this for a shorter ray. Want to see if it works?"

Nodding, Andrew took the piece and placed it over the paper pattern for one of the suncatchers. To his relief, three of the four sides matched perfectly. A trim on the chipped fourth side would make it usable. He shot Beth a wide grin. "It'll work."

She heaved a sigh of relief Andrew fully understood. The sheets of leaded glass were not inexpensive. She salvaged every piece she could to make the twelve-by-twelve-inch sheets stretch as far as possible. He knew she harbored dreams of purchasing a kiln, which would enable her to fire her own glass in all the colors of the rainbow. In the meantime, however, she had to purchase the colored glass from a manufacturer in Canada. Wasting it wasn't an option.

Beth pointed to the table holding the carbide cutting wheel. "Good! So get to hacking." Slipping off her coat, she threw it onto the display bench and moved to the box that held sizable glass scraps. She reached into the box.

"Gloves first," Andrew cautioned.

Glancing over her shoulder, she grimaced. "Bossy."

"No more than you."

She grinned.

He grinned.

She headed to the cabinet and retrieved a pair of yellow leather gloves. Waving them at him, she said, "Okay. Now cut, huh? We've got work to do."

For the next two hours, they worked in companionable silence, the *whir* of the carbide wheel and the *snip* of the pliers providing a familiar, soothing lullaby. By the time nine thirty rolled around, they had pieces for four more suncatchers, ready to be filed and fitted together into finished products.

Side by side, they organized the pieces on the worktable in readiness for tomorrow's work. He left the carborundum stone out, knowing it would be needed. But Beth picked it up and returned it to its drawer. He hid his smile. Meticulous in all areas, she would make an excellent housekeeper.

Swallowing, he focused once more on the pieces of glass laid out neatly across the worktable, shifting them around with his finger. "I'm glad these smaller projects can be done using copper foiling rather than lead caming."

Beth paused, her hand in the cabinet drawer, and glanced over her shoulder. "They do go together much more quickly, and I know they're easier to work with. But. . ." She closed the drawer, turned, and faced him. Her face wore an expression of uncertainty. "You are willing to help with larger pieces, which require the lead came, aren't you?"

Andrew felt his heart thud beneath his shirt. Her question told him he was needed. Wanted. Maybe even. . .desired. Only as an employee, he reminded himself. *For now, but maybe, in time. . .* "I'll help you as long as I can, in any way that you need." Then he felt obliged to add, "When spring arrives, though, when we need to cut the winter wheat and plant the new crop. . ."

She nodded, biting down on her lower lip. Her fine brows pinched together. "I know. Your dad will need you."

Her concern was no doubt directly related to the workload she would face alone, but his was much more personal. Being in the fields with his father could never satisfy him the way working in the studio—with Beth—could. But if Beth made a success of the studio, expanded it the way she hoped, and proved to his father a man could make a decent living at this art business, then perhaps. . .

"Well, I'll be taking the cardinal piece to Wichita tomorrow." She picked up their coats and handed his over. "Which means you'll probably be filing all alone here tomorrow. By the time I'm back, maybe we'll be able to start putting the suncatchers together, huh?"

"That's the goal." Andrew forced a lighthearted tone as he pushed his hands into the sleeves of his heavy coat. He wished he had picked up the coats first. Then he would have been able to hold hers for her while she slipped her arms into the sleeves. Maybe he would have been able to lift that ponytail from beneath the collar and find out if the strands felt as soft and silky as they looked. But she was already buttoning up, with her blond ponytail draped across her shoulder, so all he could do was open the door for her, which he did.

The wind greeted them as they stepped outside, cutting off Andrew's breath with unexpected force. He lifted his gaze to the sky, observing that the stars had been extinguished. He blew out a breath, which hung on the cold air, and pointed upward. "Uh-oh. Clouds have gathered. And it smells like snow."

Beth swung her gaze to the sky, too, her eyes wide. "Oh, no. No snow. I have to go to Wichita tomorrow, and I *hate* driving in snow."

He looked at her. "I could take you if you like."

But she shook her head. "No. I need you here, finishing those sun-catchers." She sighed, her breath creating a small cloud that a fresh gust of wind quickly whisked away. "I guess I'll worry about it tomorrow." Shivering, she hunched into her coat. "But no more talking right now. It's cold. Let's get home."

THREE

The alarm clock blared, jarring Beth from a sound sleep. She slipped one hand from beneath the covers and smacked the SNOOZE button on top of the black plastic case. Silence fell. Shivering, she pulled the covers over her head to enjoy a few more lazy minutes. She'd never been an early riser. Being her own boss meant she could set her own hours. Since she usually worked into the evening, it didn't bother her to indulge herself with some extra snooze time in the morning.

She lay in her snug nest, ears tuned for the alarm. Her windows were no longer rattling, and the tree limbs weren't clacking together. Something else occurred to her. It was *cold*. Apparently, the wind she'd heard last night had done more than interrupt her sleep. By the chill in the house, she was certain Andrew's prediction had come true. There had to be fresh snow on the ground.

Flopping the covers back, she bounced out of bed. Hugging herself, she crossed to the windows and pushed the curtains aside. She groaned. At least two inches of glistening white coated the ground, and flakes continued to fall from the sky. The wind, thankfully, had departed, but. . .the snow. . .

For a moment, Beth stood transfixed by the sight. Big, fluffy puffs drifted down from a bleached sky. The sharp contrast of darks and lights—white sky, whiter snow, stark brown tree limbs, deep green leaves, and bright red berries on a bush outside the window—teased her artist's eye.

"Wow, God," she whispered, her fingers pressed to the glass and her breath steaming the pane, "that is absolutely gorgeous. . . ."

Then frustration struck. How she hated driving in snow! Turning from the window, she hurried to the hallway and pushed the little lever on the thermostat up two degrees. The heater kicked on, sending a rush of warm air through the iron grate. She remained beside the scrolled square and enjoyed the warmth for a few minutes before forcing herself to get moving.

Mom and Henry had given her a devotional Bible for Christmas, and she started each day by reading a brief passage of scripture and an object lesson based on it. After reading, she spent time in prayer. There was still an awkwardness to her prayer time. Deep down, she believed God listened and cared. It wasn't a lack of faith that created the discomfort but more a lack of familiarity. She hadn't grown up with it. It was all so new. She appreciated being able to talk to God and found herself addressing Him at odd moments during the day, but times of formal prayer still felt stilted to her. She hoped eventually she would find an ease with the practice.

After dressing, she put on her coat and gloves, grabbed her car keys, and headed to her car. She squinted against the glare of white, listening to the squeak of wet snow beneath her feet. Snowflakes dusted her shoulders, and she swept them away with a quick flip of her hand. When she spotted the accumulated snow on her windshield, she wished for a garage where she could keep her car under cover, but fortunately the blanket of white brushed off fairly quickly. Sliding behind the wheel, she turned the ignition and sat, arms crossed, while the engine warmed up. With the defroster on full blast, it didn't take long for the remaining bits of snow on the windshield to melt into racing droplets.

Watching the droplets zigzag down the glass windshield made Beth dizzy, and she turned on the wipers to whisk the moisture away. "If I get dizzy from the water drops on my own windshield," she muttered as she put the car into DRIVE, "what will the snowflakes rushing at me do?"

She got the answer to that question as she drove the short distance from her house to the studio on the edge of town. By the time she reached the studio and pulled in next to Andrew's older-model pickup, she knew she would not be able to drive to Wichita unless the snow stopped.

Disgusted, she hurried through the back door and announced, "It's all your fault!"

Andrew, bent over the worktable, straightened and sent her a blank look. "Huh?"

"You." She pointed at him, puckering her lips into a forced pout. "You had to go and say the word *snow* last night, didn't you?"

His lips quirked. "You're blaming that on me?"

Beth threw her arms outward. "Who else can I blame it on?"

A chuckle rumbled, and he offered a one-shouldered shrug. "Sorry, but I don't have that much power."

"Well. . ." She removed her coat and threw it on the display bench. Walking over to the cardinal picture, she traced one blossom with her fingertip. "I guess I won't hold you responsible then." She turned and caught Andrew staring at her. For some odd reason, heat filled her cheeks. "What?"

He shook his head, and his ears flamed red. He jerked his head in her direction and said, "You're all dressed up. You won't want to do any grinding in that gear."

Beth glanced down. She had chosen a pantsuit and high-heeled boots in lieu of jeans and tennis shoes to make a professional appearance at the gallery in Wichita. She groaned. "I just figured I'd load up and go, but you're right—if I'm stuck here, I won't want to work in these clothes." She heaved a huge sigh and reached for her coat. "I guess I'll run home and change. If the snow clears off by noon, I can still make it to Wichita with the cardinal picture."

"You want me to grind or cut more pieces?"

Beth paused, one finger pressed to her lips, as she considered the best use of Andrew's time. "Cut." She spoke decisively, adding a firm nod. "And I'll be back in a jiffy." Grabbing up her coat, she drew in a big breath and murmured in an ominous tone, "Back into the blizzard." Andrew's laughter followed her out the door.

Per Beth's request, Andrew set aside the carborundum stone and collected the snipped pattern pieces for the suncatchers. Beth had designed the suncatcher herself, centering a cross with bursts of colored wedges seeming to come from behind it. The design was simple, but her way of choosing colors—especially glass squares that faded to a lighter shade from one side to the next—gave the piece a three-dimensional appearance. Andrew marveled at how such a small thing changed the overall impact of a design.

He placed glass squares across the worktable, then laid a paper pattern on top, holding the paper in place with his fingers while he carefully drew around it with a paint pen. When he had first started working for Beth, she had insisted he glue the pattern piece to the glass before tracing around it. Over time, she'd developed confidence in his ability to keep the paper from slipping and allowed him to skip that additional step. Not only did this shorten the length of time needed to prepare the glass for cutting, but it made Andrew swell with pride. It felt good to be trusted.

By keeping the darker color at the center and the lighter at the outside of the parts of the sunburst, a greater portion of glass was wasted, so Andrew used extra care in the placement of the pattern. "No wasted pieces," he muttered to himself. He was just finishing up the fourth piece when a knock at the door intruded.

Startled, he looked toward the back door. It wasn't locked. Were Beth's hands full so she wasn't able to get in? He darted to the door. Opening it, he found nothing but a flurry of snowflakes. The knock came again, and he realized it was coming from the front. Giving the back door a firm yank, he dashed across the floor and unlocked the seldom-used front door.

A man with melting snowflakes on his uncovered head waited on the small concrete stoop. The moment the door opened, he stepped through with a broad smile and extended his hand. His snow-covered shoes left wet blotches on the floor. Andrew was pretty sure this would aggravate Beth. He'd have to remember to ask Mom if he could bring over one of her rag rugs to put in front of the door.

"Good morning." The man spoke in a cheerful tone. "There are no hours of business posted, but I saw the lights on. I hope it's okay to come in. Are you Quinn?"

Andrew gave the man's hand a solid shake. "I'm Andrew Braun. I work for the owner. She stepped out for a few minutes, but she'll be back. You can wait."

"Thank you." He looked around the studio, his shrewd gaze absorbing every detail. "I've never been in a stained-glass studio before. It's interesting."

Andrew raised his eyebrows and followed the man's gaze, trying to see the surroundings through the eyes of someone unfamiliar with the craft. He remembered his own awe when he first started—the pleasure of combining colors and shapes to create scenes, the patience required to prepare each piece of glass to fit the overall scene, the efficiency of the flowchart of steps that Beth had posted on the wall to make certain he did things in the proper order, and finally the satisfaction of viewing a finished product.

His gaze located the cardinal piece, still resting on the display bench and awaiting packaging. He hadn't created anything that elaborate yet, but he looked forward to the day Beth trusted him with larger projects. Suddenly he wondered if this stranger was an artist, too, seeking employment. Andrew's heart skipped a beat. The man was obviously worldly. His clothing and mustache set him apart from the Mennonite men of Sommerfeld. Would Beth, who had been raised in the world, prefer his assistance?

"Are you a stained-glass artist?" Andrew blurted out the question, his words loud in the peaceful shop.

The man shook his head, the corners of his eyes crinkling with mirth. "Huh-uh."

But he didn't expound on his answer, leaving Andrew floundering. After a few more awkward seconds of silence, Andrew waved his hand toward the worktable and said, "Well, I was busy cutting pieces. If you don't mind, I'll just. . ." He backed toward the table.

"That's fine. Do you mind if I look around?"

Andrew shrugged. He had no authority to tell him yes or no. Knowing how the glass fragments flew with the use of the cutting wheel, he set aside the task of cutting and took up a stone to grind the rough edges of the glass pieces laid out on the worktable. He kept a furtive eye on the stranger, who walked slowly around the periphery of the small building, his hands clasped at the base of his spine, his expression bland.

It seemed hours passed before the sound of a car's engine alerted Andrew to Beth's return. He hurried to the back door and opened it for her.

She bustled through with a smile on her face and quickly removed her coat. In place of the purple suit, she wore faded jeans, a blue T-shirt that brought out the bright hue of her eyes, and a flannel shirt with none of the buttons fastened. How could she be so cute in such sloppy attire?

"The weatherman says this will all clear off by midmorning, so—" Her cheery patter stopped when she spotted the stranger. Handing her coat to Andrew, she walked to the man. "Hello. Welcome to Quinn's Stained-Glass Art Studio. I'm Beth Quinn."

Andrew experienced a prickle of discomfort at the ease with which Beth greeted the man. He didn't care for the way the man gave Beth a quick once-over with his eyes, perusing her as thoroughly as he had the studio. But Beth didn't seem bothered by it. Her smile remained intact.

Andrew's fingers crushed her coat in a stranglehold.

"My name is Sean McCauley. It's nice to meet you."

Beth tipped her head, tumbling her shining ponytail across one shoulder. "What can I do for you?"

Sean McCauley slipped the tips of his fingers into his jacket pockets and smiled at Beth. "I'm a shopper."

Andrew's chest constricted at Beth's light, friendly laughter.

"Well, I don't often have shoppers come by the studio. As you can see"—she held out her arms, indicating the space—"I don't have a gift-shop area at all, although I hope to expand as my business grows."

The man gave a slow nod, his mustache twitching. "Would you

mind sharing your expansion plans with me?"

Andrew bristled. How were Beth's plans this man's concern? But Beth didn't seem to see anything wrong with the question. She didn't hesitate.

"Certainly. Right now it's a fairly small working studio, appropriate for preparing pieces for craft fairs. I've been working craft fairs for the past nine months, marketing myself and my creations." She moved slowly toward the display bench as she spoke, with the man following, his gaze pinned to her face. "The craft fairs brought interest, and I was commissioned by the Fox Gallery in Wichita for this piece."

Pausing in front of the cardinal scene, she looked up at McCauley. "Are you familiar with the Fox Gallery?"

The man offered a slow nod. Andrew waited for him to say something, but he remained silent. By now, Andrew had nearly twisted Beth's coat into a knot. He dropped it on the end of the display bench as Beth continued.

"I'm hopeful this piece will garner enough interest to lead to more commissioned pieces. My heart really is in the larger works. As that opportunity opens, I want to expand the shop, doubling my work space, and build a small gallery onto the front of the building where people can come and purchase finished pieces, eliminating my need to attend craft fairs. Although it can be fun to go out and mingle with the public, the fairs take me away from the studio. I also hope to eventually have an Internet Web site offering pieces for sale and making myself available for special orders."

"High aspirations," McCauley commented.

Andrew couldn't see the man's expression, since McCauley faced the cardinal piece, but he clearly heard the note of praise. Yes, Beth had high aspirations. Her aspirations had become Andrew's in the weeks he had worked with her. He wasn't sure of this man's interest, but he sensed trouble brewing for some reason he couldn't quite understand.

McCauley leaned one way, then the other, seeming to take stock of the cardinal scene. Standing upright again, he said, "What is it, about thirty-two by twenty-four inches?"

Beth shot him a startled glance, and even Andrew found the man's accuracy impressive. Beth replied, "Thirty-two by twenty-five, but that was a great guess. Are you an artist?"

Andrew blurted out the answer. "No."

Both Beth and McCauley cranked their necks to look at him.

He felt heat build in his neck. With a lame shrug, he said, "I asked him that earlier."

McCauley's mustache twitched again. He turned from Andrew to face Beth. Holding out his hand, he said, "Let me finish my introduction. I'm Sean McCauley of McCauley Church Construction out of Kansas City. I'd like to talk to you about the possibility of making you a part of our team."

FOUR

Beth took a step back, her heart leaping into her throat. She had hoped the stranger was a gallery owner or a crafts buyer—someone who might purchase a few of her pieces for retail. But an offer to become a part of his company? Her knees felt weak, and she wasn't sure she could remain standing. Turning, she stumbled to one of the tall stools next to the worktable and propped herself against it.

"I–I'm afraid I don't quite understand what you're saying."

Sean McCauley laughed lightly, showing even white teeth beneath the straight line of his neatly trimmed, reddish gold mustache. His blue-green eyes crinkled with the broad smile. "I'm sorry. I do need to slow down a tad." Crossing to the table, he pointed to an empty stool. "Do you mind?"

With a wave of her hand, Beth gave him permission to sit. As Sean seated himself, Andrew approached and stood beside her, his steadfast presence appreciated.

Slipping his hand inside his jacket, Sean retrieved a small card, which he handed to her. "So you know I'm legitimate. . ." His tone held a hint of teasing.

Beth examined the card, then handed it to Andrew, who scowled at it as if it held an inappropriate message.

"McCauley Church Construction has been in business for nearly forty years. We have three crews, and we've been involved in the building of churches from one coast to the other. We've built everything from simple chapels to three-story complexes. There is a McCauley building of worship in every state of the continental United States."

He leaned his elbow on the edge of the table, using his finger to trace the outside edge of a rose-colored piece of glass. "We've commissioned stained-glass windows from other companies, and we have no complaints. But. . ." His smile broadened. "You've captured our attention."

Beth put her hand against her chest, rearing back in puzzlement. "Me? How?"

Sean released a chuckle. "My aunt purchased one of your suncatchers at a craft fair in Olathe—a purple butterfly."

Beth nodded. "One of my best sellers."

Sean's smile sent a spiral of warmth through her middle. "I can see why. It's a great design. My dad and I were astounded when she showed it to us. The illusion of depth. That's really quite rare in stained glass."

"I don't claim credit for it," Beth said, her heart pattering. "It's a gift from my Creator. I simply want to use it."

The approval in Sean's unique eyes increased the tempo of her heartbeat. "That appeals to me, too. As a Christian company, it's important to us to glorify God through our business dealings. You seem to be a good fit for us between your commitment to working for God's glory and your amazing ability in stained-glass art."

Andrew, always quiet around strangers, surprised Beth by inserting a question. "How would you go about putting Beth on your payroll?"

Sean shot Andrew a quick look before turning back to Beth. "You wouldn't officially be an employee of McCauley Church Construction.

We'd commission you the same way you were commissioned by the gallery in Wichita."

Andrew nodded, and Beth felt a prick of aggravation. Since when did her business dealings require his approval? Shifting on her stool, she angled her shoulders to partially block Andrew from Sean's line of vision. "How many windows are we talking about here?"

Sean shrugged. "There's no way to say. It depends on many factors." He picked up a piece of glass from the table and examined it. "Have you worked with the heavier leaded glass?" Without waiting for an answer, he continued. "What's the largest piece you've constructed? Are you willing to sign a waiver that, if the piece doesn't meet our standards of excellence, you will absorb the loss? Can you set aside other projects and focus on designing for us exclusively when under deadline?"

Beth's head spun. Although she'd tried to exclude Andrew, she now found herself turning her head to seek his advice. He stared dumbly at Sean, his mouth open slightly as though he were as taken aback as she felt. She'd get no help from him. She turned back to Sean.

"Let's try one question at a time." Taking a deep breath, she began a series of careful replies. "First, this is the weight of glass I've used so far, but my equipment can handle the heavier glass. It's just that I've done smaller projects, so I've only had need of the lighter weight. Second"—she gestured toward the display bench—"the largest piece I've constructed so far is the cardinal piece."

Sean glanced at it again. "Impressive, but small compared to what we would need for most churches."

A wave of panic pressed from Beth's chest. "What size do you need?"

Sean removed a slip of paper from his pocket, unfolded it, and handed it over. Beth looked at it, her eyes widening. The dimensions were three times the size of the cardinal piece. She showed the paper to Andrew, sucking in a deep breath of fortification when his eyebrows shot to his hairline.

Andrew whistled through his teeth. "That's a good-sized piece."

"Yes, it is," Sean agreed, "but it's smaller than some. In one of our churches, we commissioned a stained-glass window that was nine feet wide and twelve feet high."

Beth had seen projects of that size and had wondered what it would be like to create something of that magnitude. Now the opportunity lay in front of her, if she could only prove her ability.

Sean continued, speaking directly to Andrew. "The windows we've commissioned in the past have all been beautiful, but they've lacked the three-dimensional effect Beth is capable of creating. That's why I'm here." He faced Beth again. "Is it too much of a challenge?"

Before Beth could respond, Andrew cut in. "Beth can do anything she sets her mind to."

Sean's mustache wiggled as if he fought laughter, but Beth gave Andrew an appreciative smile. His confidence in her gave her a needed boost. "I'd like to try."

"Try?" Sean angled his chin to the side, peering at her through narrowed eyes. "And if it doesn't work?"

Beth squared her shoulders and met his gaze directly. "I wouldn't expect you to pay for something that doesn't please you. However, I would like to be fairly certain before I go to the expense of creating a project of the size and weight you've indicated that you would be satisfied."

"And how can we make that happen?" Sean leaned forward, his eyes sparkling.

At closer range, Beth made out a spattering of pale freckles across his nose and cheeks. It gave him a boyish appearance that contrasted with the mustache. How old was he? A few years older than herself—midtwenties probably. She momentarily lost her train of thought. But when his red-gold eyebrows rose, she realized she'd allowed long seconds to slip by without answering. She swallowed and formed a reply.

"Perhaps I could do several preliminary drawings—in color, of course—so you could see what I envision as the final project. If you approve the drawing, I'll proceed. Then, if for some reason the window is not constructed properly, you would have the option of not purchasing it. I would ask to be compensated for my expenses and time, however. Does that seem fair?"

"All but the compensating for your expenses and time."

Beth's scalp prickled. "Oh?"

Sean raised his shoulders and held out his hands. "If you were on our payroll, then yes—we might offer an hourly wage in addition to reimbursement of expenses. But as a commissioned artist, the payment comes with the delivery of a finished, suitable project. Perhaps, eventually, if this business venture proves to be mutually satisfactory, we could consider making you a permanent employee of McCauley Church Construction, but—"

"Let's stick with commissioned work." Beth heard Andrew's sigh and sensed his relief at her resistance to becoming a part of McCauley's team. She didn't understand his reason, but she knew she was reluctant to combine forces with anyone. On her own, she could call the shots. Get someone else involved, and she wouldn't be in control any longer. She wasn't ready to sign that away, no matter how large the contract.

"That's fine." Sean reached into the pocket inside his jacket once more and withdrew a packet of papers. "This is the contract my father drew up in case you were interested. Please look it over, mark any questions you have in the margin, and I'll be back tomorrow to see what you think." He stood, his smile building once more. "It's been very nice meeting you, Miss Quinn and. . ." He looked at Andrew, snapped his fingers, then added, "Andrew." His gaze on Beth again, he finished in a warm tone. "I look forward to working with you."

Beth nodded, the papers as heavy as a sheet of leaded glass in her hands. "Thank you. I'll. . .I'll give this some thought and prayer."

"Good. Until tomorrow, then." Sean buttoned his jacket and headed out the door.

Beth turned from the closed door to look at Andrew. She had considered asking him what he thought, but the glimpse of thunder in his expression sealed off her words.

In his car, the engine running and the heater blasting him with cold air, Sean flipped open his cell phone and said, "Dad," in a clipped tone. Beeping indicated the phone understood the command. He tapped the steering wheel with his fingers, impatience pinching his chest as he waited for the call to be answered.

"How'd it go?"

Sean grimaced at his father's greeting. *Don't waste time with pleasantries. Just get straight to the purpose.* He had to admit, finding out the artist Quinn was a young, attractive female had nearly set him off course. It took some effort to put his focus back where it belonged.

"She's willing to try, but I don't know. It's a pretty small studio, and she doesn't have experience with the heavier glass."

"Gut reaction, Sean. Could she do it?"

The line crackled, letting Sean know they didn't have much time before the snowy weather disconnected the service. He answered from his gut. "I think she could."

"Then follow through on what we planned."

Sean nodded. "Will do. See you tomorrow evening sometime, hopefully with signed contract in hand."

The line disconnected, and Sean dropped the phone onto the seat beside him. *Well, Lord, we'll see what happens from here.* Sean put his car in gear and angled it toward the waiting highway. He'd find a hotel down the road—maybe that one outside of Hillsboro he'd passed on the way—and spend a leisurely day holed up with a television and remote control. By this time tomorrow, he'd be on his way to securing the artist Sean was sure would be a household name in the stained-glass art industry before the year was out.

His mind hop-skipped along a pathway: Her success would mean his success; his success would mean the company's success; and the company's success would mean Dad's approval. Yes, everything would work out perfectly.

FIVE

A ndrew went back to grinding the rough edges of the pieces of glass on the worktable, allowing Beth to study the unexpected opportunity provided by the thick contract in her hands. At least, he hoped she was studying—and finding favor with—the unexpected opportunity. By her introspective expression and silent tongue, he surmised she was deep in thought.

He stayed quiet and allowed her to think while he replayed the offer made by McCauley. His heart pounded at twice the beat of the rhythmic *scritch–scritch* of the carborundum stone. If Beth took on the task of designing windows for that company, she'd be busy. Possibly wealthy. And successful.

Very successful. . .

He licked his dry lips, considering how her success would become his means of convincing his father a person can support himself with art. Beth couldn't possibly keep up with her smaller projects and the larger ones for McCauley. She'd need him full-time. Ah, yes. Andrew closed his eyes for a moment, a smile tugging at his lips. His deliverance was near.

Unless, of course, she decided not to do the smaller things at all and just focus on windows for churches. Would she be able to handle that on her own?

"Andrew?"

Beth's timid query brought him back to reality. The wariness in her blue eyes made his heart thud. "Yes?"

She flapped the contract. "In looking at this, most of the benefits are on the side of McCauley Church Construction. If I follow through on projects, meet their deadlines, and design to their satisfaction, then the benefits flow toward me. There are quite a few 'ifs,' especially since I run such a small studio. But"—she tucked her lower lip between her teeth for a moment, her brow pursed in thought—"if I meet this first challenge, if I manage to prove myself, all the plans I have for the studio could come to pass."

Andrew nodded, setting aside the stone. He spoke slowly. "You know I'll do whatever I can to help you."

"Yes, I know. Thank you."

"So. . ." Andrew's mouth went dry again. He swallowed hard. "Do you think you'll sign it?"

Beth looked at the contract again. "I want to talk to Mom and Henry about it first."

For a reason he couldn't explain, Andrew experienced a wash of disappointment.

"But for now"—she hopped off the stool and carried the contract to her coat, tucking it beneath the thick folds of fuzzy fabric—"I need to focus on these suncatchers for my craft booth."

"I can do this," Andrew blurted. "Go talk to them now."

She sent him a funny look. "Henry's at his shop. It'll have to wait until suppertime." A smile crept up her cheeks. "I've never known you to be so impatient. What gives?"

Andrew shrugged, forcing aside the eagerness that twisted in his chest. "I guess I just want to see your dreams come true. You've earned it."

Her expression became almost tender as she looked at him, and he felt heat building in the tops of his ears.

"That's really sweet. Thank you."

A twinge of guilt struck. His dreams were directly related to her dreams coming true. His wish for her wasn't exactly without strings attached. But he kept that thought to himself. He nodded to acknowledge her words, then suggested, "Instead of working on these, why don't you start some drawings and get ideas for the window so you're ready to knock Sean McCauley off his feet tomorrow?"

Her eyes sparkled as her laughter rang. "Okay. I am itching to draw." She moved to the storage cabinet with an eager bounce in her step and plucked out a pad of graph paper, drafting tools, and pencils. Back on the stool, she pushed the glass pieces aside to create a drawing space on the worktable and bent over the paper.

Andrew tried to focus on the piece of glass in his hand—he needed to be cautious not to file inside the score line—but it was hard not to watch the lines of graphite creating a geometric pattern on the paper just across the table. It was equally hard to keep his eyes off the artist.

Beth was so cute when deep in concentration. She hunched over the pad of paper, her blond ponytail slipping across her shoulder now and then only to be pushed back with an impatient flick of her wrist. Her thick lashes swept up and down, her gaze zipping from one corner of the drawing to the other. The swish of the pencil across the paper came in short, thoughtful strokes. Her lips sometimes tipped up in satisfaction and other times pursed just before she dropped the pencil and used the rubber eraser with force.

An hour slowly ticked by while Beth sketched and Andrew sanded. Snowflakes ceased their flutter outside the window. Finally,

Beth straightened on the stool, put down the pencil, and rubbed the back of her neck with both hands while emitting a low groan.

Andrew set aside the carborundum stone. "All done?"

She grimaced, stretching her arms over her head. "With a very rough draft, yes. I'll set it aside and look at it later. I need a little distance now."

Andrew nodded. He understood what she meant. Taking a break from a design allowed the artist to view it with a fresh perspective. He always needed at least three hours between first and second drafts. He jerked his head toward the window. "Snow's stopped. You could probably make that run to Wichita now."

Beth swiveled to look at the window, and her face lit. "Oh, good!" Hopping off the stool, she put the drawing pad and pencil in the drawer. Then she headed for the stack of cardboard and Styrofoam sheets they used to cushion the finished projects for travel. "I'll probably grab a sandwich at home and eat it on the way. Feel free to take your lunch break whenever you like." The squeak of Styrofoam nearly covered her words. "Do you plan to stick around all afternoon? You don't have to if you don't want to."

Andrew watched as she put a layer of foam over the top of the cardinal scene, hiding it from view. "I'll stick around. Maybe by the time you get back, I'll have one of these suncatchers put together."

She flashed a quick grin over her shoulder. "Only one? I figured a half dozen at least."

He smiled. These teasing moods of hers were fun. He just was never sure how to tease back. "Well. . .we'll see."

She laughed lightly as if he'd said something humorous and wrapped the package with wide, clear tape. Standing, she swished her hands together. "Would you mind putting that in the trunk of my car?"

"Sure." Andrew slipped his coat on, then lifted the scene and followed Beth to her car. Fresh snow clumped on their shoes, and Beth banged her feet on the lower edge of the car door opening before swinging her legs inside the vehicle. He slammed the trunk lid, then gave it a pat. "Have a safe drive."

Beth peeked out the open door and waved. "Thanks. Enjoy your afternoon." She yanked the door closed, and the engine revved to life. Andrew remained on the concrete slab by the back door, watching bits of snow fly from her tires as she pulled away. When she turned the corner from the alley, he stepped into the studio and closed the door against the chill.

He removed his coat and his boots, leaving the wet boots beside the door, and walked on stocking feet to the storage cabinet. He reached for the drawer that contained the copper foil, but he didn't open it. His gaze shifted to the drawer where Beth had put her drawing for McCauley's window.

Curiosity shifted him two drawers to the left. Feeling like an intruder, he slid the drawer open slowly. The sketch tablet came into view, showing Beth's drawing by inches. He kept sliding until the entire design was revealed. At first glance, it reminded him of looking into a kaleidoscope. Almost a starburst pattern. He lifted it out and held it at arm's length, examining it. He scowled. Although the design was pleasing in balance, something was missing.

Propping it on the cabinet, he took a step back, pulling his lips to the side in contemplation as he allowed his focus to shift from the center to the outward edges. He snapped his fingers, recognizing the problem.

Snatching up the pad, he tore Beth's sheet loose and dropped it on the worktable. He placed the pad with its clean top sheet next to her drawing. Looking back and forth from her design to the page in front of him, he began to draw.

"This is beautiful, Beth." Marilyn Fox, owner of the Wichita gallery, sent Beth a huge smile. "I'm sure the interest in this piece will be high."

Beth released the breath she'd been holding. It came out with a light giggle. "Oh, I'm so relieved. This is still so new to me."

"It won't be new for long," Marilyn predicted, giving Beth's shoulder a squeeze.

Beth nodded, thinking of the contract in the passenger seat of her car. If she ended up working with McCauley Church Construction, she would be thrown into the world of stained-glass art. Her pulse accelerated at the thought.

"Well, let's talk about your next piece for us, shall we?"

The words captured Beth's attention, and she jerked her gaze from the cardinal scene to the smiling gallery owner. "But this one hasn't even sold yet."

"Oh, it will." Her arm still around Beth's shoulders, she herded Beth into her small, cluttered office at the rear of the store. "I've been in the business long enough to recognize the keepers. And you, Beth, are a keeper." The woman's arched brows rose with her words of praise.

Beth twisted her fingers together. "I really appreciate your vote of confidence," she said, hoping her tone didn't sound as uncertain as she felt, "but I'm not sure I have the time to do another commissioned piece right now."

Marilyn sank into the chair behind her desk. Resting her elbows on the arms of the chair, she made a steeple of her fingers and stared at Beth. "Oh?"

"No." Beth stood on the opposite side of the desk, seeking an explanation that wouldn't divulge the possibility with McCauley's. She wasn't sure she should speak of it until it was final, but if she signed that contract, her time would be wrapped up in the large window. She latched onto the only certainty. "I am in the middle of making several small pieces for a crafts fair which is coming up quickly, and—"

Marilyn waved a manicured hand. "Beth, that little stuff is fine for someone who dabbles. But you are an artist. You can't afford to dabble."

In doubt about how to respond, Beth remained silent.

"Let someone else do the little stuff if you still want to have things in craft fairs." Marilyn raised one brow. "Didn't you say you had a man helping?"

Beth nodded. "Yes, and he's quite capable, but—"

"Then let him fry the small fish, and you work on reeling in the whale." Marilyn shook her head, her chandelier earrings catching the light. "Really, Beth, you have the talent to go far as an artist. The question is do you have the drive?"

"Of course I do." Beth's reply came automatically.

Marilyn's smile grew. "Good. Then let's talk about the second piece." She pointed to a plastic chair in the corner.

Beth dragged the chair to the desk and sat down. An hour later, Beth had in hand a one-page contract for a second commissioned design that would feature a cardinal on a lilac bush. Ideas for that scene competed with the image of the window for McCauley's as she drove back to Sommerfeld, and worry made her clench the steering wheel so hard her fingers ached.

"God, have I gotten myself in over my head?" She spoke aloud, feeling comfortable sharing her thoughts in the privacy of the vehicle. She sucked in a breath of apprehension. "Should I have prayed before agreeing to a second commissioned piece?" Marilyn had seemed so certain it was the right thing to do, and Beth did want to use the talent God had given her. How often should she seek the Lord's guidance in these decisions? Uncertainty made her heart race. "Oh, I hope I did the right thing."

She continued to stew the remainder of the drive, but by the time she pulled behind the studio, she had calmed herself with the reminder that she wasn't working alone. Andrew was helping. As Marilyn had said, if he assumed responsibility for the little things, it would free her to focus on the larger projects.

Although she had changed back into her suit for the trip to the gallery and it wasn't appropriate for the studio, she couldn't resist pulling in to see how much progress Andrew had made with the suncatchers during her nearly five-hour leave of absence.

She hop-skipped through the slushy snow to the back stoop and stepped inside. When she entered the studio, she saw Andrew at the worktable and smiled. But when she spotted the loose pieces of glass still scattered across the wood surface, her smile faded.

Andrew's head jerked up. "Beth. . ." His cheeks blotched red. He slapped a drawing pad upside down, creating a current that sent a single sheet scooting from the table. Beth walked over and picked up the paper. Her scowl deepened when she recognized the drawing she'd made that morning.

She looked at him, suspicion creating a sour taste in her mouth. "What are you doing?" Looking pointedly at the unconstructed suncatcher pieces, she added, "Obviously not what I had anticipated."

Andrew raised his shoulders in a sheepish gesture. "I guess I lost track of time."

Beth released a little huff. "So what are you doing?"

When he didn't answer, she held out her hand. After a moment's hesitation, Andrew slid the pad of paper across the table to her. She turned it over, and her jaw dropped.

"You're reworking my design?" Who did he think he was, sitting here doodling on something that didn't concern him rather than completing the work she'd assigned?

"Well, I looked at yours, and it seemed like something was missing—the depth just wasn't there. So I thought—"

"So you thought you'd fix it, huh?" Her voice squeaked out two decibels higher than normal. Slapping the pad onto the table, she glared at him. "I can't believe this! I leave you with a simple task: finish some suncatchers. And instead you spend the day working on a design that I fully intended to complete when I returned. This was a rough draft!" She waved the drawing. "You knew that! So why mess with it?"

Andrew opened his mouth, but nothing came out.

Beth's anger burned hotter with his lack of explanation. "Andrew, I trusted you to work on these." Her hand quivered as she pointed to the glass wedges on the tabletop. "And you let me down. If I can't trust you, then. . ." She didn't complete the thought, but she knew by the way Andrew's face went white that he understood the unspoken threat.

Shaking her head, she crushed her drawing and the pad holding his drawing to her coat front. "I'm going home now. I need to talk to Mom and Henry. I need to. . .think. You"—she backed toward the door, taking the drawings with her—"just lock up and go home."

Six

Beth pulled behind the simple, ranch-style house her mother and stepfather shared, turned off the ignition, and took a deep breath to calm her rattled nerves. Finding Andrew fiddling with her design had brought a dizzying sense of déjà vu followed by a wave of panic. She could not allow another man to sabotage her plans!

Peering through the car's window, she focused on the concrete foundation that would eventually support the two rooms Henry was adding to the west side of the house. She remembered his elation when Mom told them the doctor had detected two heartbeats. Henry's laughter echoed in her memory along with his joyous comment, "Well, Marie, we hoped to be blessed with two children. I just didn't expect to have both blessings at once!" He had immediately begun planning the addition so each of the new family members would have their own space.

Suddenly the concrete slab wavered, and Beth realized tears swam in her eyes. She brushed them away impatiently. What was wrong with her, sitting here getting all teary? Tired. That's all. She was tired from her long days at the studio. And they didn't promise to get shorter.

With a sigh, she snatched up the contract Sean McCauley had left and stepped out of her car. Henry had apparently put a snow shovel to work—the walkway was clear—so her feet stayed dry as she walked to the back porch. Although Henry had encouraged her to forgo knocking and just walk in, she didn't feel comfortable doing it. This wasn't her home. She tapped on the door and waited for an answer.

Mom's smiling face appeared in the window before the door swung wide. "Honey!" Mom tugged her across the threshold and delivered a hug made awkward by her bulky front. "I was hoping you'd stop by. Andrew said you finished the cardinal piece and it was beautiful. Did you bring it with you so I can see it?"

Beth pushed the door shut behind her, twisting her lips into a scowl. "No, I didn't even think about bringing it by. But I took some digital pictures. I'll show you after I get them downloaded."

Mom sighed, feigning a quick pout before flashing a grin. "Well, I guess that will have to do." Then she linked arms with Beth. "Come on in, then, and talk to me while I finish dinner. Do you want to stay?"

Beth sagged into a chair, plopping the contract onto the little table tucked into the corner of the kitchen. "I have something I need to talk to you and Henry about, so that'd be great. Thanks." She pushed her coat from her shoulders, allowing it to droop over the chair back, and watched her mother putter around the modest kitchen.

Her mother had changed so much since they'd left Cheyenne, there were still times when Beth did a double take. Home-sewn dresses instead of jeans and a button-up shirt; hair pulled into a bun beneath a white cap trailing black ribbons instead of tousled, loose curls; and a relaxed countenance rather than the lines of tension she'd often worn around her eyes and mouth. Returning to her childhood home had been good for Mom.

"So what did you do today since the cardinal piece was done?" Mom stirred something in an iron skillet on the stove, and the scent of peppers and onions filled the room.

"Drove to Wichita to deliver it." Beth sniffed, and her stomach turned over in eagerness. "And commissioned a second piece, this time with the cardinal in a lilac bush."

Mom sent a quick glance over her shoulder, her eyebrows high. "A second piece? That's great! A lilac bush. With those tiny flowers, that should be a challenge."

Beth flicked the stack of pages on the table with her thumbnail. "I'll probably find a piece of mottled lavender glass, maybe with some texture, to emulate the petals. I'll have to play around with it." She hoped she'd have time to play around with it.

"Sounds fun." Mom slipped a lid on the skillet and waddled to the sink. The added girth around her middle stole her usual grace, and her ankles seemed thick.

Beth frowned. "Are your feet swollen?"

Mom tipped forward, tucking her skirt against the underside of her extended belly to look at her own feet. She straightened with a soft laugh. "Oh, that's not so bad. Sometimes my ankles seem to disappear, and my toes stick out in all directions."

A stab of worry struck. "Did you do that when you were carrying me?"

Mom paused for a moment, sending Beth a crinkly smile. "Now, honey, you have to remember I've aged a bit since you were born."

Despite herself, Beth smiled. Never would she have imagined becoming a big sister at twenty-one. She teased, "Yes, I guess it's a good thing you have all your brothers and sisters, Henry's brothers and sister, plus their assorted offspring to give you a hand."

Mom tipped her head, one black ribbon trailing down her neck. "And you?"

Beth shrugged, looking at the contract. A band seemed to constrict her heart. "With all of them, you don't really need me."

A hand descended on Beth's shoulder, bringing her attention around. "Beth, you realize these babies can never replace you, don't you?"

The tenderness in Mom's eyes brought the sting of tears. Beth sucked in her lips, gaining control, before she answered. "It's just that everything is so different, Mom. So many changes. . . Sometimes it's hard to stay on top of it all."

Mom went back to the stove, turned the dial, and joined Beth at the table. She took Beth's hand, stroking her knuckles with her thumb. "You realize you don't have to stay on top of it all alone, don't you? You can ask God for help, and He'll answer every time. As for other helpers, you have Henry and me, and Andrew."

At Andrew's name, an image of him hunkered over the worktable, redoing her drawing instead of constructing suncatchers, flashed through Beth's mind. She jerked her hand free.

Mom frowned. "Beth?"

Beth shook her head. "I appreciate having you and Henry, and of course I know God is there for me. I'm still learning how to lean on Him, but I do know He's there. But as for Andrew. . ." She puffed her cheeks and blew out a breath. "I must not be a very good judge of character when it comes to men. They let me down every time."

"What has Andrew done?"

"Oh, nothing much. Just ignored my direction to put together suncatchers for the show in Salina and spent his time reworking a drawing he had no business reworking." Beth attempted a glib tone, but she heard the sharp undercurrent.

Mom's face pinched. "I'm sure his motivations were good."

Beth bounced from the chair, marching to the stove to stir the contents of the skillet. "Just like Mitch's motivations were good when he illegally 'collected' antiques for our boutique?" Vegetables and chunks of chicken caught the fury of the wooden spoon before she clanked the lid back in place. Facing her mother, she crossed her arms. "No, I'm better off working alone. That way, things get done the way *I* want them done without any misunderstandings or deceptiveness."

Her gaze fell on the contract, which lay on the table. Her heart skipped a beat. How would she keep up with everything on her own? A wave of panic struck, a silent prayer forming without effort. *God, how am I going to meet these demands?*

Mom struggled from the chair, arching her back to lift herself. With one hand pressed to her lower back, she crossed the kitchen to cup Beth's cheek with her free hand. "Honey, don't sell everyone short because Mitch made a mistake. Being alone is. . ." She heaved a sigh, her eyes drifting shut for a moment as if reliving something. "Lonely. Don't cut yourself away from everyone out of fear."

Beth felt tears sting behind her nose again. She sniffed. "I don't want to, Mom, but—"

The back door banged open, and Henry Braun entered the kitchen. His nose and ears were red from the cold, his hair stood on end, and he carried in the odors of cold air and gasoline. He bestowed a huge smile on both women. "Well, good evening! My two favorite girls." He crossed the kitchen and kissed Beth's cheek and then his wife's lips.

Beth, watching their kiss of greeting, felt a pang of envy. It must be wonderful to fully belong with someone the way her mother now belonged with Henry. She shoved that thought aside. Belonging to someone meant depending on them. And it meant being let down.

"Are you staying for dinner?" Henry asked Beth as he lifted the lid from the skillet and peeked at the contents.

"If that's okay." Beth watched Henry waggle his eyebrows in her mother's direction, his face creased in a grin. The serious Henry who had shown up unexpectedly at their apartment in Cheyenne fifteen months ago had transformed into a lighthearted, teasing man nearly impossible to resist.

"Perfectly okay." He slipped the lid in place and rubbed his stomach. "I'll try to control myself, even though your lovely mother has prepared stir-fry, one of my favorites."

Mom's tinkling laughter rang as she shook her head at her husband. Beth wondered if she should creep away now and leave the two of them alone. But Mom turned to her and pointed to the cupboard.

"Would you set the table, Beth? I'll make sure the rice is done, and then after Mr. Braun here has washed up"—she looked pointedly at Henry's hands, which he examined with mock dismay—"we can eat."

Half an hour later, the last of the rice had been scraped onto Henry's plate, and Beth's stomach ached from the second portion she hadn't needed but had eaten anyway. Leaning back in her chair, she took a sip of water and sighed.

"That was really good, Mom. Now I know why it's one of Henry's favorites."

Mom sent a fond smile across the table to her husband. "You know, he puts the title 'one of my favorites' on everything I fix, even if it's just a bologna sandwich."

Henry grinned. "That's because no one spreads mayonnaise on a slice of bread like you do—just the right amount to bring out the flavor of the bologna without overpowering it."

"Oh, Henry." Mom released an amused snort, shaking her head.

Even Beth had to laugh. Honeymooners. That's what her parents were. And at their ages! Still, she had to admit it was wonderful to see them so contented. She only wished they didn't seem so. . .complete. Where did that leave her?

Henry swallowed the final bite of rice, wiped his mouth, and fixed Beth with an intent look. "Now, your mother said you have something to discuss with us."

Beth appreciated the way her stepfather removed all teasing from his tone before addressing her. Never had Henry treated her with anything except respect and kindness, the way she had always wanted a father to treat her. Sometimes she wished she could set aside her inhibitions and accept him as readily as he had accepted her. Yet the remembrance of another father—one she'd never had the opportunity to meet—always reared up, tangling her emotions and distancing her from Henry.

But he was right: She did have something to discuss, and she did respect his opinion. She plucked up the contract, which she had placed on the floor beside her chair, and handed it across the table. While Henry leafed through it, Beth shared the details of the visit from Sean McCauley and their conversation. Both Henry and Mom listened intently, interrupting occasionally to ask a question.

Beth finished, "It looks like it would be a wonderful opportunity if I can satisfy them with that first project."

Henry looked over the top of the contract, his eyebrows high. "And all the expense falls on you if they don't like it. Can you absorb that?"

Beth grimaced. "It would be painful. It would take quite a few craft-fair sales to make up for it, that's for sure. But the risk would be worth it considering the potential payoff if they do like it. Lots more work, plus the income to expand the studio and buy the equipment I need to be completely self-sufficient."

Henry nodded and went back to reading.

"What about the gallery in Wichita?" Mom, leaning sideways to peek at the contract, shifted her gaze in Beth's direction. "Can't they keep you busy enough?"

With a shrug, Beth stifled her frustration. Being torn between the gallery opportunities and the construction company's opportunities left her feeling bruised. "I don't know. They did commission a second piece, and Mrs. Fox indicated there would be more, but it's still small scale compared to what McCauley is after."

Henry shot a startled glance at his wife. "The gallery commissioned Beth to do a second piece?"

Mom nodded, pride shining in her face. "Yes, they did. She delivered the first one, and they immediately asked for a second."

Beth wriggled on her chair, feeling as though she'd been forgotten.

But Henry set the contract aside and fixed his gaze on her. "There's no doubt this could be financially lucrative if it works out, Beth. I guess what it comes down to is what you want to accomplish with your studio. Do you want to be strictly an artist, creating your own designs on your own time clock, which gives you freedom but maybe lacks security? Or do you want the security of knowing you'll have steady jobs, putting together windows with someone else's idea at the heart, and you serving as the constructor?"

Steady, secure work opposite sporadic, unreliable contracts. Designing her own projects opposite following someone else's lead. The thoughts ping-ponged in Beth's mind, making her dizzy with the possible pros and cons of each position. Finally, she threw her hands out and huffed in aggravation. "I want the security with the freedom to create my own stuff!"

Henry chuckled softly while Mom shook her head, her lips tipped into an amused smile.

"Well, Beth," Henry said, one eyebrow cocked high, "the only way I see clear for that is if you continue doing both your own artwork *and* meet the demands of this construction company. To be honest, I'm not so sure you could handle all that on your own."

Beth sighed. "So what do I do?"

Henry shrugged. "If you want it all, hire a full-time staff."

Slumping back in her chair, Beth swallowed the groan that pressed at her throat. A full-time staff. As if workers were lining up for jobs in this little Mennonite farming community! She knew of only one person willing to dedicate time to the art studio.

It was back to Andrew.

Andrew unplugged the soldering iron and rotated his head, trying to work loose the tense kinks in his neck. The acrid taste from the solder lingered on the back of his tongue, making him wish he had one of those bottles of water Beth liked to carry around with her. Placing the soldering iron on the concrete floor to cool, he turned back to the worktable.

Satisfaction welled, bringing a tired smile to his face. It had been a hard eight hours of steady work, but seeing the suncatchers lined up, ready for the craft show, made it worthwhile. Hopefully this would make up for this afternoon, when he'd fiddled with Beth's drawing instead of doing what she'd asked him to do.

"You let me down."

Her remembered words stung on a variety of levels. He'd been taught to honor his commitments, and it created a sense of disappointment in himself that he hadn't followed through on what had been expected. Deeper than that, though, was Beth's lack of understanding that he wasn't trying to let her down—he was trying to help. There had been something wrong with her design, and he had discovered the needed element to bring out the dimension.

He wished she'd at least looked at what he'd done before flinging out an accusation and storming off. Hadn't she figured out by now that he wanted what was best for her? For them? Sighing, Andrew picked up a little whisk broom and began cleaning up the work area.

Sometimes he wondered if his fascination with Beth was unhealthy. She was so different from the other girls in the community. And it was much more than the way she dressed. She was self-reliant, a freethinker. She didn't let anybody tell her what to do. Some perceived this as pigheaded, but Andrew preferred to think of it as independent. He admired it.

And at the same time, he resented it. An independent person didn't need anybody else. Andrew wanted Beth to need him. One thing was certain: He needed her if he wanted to use his artistic abilities full-time.

His cleanup finished, he yawned and reached for his coat. Outside, full dark had fallen, letting him know without looking at a clock that it was well past his normal bedtime. But before heading out the door, he glanced once more at the worktable. Returning to the table, he took a moment to arrange the suncatchers in a neat line.

When Beth came in tomorrow morning, she would see he had honored his commitment. She'd teasingly told him to make half a dozen. He'd done it. She would see she needed him as much as he needed her.

SEVEN

A dull ache throbbed at the base of Beth's skull as she brushed her teeth. Straightening from bending over the sink, a wave of dizziness hit, and she grabbed the porcelain basin to steady herself.

"Whew, I hope I'm not coming down with something."

Her equilibrium restored, she headed to the bedroom to dress. It was early for her to be up—especially for a Saturday—but she didn't know when Sean McCauley would be stopping by, and she needed to be ready.

Her hands trembled slightly as she slipped on a fuzzy sweater, and again she wondered if she was getting sick. But then she shook her head, reminding herself of her restless night. Of course she felt wimpy this morning. It had been well after two when she looked at the clock last, which meant she'd had fewer than five hours of sleep.

"Once I get some coffee in me, I'll be fine," she encouraged herself as she sat on the edge of the bed to tie her sneakers. Bending down that way made her head spin, and she added through gritted teeth, "And I better eat something, too."

She considered going to the café for breakfast. The new owner, Henry's sister Deborah, baked the most delectable cinnamon buns.

But Saturday mornings were always busy at the café, and Beth might have to wait to be seated. She didn't want to waste time this morning. Instead, she visited her own kitchen, frowning at the limited choices.

With a sigh, she plunked a mug of coffee left over from yesterday's pot in the microwave and dropped two frozen waffles in the toaster. The microwave dinged just as the toaster tossed the waffles into the air. Leaning against the counter, she munched the dry, blueberry-flavored waffles and sipped the bitter liquid. Although it couldn't compete with Deborah's cinnamon buns and freshly brewed coffee, it filled her belly and revived her enough to go to the studio. Tucking the drawing pad containing both hers and Andrew's designs and the thick contract beneath her arm, she headed to her vehicle for the short drive.

Cars—plain ones and "worldly" ones—lined Main Street, providing evidence of the café's patronage of both Mennonite and non-Mennonite customers. Lisbeth's Café had brought in the highway traffic for more than four decades. The café was as popular now as it had been when Beth's great-aunt had operated it. Beth had chosen to build her studio on the south side of the café partly because the land had been bequeathed to her and partly because it was a great opportunity to pull in café customers when she finally built the showroom addition.

Her heart pounded as it always did when she thought of her dreams for the studio. Although she'd lain awake last night, mulling things over and over in her mind, she still wasn't 100 percent certain about signing on the dotted line with McCauley Church Construction. *God, You're going to have to clunk me hard with an answer before Sean McCauley gets to the studio. I want to do the right thing.*

She pulled her car into its usual spot behind the studio and entered through the back door. Tugging off her coat, she flipped on the fluorescent lights and then dropped her coat onto the end of the display bench. She pulled a work apron from a box beneath the bench and tied it over her clothes. Finally, she turned toward the cabinet to retrieve the copper foil and soldering iron so she could get those cut pieces turned into suncatchers.

But as she shifted, her gaze drifted across the worktable, and she froze, her eyes widening. Six suncatchers lay in a row across the tabletop, glittering beneath the bright overhead lights. She moved slowly toward the table, shaking her head. "It's like 'The Elves and the Shoemaker,' " she muttered, remembering her favorite of the Grimms' fairy tales her mother had read to her when she was small.

One by one, she touched the completed projects. She then lifted a pink cross to the light to admire the change in colors. Placing the piece back on the table with the others, she drew in a slow breath through her nose. Apparently Andrew hadn't gotten much sleep last night, either. Guilt pricked when she recalled how she had berated him for spending his time drawing instead of completing projects. He'd followed through after all.

Different emotions warred in her breast. When she saw him next, she'd thank him and apologize for being so snappy, but she would also need to talk to him about his position in the studio. He was her employee, not her partner. His job was to follow her directions. Period. No more of this acting on his own.

After retrieving cardboard and foam, she made a careful stack, sandwiching the suncatchers between protective layers, and put them in a box labeled "Salina—2/22." That done, she slid the box beneath the display bench next to the box containing butterfly designs. Recalling Sean McCauley telling her the company's interest in her stemmed from the purchase of a simple purple butterfly, her heart doubled its rate.

How quickly life can change, she thought, moving to the clean work-table and staring out the window across the snow-dusted landscape. Lost in thought, the sound of the back door opening startled her, and she whirled toward it in time to spot Andrew stepping through. He yawned as he slipped out of his coat, and she couldn't help but smile at his droopy expression.

"Rough night last night?" She deliberately affected a teasing tone.

He shrugged and didn't reply, sending her a sheepish look.

His silence told her clearly he felt uncomfortable after their last heated, one-sided exchange. Taking a breath, she formed an apology. "Andrew, I'm sorry I jumped on you like I did yesterday."

He responded with a silent nod, his lips pulled to the side.

Puffing her cheeks, Beth blew an exasperated breath that ruffled her bangs across her forehead. She shoved the strands aside and said, "Look, I got testy because I know how much I have to get accomplished and I can't"—she gritted her teeth for a moment, reality creating a knot in her stomach—"do it all alone. I need to know I can depend on you."

"You can." He finally spoke, his tone carrying a hint of defensiveness.

"Really?" She tipped her head, her eyebrows high. "To do what I ask you to do, rather than what you want to do?"

Andrew's lips formed a grim line. His dark eyes narrowed, and for a moment Beth wondered if he was going to spew angry words. She'd never witnessed him being anything but mild mannered, but she'd never pushed him quite so hard, either.

Finally, he gave a brusque nod. "You're the boss."

She fought a grin. "Don't make it sound so painful."

An answering grin, albeit a weak one, found its way to his face. "Sorry."

Beth's stomach fluttered. Remembering Henry's comment that

she would need help were she to meet the demands of the new opportunity as well as continuing to create her own artwork, she pressed. "Andrew, you realize if I sign this initial contract with McCauley, it could mean big changes around here. Can you deal with that?"

Andrew stood for a moment, his gaze aimed somewhere to her left, his jaw working back and forth as if in deep thought. She waited, wondering if she was about to be left to handle things on her own and trying to decide if it would be for the best if she was. At last, he looked at her and shoved his hands into his pockets, hunching his shoulders.

"Honestly? I'm hoping for big changes. I'd like to work here full-time, year-round. To do that, you've got to make this studio a raving success. All that craft-fair stuff, it's fun, but it won't take you places." He nodded toward the worktable, where she'd placed the contract. "That opportunity from McCauley—that's the big time. That's where I want to go. So I'll do what it takes to get there."

Beth fought a frown. While his words were spoken with conviction and he offered his assistance without hesitation, something didn't set quite right. She couldn't put her finger on it. While she processed his reply, seeking the reason for the discomfort that wiggled through her chest, a tap at the front door captured her attention.

Andrew charged past her and opened the door. Sean McCauley, his face wearing a broad grin, stepped into the studio.

"Good morning." Sean unbuttoned his jacket, swinging his smile from Andrew Braun to Beth Quinn. He let it linger on Beth. Once again, her attractiveness took him by surprise. Working with her would be a pleasure in more ways than one.

"Good morning." She walked toward him, the stiff apron crackling with the movement, and held out her hand. "I trust you had a good night's rest?"

"Yes, I did. Thanks for asking." He observed the tired lines around her eyes and refrained from asking her the same question. "And did you have a chance to look over the contract thoroughly?"

She nodded, her gaze shifting briefly toward her employee. "Yes. Andrew and I were just discussing how my signing it could alter our focus."

Sean raised one brow. "Alter your focus in a positive light, I hope."

Beth didn't answer. Instead, she turned toward the worktable, moving to the opposite side and climbing onto a stool. She pointed to another stool. "Please join me."

Sean accepted her invitation while Andrew remained rooted in the middle of the floor.

Beth seemed to wait for Andrew to make a move on his own. When he didn't, she sent a tense smile in his direction and said, "Andrew, I doubt I'll be doing any real work this morning, so you can feel free to go if you'd like."

For a brief moment, Andrew's face clouded. Then his expression relaxed, he gave a nod, and he moved toward the back door. "Fine." Sean suspected there was more the man wanted to say, but Andrew clamped his jaw and tugged on a coat. "I'll see you Monday then." He headed out the door.

Beth turned her attention to Sean. "Okay, let's talk shop."

Sean rested his elbows on the tabletop. "Before we get into the contract, would you mind telling me how you got involved in stained-glass art?" Jerking his thumb toward the outside, he commented, "Seems a rather unusual business for this area. Stained glass is pretty ostentatious. You sure won't have customers from the community."

Beth's light laugh made Sean smile. "Oh, no, I'm certain the

Sommerfeld residents won't purchase my goods. But we get quite a bit of traffic through here. The café brings in customers, and we also get an unbelievable number of gawkers."

Sean raised his brows.

Another laugh rang. "Curiosity satisfiers. People interested in the simpler lifestyle of the Mennonites and Amish who live around here."

"And that's why you built your studio here? To capture the business of the gawking curiosity satisfiers?"

"Partly." She took a deep breath, as if seeking fortification. "You see, my mom grew up in Sommerfeld, on a farm east of town. She left the community to marry my dad, and we lived in Wyoming until about a year and a half ago. Mom's favorite aunt passed away and left the café and her house to me."

"Why you?" Sean was genuinely intrigued.

A slight shrug accompanied her reply. "Mom named me Lisbeth after her aunt. I guess since Great-Aunt Lisbeth never had children of her own, she chose me to be her inheritor."

Sean got the impression there was more to the story than Beth was sharing. He waited a few beats to see if she would continue, but when she didn't, he said, "That was nice."

"Nice. . ." Beth licked her lips. "And unexpected. So, Mom and I found ourselves in Sommerfeld. I had land to build on and, with the sale of the café, funds to put up the building. Mom says it was God's way of meeting my need before I knew I had one."

Again Sean suspected he was getting the *Reader's Digest* version, but he didn't push her to give more details. For whatever reason, she was guarding herself. There would be time to get the full story when their relationship had developed further. "I see. So you always planned to have a studio?" He was puzzled by the pain that flashed through her blue eyes.

"No. Stained-glass art is something I learned when I came to Sommerfeld. But it grew on me quickly."

Her light tone made him wonder if he'd imagined the earlier signs of discomfort. He smiled. "I'm glad it did. My company can certainly benefit from your newly acquired ability."

She swallowed, her gaze jerking away for a moment before lighting on the contract. Her fingers trembled slightly as she gently flipped the corners of the pages. "Yes, well, let's hope this will be mutually beneficial."

"There's no doubt," Sean said, leaning forward. "My biggest concern at this point is whether you truly have the space to create the kinds of windows we'd need." He patted the top of the four-foot square worktable. "This won't be big enough."

She lifted her gaze to meet his. "I know. But my stepfather and Andrew could build a work surface in that open area—a platform to get the design up off the floor a bit but low to the ground to make it easier to work on larger designs."

Sean chuckled. "You've been doing your homework."

Her smile turned timid, making his heart skip a beat. "Eventually, I'd need a larger studio if I plan to construct more than one window at a time and especially if I add more equipment so I can stain and fire my own glass and have more than one cutter going, but I don't want to go to too much expense until I know for sure things will work out."

Sean smoothed his mustache with one finger, nodding with approval. Her caution impressed him. She had business savvy. From his conversation with her yesterday, he already knew she had the desire to expand her business. All necessary elements for success were in place: the drive, the talent, and the means. She was the perfect choice.

"So do you have any concerns about the contract itself?" He maintained the same light, interested tone he'd used earlier when questioning her about her interest in stained-glass art. It made for a smooth transition into business talk.

"For the most part, I'm fine with the contract. The financial compensation is fair considering the number of hours that will go into each window, and your past experience in dealing with the purchase of windows shows me you understand how much time is needed to create the artwork."

Sean nodded, smiling. *So far, so good.*

Beth flipped the contract open, her gaze scanning the printed pages. When she located what she wanted, she turned the pages around and pointed to a block of text. "But I am concerned about the clause that gives you the right to refuse the windows once completed. That leaves me holding a piece that would, in all likelihood, be unsuitable for any other purpose. The amount of time and expense going into creating it would then be lost."

"That's unlikely to happen if you meet the requirements on the first piece," he reminded her. "You're new in this line of business, so we're taking a chance on you. We need to be certain you can do what we're asking you to do."

"I understand that. It's a protective clause." Her eyes bored into his, not so much as a hint of a smile lighting her eyes. "But all the protection is at your end. How can we even the scale?"

Sean assumed the same businesslike attitude she had adopted. "We *can't* even the scale until we know for sure you can produce. Once the first window is completed to our satisfaction, you'll have proven yourself. At that point, you become an employee of McCauley Church Construction with the same rights and privileges of all other workers."

Beth sucked in her lips, observing him with narrowed eyes. "So you're asking me to purchase glass, set aside all other projects—which equates to no other means of income—until I have completed this single piece of artwork. And then it's possible you can reject it, which would leave me holding the tab."

"You make it sound so cutthroat." Sean offered a light laugh. She didn't respond in kind. He linked his fingers together, his arms on the table, and dropped all flippancy. "Look, Beth, if you're concerned your abilities won't meet our expectation, you don't have to sign that contract. I'm not going to force you. I admit this first window puts a lot of pressure on you. But when"—he purposely chose to avoid the word *if*—"you prove yourself, you stand to gain the means to turn this place into a full-blown studio. I gathered from your comments yesterday that that's what you'd like."

Her nod told him she was listening.

"If things go well, you could be the designer, hire a staff of workers to construct the windows, and turn more of your attention to being the artist behind the projects rather than the producer. That would free you up to work on your own projects in addition to ours."

Slipping a pen from the pocket of his shirt, he held it out. "We're willing to give you a chance. Sure, it might mean the loss of a few weeks and a portion of your bank account, but it can lead to financial freedom, the expansion of your studio, and your name becoming synonymous with stained-glass art. So. . .is it worth the risk?"

For a moment, he feared he'd lost her. Her brow furrowed, her chin quivered, and she blinked rapidly while holding her breath. He offered a quick silent prayer for her to push past her fears. They both stood to gain tremendously if she would just take the chance.

Beth released her breath in a *whoosh* and shook her head, her blond tresses tumbling across her shoulders. Then she jerked the contract around, flipped the pages back to reveal the last page, and picked up the pen.

EIGHT

As soon as Sean McCauley left with the signed contract in his hand, Beth paced the studio. The opportunities made available by the contract loomed in front of her. Sean's comment about her being able to hire people to put the projects for his company together while she worked on her own projects had been the deciding factor. It was the best of both worlds, and the excitement of being able to fulfill all of her dreams concerning the studio set her heart pounding in her throat.

According to the contract, she had exactly two months to complete the first project—the kaleidoscope pattern must be finished by April 1. Charging to the worktable, she flipped open her sketch pad and removed the preliminary drawing she'd made. The pad open, she glimpsed Andrew's rendition, as well. She started to put it aside, but her breath caught. She held his design at arm's length.

Her gaze jerked between the drawing in her hand and the one lying on the table. The two designs were identical through the center, but at a middle row, a circle of diamonds, the similarity ended. Andrew had modified her diamond by lowering the apex and stretching the bottom half. The simple change added a breathtaking shift in the overall pattern, making it appear that the center portion of the design stood out from the background.

Dimension. Andrew had brought the dimension to the pattern, just as he had said.

She slapped his drawing on top of hers and closed the cover on the pad. His words rushed back. *"The big time. . .that's where I want to go."* Suddenly the discomfort she'd experienced earlier found a basis. Fear struck hard, making her break out in a cold sweat. Would Andrew's desire for success lead him to undermine her as Mitch had? She shook her head, trying to set aside the worry, yet it niggled.

"Once bitten, twice shy," she murmured. Turning her face toward the tiled ceiling, she prayed aloud. "Dear God, I'm going to need help, and Andrew is the only one who has any training around here. I need to depend on him, but now I'm afraid to."

When she was a little girl, Beth had always been able to run to her mother in times of fear or doubt. Although she was hardly a child anymore, the solace of her mother's attention became a pressing need. She glanced at the wall clock. Henry would be in his shop; Mom would be home alone. It gave her the perfect opportunity to spend some one-on-one time with her mother. Something that would be extremely rare once those twins made their appearance.

A wave akin to fear hit Beth, bringing the sting of tears. The desire to see Mom increased. Grabbing up her coat, she locked the studio and headed for her car. When she knocked on the back door of Henry's house, however, no one answered. Cupping her hands beside her eyes, she peered through the window. No lights on, no movement. With a frustrated sigh, she returned to her vehicle. Where could Mom be? She rarely ventured outside of Sommerfeld on Saturdays.

Beth considered going to her own home but decided against it. She didn't want to be alone right now. Even if she couldn't be with her mother, she wanted to be with someone. *The café*, she decided, putting the car into DRIVE and turning in that direction. Although it would be less busy now than it had been during the breakfast rush, she could sit in a corner booth, eat a leftover roll, and maybe visit with one of her cousins who served tables. Not the same as being with her mother, but it beat sitting at home by herself.

The Main Street parking areas were still filled with the plain-colored, Sommerfeld vehicles of citizens doing their weekend shopping, as Beth had learned was typical for the community. She parked behind her studio and walked to the café. Only two tables were filled, both with Sommerfeld citizens. The occupants sent lazy glances in her direction, then went back to visiting with each other. But Henry's niece, who waited tables and ran the dishwasher, skipped across the floor and held out her arms for a hug.

"Hi, Trina," Beth greeted, appreciating the quick embrace. Trina had been the first person to befriend her when she arrived in town, and Beth held a fondness for the bubbly teenager.

"Hi! Haven't seen you for a while, although Andrew keeps me up on what you're doing."

Beth's eyebrows rose. Andrew spoke of her to his family? Her stomach did a funny somersault with that news. "I do stay busy," she commented briefly as she followed Trina to an empty booth.

"And it promises to get busier, huh?" Trina's eyes sparkled. "Did you sign the contract with the big construction company that builds churches?"

Beth stifled a sigh. Although she knew she should appreciate the interest expressed by her stepfather's family, at times she wished the little community wasn't quite so knowledgeable. There were no secrets in Sommerfeld. With a forced smile, she nodded.

Trina clapped her hands. "Oh, good!"

Despite the reservations that had struck when she had replayed

Andrew's comment, Beth's spirits lifted with Trina's unbridled enthusiasm. Folding her arms on the tabletop, she said, "So do you want to give up your waitressing and come put windows together for me instead?"

For a moment, Trina's sunny disposition faded. "I'd like to give up the waitressing, but. . ."

Beth waited for Trina to finish her sentence, curiosity striking at the girl's serious expression.

The girl shook her head, making the little ribbons on her cap dance, and she winked. "I'll let Andrew be your helper. He's much better at it than I would be."

A frown pinched Beth's forehead. Before she could form a reply, Trina started backing away from the table.

"I'll go tell Aunt Marie you're here."

"Mom's here?" Beth's heart leaped. She'd get to talk to Mom after all.

"In the kitchen with Mama. Do you want to come back, or should I send her out?"

Henry's sister Deborah, who now owned the café, was also in the kitchen. Although Deborah had warmed up considerably toward Beth in the months she'd lived in Sommerfeld, Beth still sensed the woman's disapproval of her worldly attire and mussy hairstyle. She made a quick choice.

"Send Mom out, please." She waited, her gaze on the doorway that led to the kitchen. When her mother appeared, Beth stood up and met her halfway across the room. Giving her a hug, she said, "I went by your house to see you. I didn't think to look here."

Mom grimaced as she walked with Beth to the booth. "I decided I could benefit from some exercise, but the brief walk has me all swollen again."

Beth glanced at her mother's feet and gasped. "Mom! You don't even have ankles!"

Mom's chuckle sounded as she peered at her own feet. "Oh, I'm sure my ankles are under there somewhere."

Beth huffed. "You know what I mean. What does the doctor say about this?"

Her mother's sheepish shrug as she slid into the booth provided the answer.

"You haven't mentioned it?" Beth's tone rose in volume, drawing the attention of nearby patrons.

Mom patted her hand. "Honey, please, it's nothing to be concerned about. Most women experience some foot swelling during pregnancy."

"But how do you even wear shoes?" It looked as though Mom's flesh spilled over the top of her simple oxfords. Beth released a shudder.

"I put them on before my feet swell. And then I don't dare take them off." Mom gave a little laugh that Beth didn't echo. "Now stop looking at me like that. I'll be fine. But I admit I'm glad to see you. You can drive me home."

"Of course I will." Beth drew in a deep breath, ready to question her mother about other discomforts related to pregnancy.

"Why were you looking for me?"

Mom's question shifted Beth's attention. "Oh, I wanted to let you know I signed the contract."

"Are you excited?"

Beth forced a short laugh. "Yes—and nervous. A lot rests on the success of this first project."

"You can do it, honey." Mom's warm hand on Beth's arm offered assurance. "You have wonderful ideas, lots of talent, and the gumption to see it through."

"And you aren't at all biased," Beth teased, pleasure spiraling through her chest at her mother's praise.

A light laugh crinkled Mom's eyes. "Of course not! I just know genius when I see it."

"Genius. Right." Beth shook her head, but she couldn't stop smiling.

"Besides, you aren't doing this alone."

Beth's heart skipped a beat. How much responsibility would everyone give to Andrew?

"Remember Philippians 4:13? 'I can do all things through Christ. . .' "

Beth finished, " 'Which strengtheneth me.' " She swallowed, pushing aside the prickle of guilt that pressed upward at her mother's reminder of Beth's ever-present help. She wondered how long it would be before thinking of God came before thinking of people.

The café door opened, allowing in a gust of cool air. Beth glanced toward the door and recognized her stepfather. She waved him over. When he reached the booth, he leaned down and gave his wife a kiss on her cheek before greeting Beth. "Hello! Andrew says the man from the construction company was by already. What did you decide?"

Beth released a snort. "News travels fast."

Henry sat beside Mom and stretched his arm along the back of the booth, his fingers grazing Mom's shoulder. "You can't blame Andrew for being excited. This affects him, too, you know."

Yes, Beth knew. Resisting the urge to scowl, she said, "I signed. So now I have until April 1 to put together a window that will knock McCauley Church Construction's socks off."

"You can do it," Henry said, but he smiled into Mom's face rather than looking at Beth. Mom whispered something that didn't reach Beth's ears.

Beth cleared her throat. "I may need your assistance. My worktable isn't large enough to accommodate a project of that size. Do you suppose you could build a platform in the open corner of the studio?"

Henry glanced in her direction. "A platform? Oh, sure, I don't know why not. When will you need it?" Immediately his attention returned to Mom's upturned face.

"I have lots of glass to order and cut first, so not right away." Beth watched her parents, unease tickling her spine. She looked away from them toward the other two filled tables. Conversations at the tables went on, oblivious to the three people in her booth.

Beth suddenly felt completely alone despite the fact that eight other people sat in the room with her. Would she ever feel as though she belonged in this community? Lowering her eyes, she stared at her jeans-covered legs draped with the tails of her flannel shirt. In her attire, she stuck out like a sore thumb from the Mennonite women in their simple, home-sewn dresses and neat caps.

Shifting her gaze slightly, she observed Mom and Henry's quiet exchange. Despite sitting directly across from her, they seemed to have forgotten she was there. Henry rested his broad hand on Mom's rounded abdomen, and she laughed softly into his face. Once again, Beth was struck by how complete her parents appeared. Unmindful of her. Unneedful of her. . .

She jumped from the booth, causing both Mom and Henry to look in her direction. "Listen, I'd better scoot. I have lots of planning to do if I'm going to get that project finished for McCauley. Henry can drive you home, right, Mom? I'll. . .I'll talk to you both later." She dashed from the café before either of them could answer.

Beth spent Saturday afternoon and evening reworking her drawing to scale until she was satisfied. Using Andrew's twist on the center row of diamonds changed her original idea, but she discovered she liked the new design much better. Using her all-in-one printer, she made several copies of the design, then set to work with colored pencils. She skipped supper to continue working, ignoring the growl of her stomach. When she was so tired her eyes no longer focused, blurring the colors together, she put the drawings aside and crawled into bed.

Her sleep that night was fitful, her dreams disconcerting. Images from the town blended with images from the city of her upbringing. Faces from Sommerfeld and others from Cheyenne kept coming and going until confusion jerked her out of sleep. Twice she awakened, her face damp, but she wasn't sure if sweat or tears were responsible for the moisture she felt on her skin.

When the morning sun crept between the cracks of the window blinds, she swung from the bed, relieved to be able to face reality instead of battling the odd, disjointed images of her dreams. With a yawn, she padded to the bathroom, then stood, staring at her reflection in the mirror. Her tangled hair stuck out in all directions, giving evidence of restless shifting on her pillow. Blue circles underscored her eyes, and her face looked pale.

"I'm a sight," she snorted. After running cold water on a washcloth, she mopped her face and then looked again at her reflection. The tiredness remained despite the thorough scrubbing.

"If I go to the meetinghouse looking like this," she spoke aloud to her dismal face in the mirror, "Mom will think I'm sick." With the thought of her mother came the remembrance of Henry and Mom in the booth yesterday, absorbed in one another. Swinging from the mirror, Beth charged to her bedroom and sank onto the edge of the mattress.

Her head slung low, she moaned, "Dear God, where do I fit in?"

She wasn't a member of the church, so she didn't belong there. Having been raised far away from the cousins who resided in this little town, she didn't blend in with them. Grown and out of her mother's house, she no longer fit there. She released a humorless huff of laughter as a childhood memory struck.

Every Christmas season, she and Mom had curled together on the sofa to watch the television version of *Rudolph, the Red-Nosed Reindeer*. She had loved to sing along with the characters. Now the lyrical question "Why am I such a misfit?" drifted through her mind, bringing both a rush of fond remembrance and a stab of pain. The words were too close to the truth.

Beth simply didn't fit in—not in Sommerfeld, not in her mother's house, not back in Cheyenne.

But she had her business, her art. Pushing to her feet, Beth straightened her shoulders with resolve. Hadn't Mom said God gave her the gift of creating beauty from bits of colored glass? Well, then, that's where Beth belonged: in her studio, creating beauty. And if the next few weeks went well, she'd have enough business to keep her too busy to worry about needing to fit in anywhere else. Her misfit days were nearing their end, thanks to the contract offered by McCauley Church Construction.

Knowing her mother would worry if she didn't show up at the meetinghouse for services, Beth laid out a modest skirt and blouse and headed for the shower. But when the service was over, she'd come home, get out her pencils again, and finish planning the window for McCauley's. By the end of the day, she'd shoot several color options to him via e-mail, and she hoped that by the end of tomorrow she'd be able to order glass.

She had one chance to carve her niche in the stained-glass world, and she wouldn't let it escape her.

NINE

Andrew shut off the cutting wheel. His ears buzzed as if the carbide wheel still screeched. He removed his goggles and peered toward the newly constructed platform where Beth sat cross-legged, scissors snipping a steady rhythm. Her shining ponytail captured the light, and as always, he found himself wondering if those strands felt as silky as they looked.

She turned and caught him staring.

Heat built in his ears, and he gestured clumsily toward the stack of glass he'd scored. "Got enough here for six more crosses and six butterflies."

A nod bounced her ponytail. "Good. I'm glad you're ahead of the game there, since my order of glass for this one"—she tipped her head toward the paper pieces scattered across the platform—"should be arriving this afternoon. That frees up the wheel for me to get to cutting."

Andrew fought a frown. She had hoarded each step of the process in creating the window for McCauley, spending every minute of the past week finalizing the colors, putting a rush order on glass, drawing the design to scale on butcher paper, and now cutting the pattern into pieces. He had hoped to at least help by cutting and fitting the glass pieces together, but apparently she intended to see this project through as a solo artist. He supposed he should be grateful she'd allowed him to help build the platform where she planned to construct her window.

Her brows pulled down in a brief scowl of worry. "I hope the glass will arrive as promised. I've got a pretty tight schedule to keep in order to meet McCauley's deadline."

Andrew considered telling her if she'd allow him to help, they could speed up the process, but instead, he glanced out the window at the sunshine-bright February day and said, "Can't see any reason why they'd be delayed."

Beth turned back to the paper spread across her lap and began snipping once more. "I sure hope not." Without looking at him, she said, "Go ahead and snap those pieces apart and then grind the edges. Hopefully by tomorrow, you'll be ready to put them together. And maybe you can ask Trina to go to Salina with you for the show so you'll have some company."

Andrew, reaching into the drawer for the pliers, jerked to attention. "You aren't going?"

She paused again to stare at him over her shoulder. "Of course not. I can't take a whole day away from here—at least not until this first project for McCauley is done. So from now until April 1, whatever shows we do are yours."

Andrew rounded the worktable to stand beside the platform and gawk down at her. "Trina can't take a Saturday off from the café." It was the only argument he could compose on short notice. He knew he shouldn't say what he was thinking: *But I look forward to those times when we go away together.* Away from Sommerfeld, Beth was more open, animated, and relaxed, which made him more open, animated, and relaxed. He relished those snatches of time.

Beth made a sour face. "Oh, I didn't think about that. Of course she couldn't." A graceful shrug bunched the blond ponytail that lay on her shoulder. "Well, you should be able to handle it on your own."

Her unconcerned comment set his teeth on edge. Andrew clomped back to the storage cabinet and snatched up the pliers.

"You could ask someone else if you prefer not to go alone."

Andrew preferred not to go alone, yet he didn't want anyone else's company. Besides, who else would be interested? His family either ignored or made sport of his art-related pursuits. Beth waited for an answer, the scissors motionless in her hand. He finally grunted, "We'll see."

She shot him a speculative look before offering another shrug and bending over the paper once more. They worked without speaking, with only the *snap* of the pliers, the muffled *clink* of glass pieces being placed on the table's surface, and the *snip-snip* of the scissors breaking the tomblike quiet. After a long while, Beth released a noisy breath and spun on her seat to face Andrew.

"What's your problem?"

Andrew, startled, raised one brow and pointed to his own chest.

A second huff split the air. "Yes, you."

"I don't have a problem." He'd lied. His chest constricted with the knowledge, yet he couldn't retract the words.

Beth crunched her lips into a scowl. "Oh, yes, you do, or you wouldn't be so sullen." Plopping the scissors onto the wooden platform with a solid *thunk*, she folded her arms and glared at him. "Come on, spit it out. Neither of us will be able to focus until you do."

Andrew's heart set up a thudding he feared could be heard. He disliked conflict. How often had he held his tongue at home, even at his age, when his father forced his opinions on him? He'd been raised to honor his father and mother, so he did. He'd been raised to believe confrontation dishonored God, so he avoided it. Now he looked at

Beth, who sat waiting, her pretty face pinched with frustration. She gave him an opportunity to speak his mind, to share his thoughts, but words failed him. All he could do was give a helpless, wordless shrug.

Throwing her hands outward, she filled the silence. "Andrew, things are changing here. For the better, I hope. I realize we've done most everything together, but right now, I have a huge task I have to tackle on my own, proving to Sean McCauley and his father that I am capable of putting together a window that will meet their expectations. What that means is I have to concentrate solely on this project."

She gave the platform a slap with her palm that sent a few cut pieces scooting across the wooden surface like ducks skidding across a pond. "But I can't afford to just ignore the other commitments I've made—namely, the second cardinal piece for Fox's studio and the two craft fairs between now and McCauley's April 1 deadline. People are waiting for those stained-glass projects. And I can't do it all without your help."

Andrew swallowed and managed to give a nod. He would help. That wasn't the issue. He wished he could get his tongue to express the issue, which was his desire to be needed for more than someone to work on her secondary projects.

She went on, her tone rising in intensity. "Once this project is completed and McCauley extends the contract beyond the conditional one I signed, I intend to be the designer rather than the producer. At that point, I'll want you to put together the windows I design for the churches. I'll probably even hire a couple more people to work with you, which will free me up to focus on one-of-a-kind pieces for galleries. I can really broaden the scope of the studio that way.

"But"—for the first time, her fire seemed to flicker—"none of this is going to happen if you aren't going to be around. So. . .what's the plan, Andrew?"

To become so indispensable you lean on me at work and home. But of course he couldn't say the words out loud. He sat stupidly, perched on the stool like a crow on a fence post, but unlike a crow, he couldn't manage to release so much as a squawk. Looking at her with his lips clamped shut and his thoughts racing, he carefully processed everything she'd said.

Her choice of the word *I* rang too prominently in his mind for him to feel completely secure, yet he replayed her comment about him eventually putting together the windows for McCauley. His heart sped up, making his breath come in spurts. That meant full-time work. Which meant supporting himself with art. His hands quivering, he rubbed the underside of his nose and swallowed.

She had asked him the plan. It seemed she already had one mapped out, but he wouldn't oppose it if it meant the fulfillment of his dreams. He opened his mouth and forced a reply past his dry throat. "My plan is to help you get this studio going."

Her eyes narrowed to slits as she seemed to consider his brief response. "Even if it means doing all the little stuff on your own until April?"

He felt as though his tongue stuck to the roof of his mouth. Dad might have different ideas about his time in another few weeks. He'd be needed to help in the fields by the first of March for sure. But somehow he'd make time for Beth's "little stuff," as she put it, and bide his time until he could prove to his father this art studio had the capability of supporting a family.

"Whatever it takes," he said with conviction.

Beth nodded. A smile curved her lips. "Thank you. That's what I hoped you'd say. Now"—she pointed to the idle pliers in his hand—"finish snapping, and get to grinding. We've got work to do."

Andrew followed her direction, and at noon, she suggested he go to the café and pick up sandwiches. By the time he returned, she had finished cutting the design apart and was reconstructing it on the platform. Slender coils of butcher paper—the pieces removed by the scissors to allow for the width of the lead came—lay in tumbled heaps around the wooden platform, giving the illusion that someone had thrown confetti. He supposed that was apt, considering the party that would take place when the project had served its purpose in securing future contracts with McCauley.

For a moment, he stood, paper sack in hand, and watched her carefully secure each labeled pattern piece with a roll of masking tape. The look of concentration on her face made him hesitate to interrupt her. Always zealous when it came to her work, she'd been almost obsessed this past week. He admired her hardworking attitude, and he wondered if she would be as fervent in other aspects of her life. . . such as relationships.

A lump formed in his throat with that thought, and he cleared it, making Beth jump. She whirled on her knees and stared at him with wide, blue eyes, a strand of hair framing her cheek.

"Oh! You're back." She pushed off from the platform and stood, brushing off the knees of her jeans with both palms. "You should have said something."

He grinned. "You were busy."

She glanced at the array of snipped paper and frowned. "Yeah." Turning her gaze to the window, she sighed. "But I'll be out of things to do in another hour if that glass doesn't arrive."

"Here." Andrew reached into the bag and retrieved a sandwich. Holding it out, he said, "Take a break and eat. It will take your mind off the missing glass."

She flashed a quick smile, took the sandwich, and sat down on the edge of the platform. After a moment's hesitation, Andrew perched next to her, even though she hadn't offered an invitation. Her smile told him it was okay, and heat once more built in his ears. He blurted, "Should I pray?"

She gave a wordless nod, and he bowed his head and asked a brief blessing for the food. He ended, "And let the glass come, please." When he raised his head, he found Beth's smiling face aimed at him, which only increased the warmth in his ears. He turned his attention to his sandwich.

He finished before her and stood, stretching his tense muscles. Accustomed to hard work, he always found it interesting that his muscles complained more about sitting still than they did from a long day in the fields. The hunching over, he decided, made things tighten up. If he was going to be an artist, though, he'd need to get used to it.

The kinks worked loose, he sat back on the stool and picked up a carborundum stone. Just as he began grinding, Beth set aside the remainder of her sandwich and picked up the roll of tape.

"You should at least finish eating," he admonished. While he admired her slender figure, she needed the energy to keep working.

"I'll finish it later." Swinging her ponytail over her shoulder, she sent a quick grin across the room. "When this project is done."

He snorted. "You'll waste away by then."

She imitated his snort. "Not likely. It's only until April."

"That's two whole months," he reminded her, warming up to the teasing and surprising himself with the ease he found in playfully sparring with her.

"You mean *only* two months." A slight frown marred her brow. "That's really not much time at all." Slapping her knees, she stomped to the window and peered outside. "Oh, where is that glass?"

Andrew set aside the carborundum stone and crossed to stand behind her, looking past her head to the road outside. "My mother always said a watched pot never boils."

If he thought his lighthearted comment would bring a laugh, he was wrong. "It's got to get here soon." She rested her hands on the windowsill and strained forward, her shoulders tense. "I've got limited time, and I must meet that deadline."

His hands twitched with desire to squeeze her shoulders and offer comfort. He put his hands in his pockets. "I could help."

She spun to face him, shaking her head adamantly. "Huh-uh. I told you. This project is mine. After I've proven myself, then I'll let you work on windows for McCauley. But this one. . ." Her gaze drifted to the paper pieces forming the design. "This one is all mine."

"Then work on your cardinal piece," he suggested. "It'll occupy your time."

She stared at him for a moment, her brows low and lips tucked between her teeth. He wondered if she would start spewing frustration. Her mood swings reminded him of a mule he'd had when he was a boy. Old Pokey nosed you with affection one minute, then bruised you with a nip the next. Despite the animal's sometimes irascible nature, Andrew had always been fond of Old Pokey. He'd felt as though he'd accomplished something when the mule greeted him with a happy bray.

"I suppose I could. . . ." Her musing tone was cut short by the sound of an engine's roar. She jerked toward the window, once more nearly pressing her nose to the glass.

Andrew tipped sideways to look, too. A shipping truck bearing the logo HALE'S SHIPPING AND TRANSPORT came to a groaning halt in front of the studio.

Beth grinned at him, her nose crinkling impishly. "I guess sometimes a watched pot does boil!"

With a chuckle, he headed across the room and grabbed up his coat. "I'll help the driver unload."

TEN

Sean McCauley leaned back in his desk chair, wincing at the *squeak* of the springs. As a kid, he had never cared for high-pitched noises. His brother, Patrick, had teased him by stretching the mouth of a balloon and releasing its air in ear-piercing squeals. He had played basketball in high school, but the squeak of sneakers on the polished floor jarred his concentration. Even as an adult, the screech of a saw or the squeal of brakes was enough to set his teeth on edge. He supposed that was why he'd chosen the architectural side of construction rather than being part of the assembly crew.

Sean glanced at his computer screen, smiling at the most recent e-mail from Patrick.

> *Hey, little bro! Had some awesome tamales in a café on the border this evening. Thought about you and wondered if you were eating a cold bologna sandwich—ha! Tell Dad things are on schedule and that glitch with the plumber is all fixed now so he doesn't need to worry. I'll touch base again tomorrow.*

As an assembly crew foreman, Patrick traveled all over the United

States. Each day since he'd arrived in Columbus, New Mexico, he had sent Sean an e-mail raving about some unique feature from landscape to customs to food. Patrick, the older of the McCauley brothers, had always loved to pester and tease, and his daily e-mails were his way of letting Sean know exactly what he was missing by being stuck in the little office he'd set up in the smallest bedroom of his 1960s unpretentious ranch-style home.

What Patrick didn't realize, however, was that Sean was perfectly happy in his office. He loved the planning side of construction—meeting with church committees, drawing blueprints, finalizing dreams. His prayer was that the churches he designed would be attractive, inviting, usable buildings, but mostly that they would serve as places of growth and worship for the members of the community in which they were built.

His gaze shifted to the blueprint that lay on the drafting table in the corner. A small town outside of Salina, Kansas, had requested his services in planning a church building. Their original building, erected in the early 1900s, had burned to the ground nearly a year ago, and the congregation currently met in the high school gymnasium. They were eager to build, but the congregation was split between re-creating the chapel they'd lost and building a more modern facility.

Sean viewed this as his biggest challenge thus far, and he had an idea for a compromise he believed might meet the desire of the entire congregation. But it involved Beth Quinn, and he wasn't sure he could ethically involve her until he knew for sure she would be working long-term with McCauley Church Construction. He reached back to massage his neck, bringing another complaining *squeak* from his chair's springs.

Grimacing, he pushed himself out of the chair and crossed to the office closet, where he kept a can of lubricant. A few well-placed squirts insured the chair's noise-making days were over for the time being. He put the lubricant away, then crossed to the drafting table and looked down at the drawings.

The congregation had limited funds—they hoped to keep the cost equivalent to the insurance settlement—and building costs had increased since the policy had been purchased. Extravagance wasn't possible, but Sean hoped he could squeeze in one small splash of ostentation.

"And when it comes to splashes of ostentation. . ." He could use an artist's input on whether his idea would work or not. Only one artist came to mind. Moving from the table to his desk, he clicked a few buttons on the computer keyboard, bringing an address book into view. He gave a one-fingered *click* on Q, and Beth Quinn's telephone number popped onto the screen. In short order, he punched in the series of numbers on his cell phone and then waited, rubbing his lips together in anticipation of hearing her voice.

"Quinn's Stained-Glass Art Studio."

That was not Beth's voice, and a horrible racket came from the background. Sean frowned. It sounded as if a dentist were drilling a mastodon's teeth. The fine hairs on the back of his neck prickled. He raised his voice to block the unpleasant sound. "Is this Andrew?"

"Yes. May I help you?"

"This is Sean McCauley. Is Miss Quinn available?"

"Oh." The tone took a turn, a bit of cold air seeming to whisk through the line. "Yes. Just a moment, please." A slight *thunk* was followed by a wheeze as the grinding sound came to a halt. Muffled voices let Sean know Beth was on her way. Finally, the voice of the person who had filled too many of his thoughts lately came through. "Hello, this is Beth."

"Good morning, Beth. Sean McCauley here. How are you today?"

"Busy," she replied with a light laugh. "I have a lot of glass to cut for a large stained-glass window."

He smiled. "Glad to know it's coming along. Listen, I need to be in your area early next week. I wondered if I could swing by, check on your progress, and discuss a different project with you."

"A different project?"

Did he detect a slight note of panic? "I'd like your input as an artist," he said. "This is a window that might not come to pass for reasons too complicated to explain over the phone, but if it's a possibility, I'd like to be able to present the idea to a church planning committee."

"Oh, I see." A slight pause, then, "Sure. You can stop by. I'm here pretty much around the clock these days, so feel free to just pop in."

"Great. I'm guessing it would be around nine in the morning on Monday. I have a meeting in Carlton at noon. Will that give me time to get there?"

"Let me ask Andrew. He's more familiar with the towns around here." Her voice became muffled, as if she had shifted the receiver away from her mouth. "Andrew, how far is Carlton from here?" A mumbled tone answered, and then her voice came clearly through the line once more. "Andrew says it's less than forty minutes from here, so that should give you plenty of time."

"Okay. Nine it is then."

"Fine. I'll see you Monday." The *click* indicated she had disconnected.

Sean stared in surprise at his telephone for a moment before bursting into laughter. Beth Quinn was all business. Placing the cell phone on the corner of his desk, he tapped his lips with one finger, his laughter fading. He needed her to take her business seriously if he was going to be able to use her services regularly. So why did her abrupt departure leave him feeling slightly disappointed?

Beth moved directly back to the cutting wheel, slipped her goggles into place, and reached for the switch.

"So he's coming to check up on you?"

Andrew's voice, carrying a hint of something—rebellion, maybe?—gave her pause. She moved the goggles to the top of her head and gave him her full attention.

"He's coming because he has a meeting with some people in Carlton and needs my advice before he goes."

Andrew's eyebrows rose. She'd seen that look before when Sean McCauley's name had come up in conversation. If she didn't know better, she'd think Andrew was jealous of Sean. But how ridiculous would that be? Her relationships with both men were business only. An odd sensation wiggled down her spine. At least from her end, they were business only, weren't they?

Giving a shake of her head to dislodge that thought, she pulled her goggles down and suggested, "If he is checking up on me, I want to have progress to show him, so I'm going to finish cutting. How are the butterflies coming?"

Andrew held up the soldering iron. "Almost done."

"Good." Beth flipped the switch on the cutting wheel and focused on her task. The *whir* of the spinning wheel changed to a high-pitched *squeal* when she pushed the heavy glass beneath the carbide wheel. Brow pinched, lower lip tucked between her teeth, Beth concentrated on following the lines she'd drawn on the glass.

Making straight cuts was simple; the curved ones required complete concentration. But as she guided the glass with glove-covered fingers, she found her thoughts wandering. Andrew's behavior over the past few days had begun to concern her. He remained his usual helpful and hardworking self, but at times he exhibited a protectiveness—an almost territorial attitude—that created a niggle of discomfort. This studio was hers and hers alone. He was an employee. But his actions made her feel as though he saw himself as much more than mere employee.

Sliding the blue glass free, she reached for a second piece, and her gaze drifted across to Andrew. He sat at the worktable, guiding the soldering iron along the lines of copper foil. She felt a little better seeing him engrossed in his task. Maybe she'd only imagined his change in demeanor. Yet something told her she hadn't. Still, worrying about it wouldn't get the glass cut.

Keep me focused, she prayed silently and aligned the mark on the glass with the wheel. For the next two hours, she repeated that simple prayer a dozen times. It helped. By the time noon rolled around and she let the wheel wheeze to a stop, she had the glass scored for at least a third of the McCauley window.

"A good morning's work."

She almost didn't hear Andrew's approving voice over the whine in her ears. It always took awhile before the sound of the saw ceased its echo in her head. Mom had suggested earplugs. Beth was beginning to think that was a good idea. Crossing to the worktable, she fingered the line of butterfly suncatchers with the tip of a gloved finger.

"You, too. Thanks for finishing these up."

"That's my job."

The words were glib, yet Beth once again sensed an odd undercurrent. Dropping her gloves on the worktable next to her goggles, she pushed aside the twinge of worry. "When we get back from lunch, I'll help you pack these; then we can snap and grind the pieces I scored this morning."

Andrew, whisking a small broom over the surface of the worktable, shot her a startled look. Before she had a chance to question him about it, he said, "Do you want to go to the café for lunch? Trina told me Aunt Deborah planned chili and cinnamon rolls for today's special."

Beth's stomach growled on cue, and she laughed. "I'll never pass up Deborah's homemade rolls, but I need to run by the house and check my mail. Marilyn Fox e-mailed me—"

"Is she checking up on the lilac piece?"

Now Beth was certain she'd heard an edge in Andrew's tone. The "checking up" comment had been made earlier in reference to Sean. Apparently, Sean McCauley brought out a rather unattractive side to Andrew. With a pointed look, she said, "No, she only wanted to let me know the cardinal-and-dogwood piece sold and she'd be sending a check." She gentled her voice as she concluded, "I don't want to leave something like that in my box for long."

Andrew nodded. "That's fine. Grab your jacket. We'll take my truck."

For a moment, Beth hesitated. What had happened to asking what she preferred? Although his words weren't exactly a directive, she sensed a command in the tone that made her want to dig in her heels. Then she gave herself a mental shake. What was wrong with her these days, reading more into everything Andrew said and did?

"Okay. That sounds fine." She followed him out, and he opened the passenger door for her. She had to admit it was nice having a man perform little courtesies for her. Mitch had never been one to, as he put it, "pamper" her. He said she was capable of opening her own doors, carrying her own packages, and filling her own gas tank.

During the months of their relationship, she had never questioned it. She'd seen it as his confirmation of her strength and independence, and she found no fault in it. She had rather liked having Mitch treat her as an equal rather than someone weak and in need of looking after. Since coming to Sommerfeld, though, she'd seen a different relationship between men and women. Henry's tender care of her mother, almost a doting now that she expected his babies, often raised a desire in Beth to be treated in a like manner by a man.

At other times, she feared that much attention would smother her.

Risking a glance at Andrew as he drove slowly toward her house, she wondered if he would emulate his uncle in how he treated his wife. In all likelihood, yes. Most of the Mennonite men were more like Henry than like Mitch. Certainly that would include Andrew.

He pulled up beside the mailbox, put the truck in PARK, and opened his door.

"I can get it!" Beth's voice burst out more loudly than she intended. He sent her a puzzled look. "I mean," she added lamely, twiddling with the door handle, "there's no need for you to run around the truck when the mailbox is on my side."

Slowly he closed his door, offering a nod. "All right."

She popped the door open, dashed to the corrugated metal box, and peeked inside. Three envelopes, including the one from the Fox Gallery, waited. She snatched them out and slid back into the warmth of the truck's cab. "Got it."

She slipped the envelopes into her purse as Andrew turned the truck around and headed back to the studio. After parking behind the studio, they walked together to the café. Even though Beth was in the lead, Andrew reached past her and opened the door, gesturing her through. She offered a wavering smile of thanks as she unzipped her coat.

Trina bounced over the moment they slid into a booth, her smile bright. "Two specials?"

"Yes, please, and two coffees with cream and sugar." Andrew answered for both of them, giving Beth a rush of frustration. She could place her own order!

"Be right back," Trina promised and dashed to the counter, which held coffee mugs and a brown plastic carafe.

"Coffee okay?" Andrew's quirked brow and hesitant tone smoothed Beth's ruffled feathers. He meant well.

"Sure, it's fine." Leaning back, she sighed. "It always smells so good in here."

Andrew sniffed deeply, his nostrils flaring. "Deborah's a good cook. As good as your great-aunt was, I'd say." He gave a quick glance around. "At least, it's just as busy in here as it always was when Miss Koeppler ran it."

Beth glanced around, too. Deborah had made no changes in decor. The same simple tables, plain walls, and tiled floor that Great-Aunt Lisbeth had installed when she opened the café in the mid-1960s gave the feeling of stepping back in time when one entered the café. If Beth had chosen to keep the café, she would have updated everything. But apparently the decor didn't put anyone off, because the café maintained a steady flow of business.

Trina bustled over with two steaming mugs and a little silver pitcher of creamy white liquid. "There you go. Chili and cinnamon rolls coming right up." She zipped off before either Andrew or Beth could thank her.

Beth chuckled fondly. "That Trina is a real go-getter."

Andrew frowned slightly as he gazed after Trina's departing back. "Yes, she is. . . ." He looked at Beth, and his expression cleared. "You were real smart to build your studio next to the café. When you finally get your showroom up and running, the business from here should just trickle over."

Beth smiled. "That's the plan." She leaned forward, propping her chin in her hands. "But in the meantime, the craft fairs will get my name out there and bring in money."

Andrew's brow crunched into a curious scowl. "You pay me a wage for helping, and I know you have other expenses. Those craft fairs don't make that much. So how are you keeping things afloat right now?"

Beth straightened in her seat, setting her lips in a firm line as she contemplated not answering at all. Since when did an employee stick his nose into an employer's business? The feeling that Andrew was becoming too territorial returned, flooding her with indignation. She formed a response. "As long as you're getting paid, you shouldn't need to worry about it."

His face blotched with color.

At his obvious embarrassment, Beth experienced a pang of remorse. He'd been a good friend, and without his help, she probably wouldn't be enjoying her current success. She forced a casual shrug and said, "I have a couple of credit cards I've been using to get things going."

Andrew's expression told her clearly he disapproved of her means of staying afloat.

The fine hairs on her neck bristled at his silent, condemning look. "But I'll be able to pay them in full and still be ahead financially when I finish the window, so it's not a big deal."

"Using credit cards is borrowing trouble," he said, chin tucked low and brows pinched.

"Well, it isn't your trouble," she snapped, "so don't let it worry you."

He jerked upright, his ears glowing bright red, and he shifted to peer across the café rather than looking at her. Regret flooded her. To be honest, the growing amount on her card concerned her, too, and his comments only increased her worries. But she shouldn't take her anxieties out on him, even if his comments were unwarranted.

She opened her mouth to apologize, but Trina interrupted, delivering crock bowls filled with thick, aromatic chili and a plate of cinnamon rolls. By the time she'd asked a silent blessing, Beth decided it was less awkward to leave the topic of finances closed.

She couldn't, however, set aside the feeling that Andrew was assuming a bigger interest in her affairs than was prudent. For either of them. She would need to find a way to communicate where he fit in Quinn's Stained-Glass Art Studio.

Eleven

Andrew placed the paper pattern on a piece of mottled lavender glass and slowly drew around it with a marker. His gaze was fixed on the tip on the pen by necessity—multicolored, textured glass was twice the cost of smooth, single-colored, and he didn't dare make an error in marking—but his ears were tuned to the quiet conversation taking place at the platform.

Beth sat on the edge of the raised wooden box with Sean McCauley beside her. At least the man kept a respectable distance, although he tended to lean his head close to hers occasionally to peek at the sketch pad she held in her lap. Every time his reddish hair drew near Beth's shining blond locks, a band seemed to clamp tighter around Andrew's heart. That's why he'd stopped looking. But he couldn't ignore the mumbled voices, the soft laughter, the sound of two people talking as if completely at ease with one another. The way he wished he and Beth would talk.

His chest tightened another notch.

How did a man get completely comfortable with a woman? The only woman with whom Andrew was able to communicate easily on a consistent basis was his cousin Trina. Of course, at seventeen, she was barely a woman, and she'd always been like a little sister. It was hardly the same thing. He hated how he got tongue-tied and hot in the ears when conversing with a woman.

It had taken weeks for him to grow comfortable enough to talk to Beth without her speaking first. He had even been able to tease with her a little. He liked it—the playful sparring. It reminded him of Uncle Henry with his wife, Marie. Even though they were old already—entering their forties—they acted like young teenagers and bantered good-naturedly. Every now and then, he'd been able to do that with Beth. Until McCauley came along. That had changed things between them.

Setting aside the piece of lavender glass, he risked a quick, sidelong glance at the pair at the platform. Beth's attentive expression, the slight curve of her rosy lips as she listened to whatever McCauley was telling her, brought a rush of jealousy so strong Andrew's hands quivered. When he picked up a piece of green glass, the thick square slipped from his grasp and clanked against the worktable.

Beth's gaze swung in his direction, her brows high.

He held up both hands as if under arrest. "Nothing broken. It's okay."

She offered a brief nod, then returned her attention to McCauley without a word. The band around Andrew's chest nearly cut off his breath. Sucking air through his nose, he forced his hands to cease their quivering and picked up the pen. *Don't look at them, don't listen to them, just focus.* But a burst of laughter sent the pen squiggling across the square of glass. Quickly, he snatched up a dry erase marker from beneath the worktable and scribbled it over the errant mark. A firm scrub with a paper towel removed every trace of the black line, and he blew out a relieved breath.

A glance in the direction of the platform confirmed Beth had witnessed his error. His ears burned. He wished McCauley would hurry up and leave so things could return to normal! But, Andrew realized as he bent over the table to move the marker slowly around the paper pattern, things would be forever changed with this new contract of Beth's. McCauley would be a permanent fixture.

He felt as though he stood in the middle of a seesaw, with the board waffling up and down and carrying his thoughts with it. Having McCauley as a permanent fixture meant the success of the studio, but it also meant having Beth's attention claimed by the other man. So did Andrew want success, or did he want Beth?

His hands stilled and he turned to examine his boss. The internal seesaw froze in place perfectly parallel to the ground. He wanted both. And his father would not approve of either.

Sean sensed Andrew's gaze boring a hole through him. It took Herculean effort not to shift his head to meet it and send the man a glowering frown. Andrew's protective act, while perhaps endearing to Beth, made it difficult for Sean to focus on Beth. And Sean was discovering a deep desire to focus solely on Beth.

"Do you mind if I take this sketch with me?" Sean pointed to the pad in her lap.

She wrinkled her nose as if uncertain. "It's just preliminary based on your description. I can't imagine it would be very impressive. If I had a photograph of the old church, though, I could make a much better drawing."

Sean battled a grin. He admired her perfectionism—it would serve him and his company well. "And if they like the idea, I'll bring you a photograph. But I need something to show them the potential. So. . . may I?"

Only inches from her, he could see his reflection in her irises. As he stared into the deep blue depths of her eyes, some emotion flitted through—mistrust? Confusion? Before he could fully process it, she lowered her gaze, ripped the drawing from the pad, and thrust it at him.

He took it, his forehead creasing into a slight frown at her abrupt action, but then he offered a smile. "Thank you." Slipping it into the leather folder that rested against his leg, he said, "I know this will help the committee see what I envision. We can worry about a detailed, accurate sketch after we've gotten their approval to proceed."

Beth nodded, swinging a quick glance in Andrew's direction. Sean turned his head in time to see Andrew give a nod of approval. He voiced what he assumed the pair were thinking: "If this committee approves you creating a window that resembles the original church building, you'll have two major projects to complete. Pretty exciting, isn't it?"

Beth's wide-eyed expression didn't appear as much excited as terrified. She chuckled softly, rubbing her finger beneath her nose. "Andrew and I will have to burn the midnight oil to stay on top of everything."

Andrew's grin let Sean know he wouldn't mind burning the midnight oil with Beth. A stab of jealousy pinched Sean's chest, but he forced a smile and pushed to his feet, bouncing the leather folder against his trouser-covered thigh. "I have confidence you'll be able to handle it."

Beth rose, too, holding her hand toward Sean. He took it, her palm cool and smooth, and gave her fingers a gentle squeeze. "Thanks again for spending your morning with me, Beth. I know you have things to do, so I appreciate the time you took to help get this idea solidified in my head."

Her hand still in his, her gaze flitted toward the mess on the platform that would eventually turn into a stained-glass window. Another soft laugh tripped out, almost nervous in its delivery. "The hour I spent with you means I have to make it up this evening."

That wasn't exactly the response he hoped for. "I'm sorry."

Her startled gaze met his. "Oh! I didn't mean—" Her face flooded with pink, and she jerked her hand free from his grasp. "I wasn't complaining. Really. This time we spent—it's an investment in my future, so it's worth it."

"Good." He remained rooted in place, peering into her eyes and gaining courage. There was something more he wanted to ask. Nibbling his mustache, he wished Andrew would leave the studio.

Beth stood silently, too, her hands tangled in the tails of her sloppy work shirt.

Finally, Sean blurted, "I wondered. . ."

She tipped her head. "Yes?"

"Well, after I meet with the committee in Carlton, I might need to meet with you again. If they like this stained-glass window idea, I'll ask for a photograph right away, and I could drop it by so you'd have it to work from. And maybe we could. . ."

Her eyes shot briefly toward Andrew. Sean looked sideways to find Andrew staring boldly in their direction. Simultaneously, he and Beth shifted, their shoulders coming together with Andrew at their backs. He was certain she smirked. Maybe she didn't find the Mennonite man's protectiveness as much endearing as annoying.

In a whisper, she said, "We could. . . ?"

Sean cleared his throat. "We could talk over dinner. I've heard the little café here in Sommerfeld is good. Could we meet there at, maybe, six thirty?"

Sean was certain that disappointment twisted Beth's lips, giving him a rush of satisfaction despite her negative response. "I'm sorry.

The café is always closed on Mondays." From behind them, Andrew coughed. A contrived cough, Sean was sure. He resisted looking at the man.

"Oh." Sean smoothed his mustache with two fingers, observing Beth's attention on his motion. "Well, then, I could take you into Newton. I'm sure something will be open there." He winked. "Unless you really do need to stay here this evening and make up the hour I stole from your day."

They laughed softly together. Beth answered quickly. "Dinner out sounds great."

"Good. Will you be here or at your house?"

Andrew cleared his throat loudly. "Beth, is dinner out a good idea?"

Both Sean and Beth turned to face Andrew. Although his face appeared deeper in hue, he spoke in a bold, authoritative tone. "If you go out, you'll end up leaving earlier than usual to. . .gussy up." The man's neck blotched purple. "That's even more lost time. Can you afford it?"

Sean fought a laugh as Beth glared at Andrew, her jaw set in a stubborn angle. Without responding to her employee, she turned her face to Sean. "I'll be at my house. When you come back into town, just turn left off of Main Street onto First. I'm on the corner of First and Cottonwood, one block west of Main. The white bungalow. I'll have the porch light on."

A "harrumph" actually came from the worktable. "All the porch lights will be on by then," Andrew said. He swung a pair of goggles in his hand, a silent message that he had work to do.

Beth drew a deep breath, her eyes spitting fire. But when she looked back at Sean, a smile washed away the fury. "It'll be the white bungalow with the wraparound front porch, spirea bushes under the front window, *and* a porch light on. Does that help?"

Sean chose to ignore Andrew's second, softer snort. "I'm sure I can find you. Sommerfeld isn't that large."

"True enough."

They shared an amused grin, and Sean found himself tempted to lean forward and place a kiss on her softly curving lips. The sound of the cutting wheel split the air. Beth gave a start, and Sean jerked backward, bumping his heels on the platform. He caught his balance, swung a wide-eyed look toward Andrew, then took a stumbling step toward the door.

"Six thirty," he hollered over the sound of the cutter. His jacket draped over his arm, he headed out the door.

Beth paced the living room floor, the heels of her black dress boots clumping against the carpet. Despite her efforts to set aside the aggravation, she still stewed about Andrew's rudeness hours ago. She wondered if Sean would show up after his abrupt departure from the studio. Recalling how he practically ran for the door without bothering to put on his jacket made her blood boil. She and Andrew really needed to have a talk.

Mom had always told her to think before she spoke, especially when she was upset or angry. That advice had kept her silent over the past week. Whenever the urge to confront Andrew arose, it came with a wave of frustration or anger, and she didn't want to dishonor God by being unkind. So she'd wait, and then she'd forget. Until the next time he irritated her. She felt caught in a merry-go-round and didn't care for the sensation.

What had gotten into him, anyway? His first weeks in the studio, he'd been the model employee, following her directions, working meticulously and quietly, showing up early and expressing a willingness to stay late, and offering her endless support. But lately? It seemed he was trying to rise to the top and wanted to use her as the stepping stool to get there. What had brought about the change?

Her pacing ceased, her heart firing into her throat as realization struck. Andrew's attitude change coincided with Sean McCauley's visit to her studio. But why? Before she had a chance to explore the reasoning behind Andrew's behavior, a tap at her door signaled the arrival of a visitor. Charging to the front door, she swung it open and returned the smile Sean McCauley offered.

"Right on time," she said, glancing at the silver watch that circled her wrist.

"And you're ready to go." His eyes glowed with approval.

"Yes, well, punctuality has been drilled into me from an early age." She underscored her words with a light laugh, reaching for her coat, which hung on a hall tree beside the front door. "My mother always said—"

Sean plucked the coat from her hands and held it open. For a moment, she stared at the coat, her heart tripping through her chest at a pace far above normal. Then turning her back to him, she slipped her arms into the sleeves and finished her thought in a reedy tone. "Being late is disrespectful. Respectfulness has always been one of her favorite virtues."

"I think our mothers would get along well then."

She faced him, sliding her hands behind her neck to release her hair from the coat's collar. His gaze seemed to follow the tumble of her curls across her shoulder, and a surprising warmth filled her cheeks. "So, have you decided on a restaurant?"

He shrugged, grinning. "I'm the new one around these parts, so you choose."

"A place called the Apple Barrel is right off the highway on the outskirts of Newton, and they have a good variety of menu choices."

"That'll do. Let's go." He held the door open for her, and as she passed through, she felt his hand lightly press the small of her back. The whisper touch sent a shiver of pleasure up her spine and a wave of heat to her face. The chill evening air whisked across her, cooling her cheeks. She hugged herself and danced in place while waiting for him to unlock the car door.

His smile as he popped the car door open for her sent a second rush of fire through her face. While she waited for him to round the car and get behind the wheel, she reminded herself this was a business dinner, not a date. But her jumbled nerves didn't settle down until midway through the meal.

Sean carried a seasoned french fry to his mouth, bit off the end, and chewed, the movement of his mustache oddly fascinating. Beth wasn't unfamiliar with facial hair—Mitch had deliberately waited days between shaving to give himself a rugged Indiana Jones appearance—but Sean's neatly groomed, red-gold mustache was a far cry from Mitch's dark shadow.

An image of Andrew's clean-shaven face with its square chin and firm jaw popped into her mind, competing with the mental pictures of Mitch and the real-life view of Sean across the table. To rid herself of the parade of images, she approached the purpose of their time together.

"You haven't told me whether the church committee was interested in your idea."

Sean's face lit up. "Ah, my idea. . ." He used his napkin to wipe his mouth and hands, set the wadded paper square aside, and leaned forward, eagerness in his bearing. "They liked my idea very much and would like to see an official sketch of the proposed window."

Two major projects in quick succession! Beth caught her breath. "Wow!"

Sean laughed, his teeth flashing. "Wow, indeed. They gave me a copy of their church directory, which has photographs of the church building for you to use in creating your sketch. The photos are black and white, so I also have a description of the building to help you decide on appropriate colors."

Beth put down her fork. "You must be a great salesman."

Sean shrugged, grinning. "I know my business." The statement, while confident, didn't sound cocky. He placed his elbows on the table edge and linked his fingers together. "I've been praying for quite a while about this particular project. The committee was so firmly divided into two ranks, I knew I'd need to find a way to bridge their different goals. Having a modern building with a beautifully crafted Beth Quinn window serving as a reminder of the original building turned out to be a compromise they could accept."

"I'm so glad." Beth realized she was pleased for two different reasons. First, it offered her another opportunity to build her business. And second, Sean indicated he had prayed about the project. His easy acknowledgment of consulting God gave her a feeling of security and increased her admiration for him.

Sean reached across the table to cup his hand over hers. "And I'm so glad we're in this together. I think you are going to be a wonderful asset to McCauley Church Construction. Making use of your skills is one of the smartest moves I've made."

The feeling of security instantly fled.

TWELVE

Sean observed Beth's smile fade, her eyes taking on a wariness he'd witnessed on earlier occasions. But he had no idea what had caused the change. Removing his hand from hers, he reached for another french fry and a different topic.

"So, tell me about your family. You mentioned you grew up in Wyoming even though your mom was raised in Sommerfeld. Do you have any brothers or sisters?"

Beth's gaze narrowed, as if she were trying to read more into his question than what existed, but after a moment, her expression relaxed and a slight smile teased the corners of her lips. "Not quite yet."

Her cryptic reply raised Sean's eyebrows. "Not quite yet?"

Her grin grew. "My mother is expecting twins in mid-May."

Sean whistled through his teeth. "Wow! Why'd she wait so long to have more children?" He realized how abrupt the question sounded, but to his relief, Beth didn't appear insulted.

She took a sip of her cola and shrugged. "My father died in an accident before I was born. It was just Mom and me during all of my growing-up years. Then when we returned to Sommerfeld, Mom's childhood sweetheart started courting her again. They married a little over a year ago. Henry had never married, so having a family was important to him. They were both thrilled when they found out Mom was pregnant."

"I bet." Sean tried to imagine being in his early twenties and becoming a big brother. The picture wouldn't gel. He observed, "She must have been pretty young when she had you."

Another casual shrug lifted Beth's shoulders. "Eighteen when she married my dad, nineteen when she had me."

"And widowed at nineteen." Sean felt a rush of sympathy toward this woman he didn't know. "She must be very strong."

"She is." Beth's eyes glimmered briefly. "She's a wonderful mom."

Sean nodded. She must have been a good mother to have raised such a strong, capable daughter. His admiration for Beth grew with the knowledge of what must have been a difficult childhood. "And now she'll be a mom again." He shook his head, chuckling. "Twins, huh? That'll keep her busy."

Beth offered a silent nod, lifting a bite of salad to her mouth.

Gesturing with a french fry, Sean said, "It's good you're close by. You'll be able to help her."

"Oh, she's got lots of family around for that. I'll be busy in my studio."

The glib tone seemed to carry an undercurrent Sean was tempted to explore, but he decided their relationship was too new to go digging below the surface. So he threw out another question. "Have you ever thought about relocating your studio?"

Beth's fork froze between her plate and her mouth. "Why do you ask that?"

There was no denying the challenge in her tone. He frowned slightly. "Curiosity. I know you said you hoped to garner some of the café's business when you open a showroom, but I would imagine in a small town like that, you're still limiting yourself. A larger city might hold more opportunities for you."

Beth put her fork down without taking the bite. "Did you have a city in mind?"

Sean's frown deepened. The defensiveness she presented at times seemed so alien to her soft appearance. What brought about these mercurial mood swings? "Not particularly. Although remaining in Kansas would be good if you plan to ship projects throughout the United States. It's centrally located."

"Well"—she picked up the fork again—"Sommerfeld is in central Kansas, so I think I'll just stay put." She chewed the bite of lettuce, swallowed, and then continued. "Besides, you haven't been around in the warmer seasons. Between the farmers' market, carriage rides, and café, plus the demonstrations for wheat-weaving, quilting, and harness-making, Sommerfeld teems with activity on the weekends. And all of those tourists are prime candidates for exploring my showroom."

He swallowed a chuckle. Her fervent defense of Sommerfeld was almost amusing in its intensity. He wondered briefly whom she tried to convince: him or herself. Biting off the end of a french fry, he raised his brows to indicate interest. "Harness-making demonstrations and carriage rides? I thought the Mennonites had converted to using automobiles."

"Most in Sommerfeld have," Beth said, "but their Amish neighbors have not. They combine forces for these weekend events, since the visitors are mutually beneficial."

"I see." Sean chewed and swallowed thoughtfully while Beth pushed the remainder of her salad around on her plate with the prongs of her fork. Something struck him. "You don't claim to be Amish or Mennonite. You must feel like an odd duck in that community."

She dropped her fork with a clatter against the plate. Fixing him with a steady look, she took in a deep breath through her nose. "Sean, I'm not moving my studio. My mother is settled in Sommerfeld, and she's my only family. I've told you several reasons why my location works for me. Please do not continue to try to influence me to go somewhere else even if it's more convenient for you. 'Odd duck' or not, I won't disrupt my life again for any man."

Ah. Suddenly the wariness, the defensiveness, the mood swings all made sense. Setting the french fry down, Sean pushed his plate aside and said softly, "So what was his name?"

Beth's cheeks streaked with pink. She fiddled with her napkin, her eyes downcast. "Whose name?"

He released a low, light chuckle. "The man who disrupted your life."

The red stain in her cheeks deepened. She shot him a stern look. "That isn't important." Flopping her napkin over her plate with one hand, she lifted her glass with the other and took a long draw that helped return her face to its natural color. She put down the glass, jiggled it to make the ice clink, then set her chin at a proud angle. "I believe the purpose of this evening was to discuss the church window. So let's get to it, huh?"

Her meaning was clear. Her personal life was *her* personal life, and he would need to keep his distance. Well, he'd follow her lead. . .for the moment. He could stick to business for now. But as their business relationship grew, he fully intended to pursue her on a more intimate level. Beth Quinn was far too intriguing for him to remain forever distanced.

Beth yanked open the drawer containing goggles and snatched up a pair. The rubber headband caught on something, and when she gave a hard jerk to free the goggles, the band snapped against the side of her thumb.

"Ouch!" She sucked the stinging spot. The back door swung open, and Andrew stepped through, catching her with her thumb in her mouth. She swung her hand abruptly downward and slammed her wrist on the edge of the open drawer. With another yelp, she thumped the drawer shut with her hip. The tail of her shirt caught in the drawer, holding her captive.

Releasing a loud "Uh!" of aggravation, she grabbed her shirt and tried to jerk it free, only to hear the flannel tear. She puffed her cheeks and blew a noisy breath toward the ceiling.

Andrew's laughter rang, filling the room.

For one brief moment, she glared at him. Then she felt a grin twitch her cheeks. How ridiculous she must have looked first with her thumb in her mouth and then attached to a drawer by her own shirttail. Imagining it from his viewpoint, her frustration evaporated, and she couldn't help but laugh, too.

He strode forward, pulled the drawer open a few inches, and removed the tattered tail of her shirt. He stuck his fingers through the tear, chuckling. "And how is your morning?" Dropping the fabric, he grinned at her.

"I think you already know the answer to that," she retorted in a saucy tone, but she smirked. His easy laughter and teasing comment gave her heart a lift. With an exaggerated sigh, she added, "I hope this start isn't an indication of how the whole day will go."

"Stay away from the drawers, and you should be okay," he advised.

She teasingly held up her hands and took one giant sidestep away from the storage unit.

Andrew grinned at her, but then his brow pulled down. He

crossed his arms. "Did you get any sleep last night?"

"That obvious, huh?" She moved toward the worktable, forcing him to shift back a few feet. The truth was, she'd gotten little sleep. Her mind had kept replaying bits of her dinner conversation with Sean McCauley. Even after prayer, she felt troubled by his seeming overzealous interest in her studio and subtle attempts to convince her to relocate.

If only he weren't such a handsome package, it might be easier to set thoughts of him aside. Unfortunately, the feminine side of her felt drawn to his boyish charm and obvious intelligence. But, she told herself firmly, he wasn't worth losing sleep over!

Andrew leaned against the opposite side of the worktable and watched her slide the goggles into place. "Did McCauley keep you out all night?"

The easy camaraderie she'd felt only moments before now swept away. "No!" She slapped the goggles onto the tabletop and pointed at him. "And don't even think of mentioning something like that to anyone in your family! My mother doesn't need to be worrying about me."

Andrew drew back, his eyes wide. "I—I don't talk about you to—"

"Oh yes, you do. But not this time, Andrew." Her anger grew, tiredness and frustration welling up to spew like steam from a boiling pot. "In fact, not ever again, for any reason. Do you know how tiresome it is to have everyone knowing my business? To go to the café for a cup of coffee and have people mention things that don't concern them at all? I don't like being the topic of gossip. If you're going to continue working here, I've got to be able to trust you. And that means *you— don't—talk*."

She glared into Andrew's stricken face. Guilt smacked her. What was she doing, haranguing him in such an unprofessional manner?

Her mother's admonition to think before she spoke came back to haunt her, but it came too late. She couldn't take back the words she'd just poured out.

The expression on Andrew's face, however, made her wish she could.

She closed her eyes, asking God to calm her racing heart and tumbling thoughts. When she opened her eyes, she found Andrew still leaning on the worktable, seeming to examine his hands. She reached across the table and tapped his wrist. When he raised his gaze to meet hers, she spoke.

"Andrew, I'm sorry I snapped at you. I am tired. It's not because I was out all night—I was home by nine o'clock." Why she felt the need for him to know that, she wasn't sure. She only knew she felt compelled to assure him. "But I had a lot on my mind, so I didn't sleep well, and I guess I'm grumpy."

His expression didn't change.

She sighed, fluttering her eyelashes and peeking at him out of the corners of her eyes. "I'm grumpy a lot?"

He sucked in his lips—an obvious attempt to stop a grin from growing.

Now that he'd lost the hurt look, she stopped goofing around and faced him squarely. "I really am sorry. I do get aggravated when Trina or Henry mention things they could know only if you told them. It makes me feel like people are talking behind my back."

Andrew straightened and placed one hand against his chest. "I don't talk about you out of maliciousness. It's because I'm excited for the things happening here for us."

Beth's antenna went up. She carefully tempered her tone. "You mean for *me*. It's my studio, Andrew, not ours."

His ears glowed. "That's what I meant."

She nodded slowly. "I hope so. I need your help on projects, and I need McCauley's contracts to get everything up and running around here, but both of you are going to have to understand that the studio is *my* business. It's going to stay that way."

Andrew remained silent, his narrowed gaze pinned to hers. She held her breath, waiting for him to tell her she was out of line in her expectation.

"Okay. You're the boss."

At his flat comment, she nearly sagged with relief. Although his words were pushed past a tense jaw, she hoped she'd made herself clear about where he fit in the studio. She also hoped it would be the end of his possessiveness concerning the studio. And her.

"Great." She slid the goggles back in place. "I've got to sand the edges of these pieces for the McCauley window. With the number of pieces involved, I speculate I'll be sanding all week."

"And you need me to. . . ?"

She nodded toward the cutting wheel as she picked up the carborundum stone and began whisking it across the edge of a piece of cornflower blue glass. "It wouldn't hurt to make up a few more crosses and butterflies. The e-mail I got from the organizer of the President's Day Extravaganza said they expect a great turnout. I'd rather have too many than not enough."

Andrew's jaw dropped. "The craft show—it's this Saturday."

Beth's hand paused. "Yes. We've had it on the calendar for months."

He slapped his forehead. "I didn't make the connection."

Beth put the stone down. "What's the problem?"

"The men are meeting at Uncle Henry's on Saturday to put up the walls and roof for his addition. They want to get it going before the farmers need to be out in the fields. I had hoped. . ."

Beth didn't need to hear the remainder of his sentence to know what he'd hoped. But she'd already lost time this week with the meetings with Sean. She couldn't take Saturday off to man her booth, yet she counted on those sales to cover the expense of having made the suncatchers plus expenses involved with keeping the studio open. Andrew already knew all of that; she wouldn't spell it out for him. She simply waited for him to decide what to do.

With a sigh, he gave a nod. "There will be plenty of men around to help with the addition. I'll go to Salina like we'd planned."

"Good."

Andrew turned toward the drawer that contained the patterns, and Beth leaned over her pieces of glass. As she whisked the stone along the edge of the diamond-shaped piece, her thoughts skipped ahead to Saturday. She had fully intended to work all day in the studio. But after the community—organized by Henry—had rallied around her in erecting the building that housed her business, didn't she have an obligation to help in the construction of the room addition?

Once more the question stabbed her heart: *Where do I fit in?*

THIRTEEN

Beth and Andrew worked in quiet amity the remainder of the week—Beth grinding until her fingers ached from gripping the glass and stone, and Andrew constructing another dozen suncatchers. Sean McCauley called twice to check on progress and forward a couple of questions from the church in Carlton. Each time, Beth sensed Andrew's disapproval, which gave her a slight feeling of unrest, but she managed to sweep it away. On the Saturday morning of the craft show, she watched him load the boxes of foam-cushioned suncatchers into the back of his pickup truck.

As usual, he'd dressed in his Sunday suit for the fair. In his workday clothes of dark trousers, solid button-up shirt, and suspenders, he could blend in with farmers outside of Sommerfeld. But the black homemade suit with no lapels on the jacket, a light blue shirt buttoned to the collar, and the black, flat-brimmed felt hat marked him as Mennonite. Each time they'd attended a fair, his attire had drawn curious gazes and a few bold questions. She'd recognized his unease in fielding queries about his "Amish" clothing in the past, and she had frequently explained the differences between the Amish and Mennonites who lived in Sommerfeld. Today he'd have to answer questions himself, and his silence told her he wasn't keen on going alone.

"It's too bad Trina can't go with you." Beth knew Trina was the favorite of many of her cousins, Andrew included. Her bubbly personality added a healthy dose of fun wherever she went.

Andrew grunted. "Yeah, I'd like that, but Aunt Deborah would never let her loose from the café. Especially today, with half the town turning out to help Uncle Henry. Aunt Deborah plans to take lunch over for all the workers, and she'll need Trina to get it accomplished."

"Sure seems like Kyra or someone might have been willing to take Trina's place," Beth mused. Kyra, one of Beth's many cousins, often helped out in the café.

"She *is* helping," Andrew said, giving the hatch of his pickup a firm slam. "Aunt Deborah needs both Trina and Kyra today."

"Oh." The crisp air tugged strands of her hair free of her ponytail and whipped them beneath her chin, tickling her. She shoved the errant strands behind her ear and squinted up at Andrew. Beneath the brim of his hat, his shadowed eyes appeared uneasy. "Well, I'm sorry you have to go alone, but you look very handsome."

The instant the word *handsome* slipped from Beth's tongue, embarrassment washed over her. It increased when she saw his ears turn bright red before he ducked his head, pulling his hat brim lower. But it was true. Andrew, with his close-cropped hair, dark eyes, and solid frame, was a handsome man. The unpretentious clothes in some odd way seemed to accentuate his rugged attractiveness rather than detract from it. Maybe if he realized it, he would set aside some of his insecurities and feel more confident.

So she ignored the awkwardness of the moment and added, "I am positive you will single-handedly sell out of suncatchers and bring back orders for more."

He chuckled, a low, throaty sound that made Beth smile. "Whatever you say, boss."

She laughed out loud, then waved as he climbed into his pickup and drove out of the alley. Turning toward the door of the studio, she heard a sound, an echoing, sharp ring. A hammer hitting a nail. Then came another, followed rapidly by two more. The rings came in closer succession, taking on the semblance of off-pitch bells, and Beth realized it was a chorus of hammers.

The men were already at work on Henry's addition. She quickly stepped into the studio and closed the door, but even behind the steel door, the sound of clanging came through. Guilt hit hard. She should be helping like everyone else was. The rooms were for her new siblings. What would people think if she didn't come?

She walked to the platform and looked down at the array of glass pieces waiting to have their edges ground. The grinding was taking much longer than she had anticipated given the weight of the glass and the number of pieces. She rubbed the calluses on her thumbs, grimacing at the roughness of her hands.

Maybe she'd wear gloves today, even though it was harder to control the carborundum stone with the bulky leather. Or maybe she'd use her credit card and purchase an electric grinder, even though she worried she'd ruin some pieces while learning to operate it.

Clang! Clang–clang–ring!

The hammer sound called to her. She drew a deep breath, debating with herself. Her gaze went from the scattered pieces of the glass to the window then back to the glass. With a disgruntled huff, she marched to the radio in the corner and snapped it on. Music covered the hammer rings. Returning to the platform with carborundum stone in hand, she plunked down and lifted a red diamond.

But the moment the stone touched the glass, the image of a

hammer connecting with the head of a nail intruded. She knew she would not be able to focus unless she at least made an appearance at the house.

After bundling up in her heavy jacket and scarf, she decided to leave the car and walk. It was only six blocks, and the late February morning was crisp but not unbearably cold. The clear sky seemed to echo the choir of nail strikes, making Beth's ears ring. Halfway there, she picked up the sounds of voices and muffled laughter in addition to the ringing of hammers. For some reason, the mingling sounds made her chest feel tight.

When she rounded the final corner and glimpsed the clusters of townspeople, the tightness in her chest increased. The women, with their skirts showing beneath the hems of plain wool coats and their heads covered with simple white caps, made Beth feel slovenly in her faded blue jeans and short suede jacket with her ponytail tumbling over her shoulder. Her steps slowed, and she considered returning to her shop.

But a masculine voice called out, "Beth!" Heads turned. She'd been spotted. Lifting her hand to wave at Henry, who smiled from his perch on a roof rafter, she closed the remaining distance between herself and the group where her mother stood.

"Hi, honey!" Mom greeted her with a hug and a press of her cold nose to Beth's cheek. "I'm glad you came by. Look at that!" Mom's breath, released on a sigh, hung in the morning air. "It never ceases to amaze me how well they work together."

Beth's gaze followed her mother's to the addition. Already the studs clearly marked the peripheries of the room, and the rafters connected with the existing roof. At least a dozen men swarmed over the skeleton, adding crossbars and securing the rafters to the wall studs. More applied saws to lengths of wood laid across sawhorses or unloaded Sheetrock and plywood from the backs of pickup trucks.

"By noon," Mom continued, her arm around Beth's waist, "they'll probably have the roof sheathed and ready for shingles."

A woman on Mom's right released a snort. "Not if Nort Borntrager has anything to do with it. Look at him over there, leaning on the Mullers' car hood as if he's already earned a break."

"And I saw him eating buns instead of unloading lumber," another contributed.

As they watched, the man pushed himself free and ambled toward the sawhorses. He stood, hands in pockets, watching the wielder of the saw. A yawn nearly divided his face.

The cluster of women clucked their disapproval. One said with no small measure of sarcasm, "That Nort, he's so slow you have to look twice to see him move."

The women all chuckled, and even Beth fought a grin. Someone like Nort, who watched rather than worked, was the exception rather than the rule when it came to the hardworking attitude the Mennonites possessed. But then she swallowed her grin, her hands clenching within the pockets of her trendy jacket. What might these women say about her when she wasn't in earshot?

She ducked her head, taking in the sea of skirts surrounding her denim-clad legs. Discomfort pressed harder. Just as Nort's laziness set him apart, her attire set her apart. Once more, the feeling of being a misfit washed over Beth. Her heart pounding, she raised her gaze to her stepfather, who straddled a rafter and swung his hammer with precision. A glance to the side confirmed her mother also watched Henry.

By joining the church and marrying Henry, Mom had reestablished her place in the community. Beth knew her mother had never been more content than she was in her role as Mrs. Henry Braun, accepted resident of Sommerfeld, Kansas. Jealousy hit, surprising Beth with its intensity. As much as she wanted to feel as though she belonged, did she want everything else that would be required to be accepted here?

She tried to envision herself in the head covering and simple dress of the Mennonite women, and she nearly laughed out loud. No doubt she'd look ridiculous! She squirmed within the confines of her jacket and ducked her gaze once more. The sight of her mother's legs next to hers gave her a jolt of concern.

"Mom, you're all swollen again."

The hand at Beth's waist slipped away, and Mom tucked her coat beneath her belly to look at her feet. She grimaced. "Oh, goodness, and I've hardly been up. Well"—she flipped her hands outward in a nonchalant gesture—"at least I'm consistent. This puffiness has become the norm."

"But it isn't normal, is it?" Beth pressed, worry making her heart thud in tempo with the hammers that continued to pound.

One of the other ladies in the group shook her head and pursed her lips at Beth. "Now, young lady, don't fuss at your mother. We check on her every day, and she always says she feels fine. A little swelling isn't uncommon."

Beth bristled at the implication that she didn't check on her mother as frequently as she should. She also didn't believe one would call what she was seeing a "little" swelling. Mom's legs looked puffy from the knees down, and the flesh extended over the tops of her brown oxfords. It looked painful and worthy of great concern.

She clamped her jaw and didn't answer. These women already saw her as an oddity who was too headstrong for good sense. She wouldn't argue and give them fuel for gossip about her. Instead, she offered a brief nod and looked back toward the workers.

She easily located Henry. From the back, his dark hair and broad shoulders reminded her of Andrew. How much Andrew resembled his uncle. Along with the thought of Andrew, a recurring idea teased the back of her mind. If she were to marry into the community, as her mother did, she would belong. *Really* belong. Remembering his formal bearing this morning and her comment on his handsomeness, she felt color flood her cheeks.

"Mom," she blurted out, jerking sideways two steps, "I'm going to head back to the studio. I have work to do."

The disapproving raised brows and pinched lips of the women standing nearby made Beth's face grow hotter.

"But I'll go to the café at noon and help Deborah carry lunch over, so I'll see you then, okay?"

Some of the women gave small nods of approval, their expressions softening. Beth wasn't sure if this pleased or aggravated her.

Mom moved forward on her swollen feet to offer a quick hug. "All right, honey. Enjoy your day."

Beth turned and fled.

Sean hung up the phone and stifled a frustrated groan. He replayed his father's parting comment: *"You're sidetracked, son. Focus. We've got deadlines to meet."*

He'd like to argue with his father. He'd like to say he was just as on top of things as he'd always been, but he knew it wouldn't be the truth. And he admitted only to himself, *sidetracked* wasn't a strong enough word to describe what had happened. He'd been completely derailed. By a blond-haired, blue-eyed, cleft-chinned artist whose sole focus was her art. Ever since their "business dinner" a week ago, he'd had a harder time setting aside thoughts of Beth. Despite the original intention, it hadn't been a business meeting, and Sean knew it.

Shaking his head, he looked toward the ceiling. "God, I prayed we'd find a dependable artist with a heart for You who would be willing to use his talents in our company. Did You have to send me to a woman too pretty and independent for her own good?"

He didn't get a reply. But he didn't expect to. God worked in mysterious ways, as Sean well knew, and he'd learned long ago to simply trust His judgment. But that was easier when it didn't affect every aspect of his life. He could not get Beth Quinn out of his mind.

Their relationship—such as it was—was only weeks old. They'd had little face-to-face contact, although he communicated with her daily by e-mail and weekly by telephone. How had such minimal connections managed to keep her in the forefront of his thoughts? He saw the checkout girl at the local grocery store more regularly than Beth. But the checkout girl didn't have that endearing cleft in her chin.

He pushed away from the drafting table and stormed to the kitchen, where he yanked open the refrigerator and grabbed a can of cherry-flavored cola. Popping the top, he stared at the silver ring and for the first time contemplated placing a gold ring on a woman's finger.

Without taking a sip, he plunked the can on the counter and spun toward the window. Looking across his neatly trimmed backyard, he tried to imagine working side by side with someone under the sun, putting in a garden—tomatoes, cucumbers, and green beans, like his parents did every year. Turning a slow circle, he envisioned sharing the cooking duties, sitting down with someone and holding hands to pray, loading the dishwasher after someone else rinsed the pots and plates.

In each case, the someone had a face. Beth.

He shook his head, grabbing up the can to take a long draw that did little to cool his racing thoughts. Hadn't she made it clear she had no interest in leaving that little town called Sommerfeld? Imagining her in his yard, his house—his *life*—was a waste of time.

"An exercise in futility," he said aloud, then drained the can. He dropped it into the recycling bin before returning to his office. Sliding into the chair at his tall drafting table, he picked up his pencil and T square and bent once more over the drawing pad. Although the final drawing would be done on computer, he always did hand sketches first. Applying the pencil to paper somehow made the building more real to him than when he created it on a computer screen. As his eyes followed his line of lead on the page, he suddenly pictured Beth's hand forming the peak of the little chapel from Carlton.

He sat straight up and slapped the pencil against the pad. "What will cure me of thinking of that girl?" he exclaimed to the empty room.

Oddly enough, a voice from his past offered a solution. His grandfather, for whom he'd been named, had once proclaimed, "The best cure for any ill is the hair of the dog that bit ya." Sean remembered how his mother had shaken her head in disapproval, and he'd learned later that often that statement was used in reference to imbibing. While neither of Sean's parents ever partook of alcoholic beverages, nor had Sean, that saying now seemed to offer a solution to his dilemma with Beth.

Perhaps a quick phone call. Hearing her voice, being reminded of how focused she was on her own work, would help him put his attention back where it belonged. Yes. He slid his cell phone from his pocket and flipped it open. Just a few minutes of conversation would certainly get him back on track.

He scrolled to Beth's number, pushed the TALK button, and lifted the phone to his ear.

FOURTEEN

Andrew glanced up as Beth placed the telephone earpiece on its cradle. The slight frown on her face captured his attention.

"Everything okay?" The question formed without effort. He knew she'd been talking to Sean McCauley—she used a different tone when she spoke to that man, a tone that always ruffled Andrew's feathers as much as he tried not to let it.

"Yes." Beth walked slowly to the platform, where she stopped, staring down at the pieces of glass that would form McCauley's window. But she didn't crouch to resume working.

Concerned, Andrew stepped beside her. He resisted touching her arm. "Are you sure? You don't look too happy."

Beth sighed and tipped her head to look at him. Andrew was struck by the circles under her eyes. Doing this window on her own was taking a tremendous toll. When would she realize she didn't need to carry this project alone? He waited for her to say something, but she remained silent, simply looking at him as if she expected him to do something, say something. But he stood motionless and silent, as well.

A second sigh escaped, and her attention returned to the window. Then, in a matter-of-fact tone that took him by surprise, she said, "Do you suppose you could take a break and go after another two dozen horseshoe nails?"

Andrew gave his head a quick shake. He felt as though he'd missed something between the phone call and now. "Horseshoe nails?"

"Yes." Still with her eyes aimed downward, she added, "I'll be needing them before too long."

He stared at her profile, trying to read beneath her bland expression, but he wasn't well enough versed in females to figure out what she was thinking.

She laughed lightly. Not a humorous laugh, but one that had a frightened ring to it. "Sean plans to drive over in the middle of next week to talk to the Carlton committee. He said he'd stop by and take a few pictures of the progress here." Crossing her arms, she sent Andrew a brief sidelong look. "Think he'll be pleased or disappointed?"

Andrew looked down at the makeshift design on the platform. Even though the pieces weren't connected and lay in a haphazard display of shapes and color, he could imagine the finished product. The window would be beautiful when completed. "Why would he be disappointed?"

"Because I'm not far enough along." The tinge of frustration came through. "I've got to pick up the pace."

Andrew took her arm and turned her to face him. Boldly, he brushed her cheek with his thumb right below her eye where the pale skin showed a hint of purple. The slight contact with her skin catapulted his heart into his throat. "The pace you've set now is doing you in. Have you looked in a mirror lately?"

Jerking her arm free, she stepped away from him and glared upward. "Thanks a lot."

Andrew realized how insulting his words must have been. He'd only meant to express concern for her obvious tiredness. Why couldn't he ever say the right thing when it came to Beth? "I didn't mean it that way."

He would have explained, but she shook her head, her bright hair swinging across her shoulders. "Forget it. I'm tired and testy, and I'm worried that this window isn't going to be done. I've used half my time already, and I'm not halfway there."

It was on the tip of Andrew's tongue to say, "Let me help," but he knew she would only rebuff him. Instead, he said, "You're on the downhill slide. The cutting and grinding always takes longer than soldering."

"But with lead came?" Panic underscored her question. "I'm so used to the smaller projects. I've only used lead came once—on the cardinal piece."

"And you did great." Andrew was relieved when the furrows in her brows relaxed. He straightened his shoulders, determined to make up for his previous comment. "You will this time, too."

The furrows returned. "But on time?"

Andrew gave a firm nod. "On time. I'll pray about it."

To his puzzlement, her cheeks flooded with pink, and she lowered her gaze. She sat back on the edge of the platform and reached into the box of cut glass pieces near her feet. Andrew knew her focus was fully on the project. He'd been forgotten. He cleared his throat as he backed away from the platform. "I–I'll go get those nails now."

Her nod provided her approval. He headed out, leaving his jacket on the hook. The ground was mushy from the end-of-February snow that had fallen two days ago followed by the beginning-of-March sun. He crossed the ground with wide strides, reaching his truck quickly, and slid into the cab. It felt good to close the door on the wind, which carried a bite despite the clear sky and bright yellow sun beaming overhead.

The sight of that sun sent a stab of worry through Andrew's chest. March had arrived, and Dad was pressuring him to use his hours on the farm instead of in the studio. It was hard to convince Dad that making suncatchers was more important than tending to a money crop. He jammed the key into the ignition and started the engine with a firm press of his foot against the foot pedal. The rev of the engine vibrated away thoughts of Dad and winter wheat.

The drive to Doug Ortmann's farm took him past Uncle Henry's shop and house. He felt a stab of regret when he saw the neat addition on the side of the house. Taking care of Beth's business had kept him from helping, but the walls had gone up without him. His father hadn't been any happier than Andrew had been about missing the workday, and Dad hadn't minded saying so. He'd also made a suggestion Andrew approved—helping to spackle and paint the inside walls to make up for not being around on construction day. On the way back to the studio, Andrew would stop at the shop and let Uncle Henry know he would do that.

He left the town and turned left at the first country road. The Ortmann farm waited at the end of a mile-long lane that was nearly impassable thanks to the soft ground. Andrew kept a steady, slow speed, gritting his teeth when the tires slipped in the mud. When he reached the graveled area in front of the house, he released a whoosh of breath.

As he stepped around the hood of the truck, the door to the house opened and Livvy Ortmann stood framed in the doorway. Andrew had known Livvy since they were toddlers, but between him being tongue-tied and her being shy, he didn't think they'd exchanged more than a dozen words in all their growing-up years. He wished briefly that her dad or one of her brothers had opened the door. But he couldn't just walk out to the barn now that she'd seen him. He headed for the porch and stopped at the base of the steps.

"Are you looking for Dad?" She wore a flowered apron over her blue dress, and she tangled her hands in the square flap of cloth, wrinkling it.

Andrew nodded. "Beth Quinn needs some more horseshoe nails."

Livvy lowered her face for a moment, her lips puckering in an odd way. "Dad went to Hillsboro to look at a trailer, but he keeps the nails in the tack room. I can get some for you."

Andrew backed up one step. "No. That's okay. I know where he keeps them, and you'll get yourself all muddy if you come out. It's a mess."

A soft warmth lit her eyes at his comment, but he didn't understand why. She moved forward, allowing the screen door to close behind her. "How many do you need? So I can tell Dad what you took."

Andrew pushed his hands into his pockets. "I'm getting twice as many as last time, a couple dozen. Think that'll be okay?" The question wasn't necessary. Hadn't Doug Ortmann told him he could come back for more?

"Sure. Get what you need. Do you need a little sack?"

Andrew grimaced. He hadn't brought anything along in which to carry the nails. But an unexplained desire not to detain Livvy made him give a shrug. "Nope. I'm okay. Thank you."

"Sure. Good-bye, Andrew."

He felt certain she sounded sad when she offered the farewell. But she slipped so quickly back into the house, he couldn't see her face to confirm it. With another shrug, he headed for the tack room at the back of Ortmann's horse barn. As he passed the stalls, a soft mewling complaint captured his attention. He glanced to the side and spotted a gray and white cat, half grown, crouched in the hay.

He stopped and looked closer. One of the kitten's eyes was crusted over. As he watched, it raised its back paw and scratched at the eye.

"Hey, now, don't do that," he chided. "You'll only make it worse."

The little cat rolled to its side, pressing its face into the hay.

Sympathy rose in Andrew's chest. The poor thing must be suffering. Immediately, he thought of his cousin Trina and her love for small creatures. The last time he'd talked with his young cousin, she'd expressed the desire to have something to do besides work at the café all the time. Trina would want to doctor this little kitty back to health.

Andrew hurried on to the tack room, jammed his shirt pocket full of nails, and headed back to the house and banged on the door. Livvy answered again, her lips tipped into a bashful yet welcoming smile.

The smile unnerved him. "Is anybody else here?"

Her face fell. "No. The boys are at school, and Mom's visiting the Erlichs. What do you need? W-weren't you able to find the nails?"

Andrew touched his bulging pocket. "I found them. But I also found a cat with a bad eye."

Livvy nodded. The white ribbon trailing from the right side of her cap caught on her shoulder. She flicked it loose before replying. "Yes. One of Ginger's kittens. We don't know what he got into."

"Trina could probably cure it," he said, "but I don't want to take it without permission."

He was certain Livvy looked at him with approval. His ears grew hot.

"You can take him. Dad won't care—he thinks cats are more of a nuisance than they're worth, but they keep the mouse population down in the barn."

It was the lengthiest speech Livvy had ever delivered directly to him. He wasn't sure what had brought out this talkative side, but it increased his feeling of unease. He didn't want to stay and chat more, but he needed something from her. "I'll take him, but do you have a box to put him in so he won't get under my feet in the cab?"

Without a word, Livvy stepped back into the house, closing the door behind her. Andrew wasn't sure if she would come back or not, but he waited, hoping. In a few minutes, just as he was deciding to let the cat run loose in the cab, she returned.

"Here." She thrust a square box marked with black-and-white bottles of ketchup at him. "I had to empty it. It had Johnny's rock collection in it."

Andrew peered inside. Small bits of grit peppered the bottom. He moved to the edge of the porch and shook the bits onto the ground. Looking over his shoulder, he asked, "Will he mind me taking it?"

Another grin lit her face. "I just put the rocks in another box in his room. My brother has dozens. I doubt he'll even notice it's missing."

"Okay, then. Thanks." Andrew bounced the box against his knee as he headed back through the muck to the barn. To his relief, the gray and white cat was still stretched out in the hay and didn't resist as he lifted it. It took some doing to get it into the box and fold the flaps down over it, though, and he worried all the way back to town that the scrabbling paws would manage to pop the top loose before he reached the café. The cat yowled as if its tail was on fire, and Andrew wondered at the wisdom of carting it back.

He drove straight past Uncle Henry's, deciding that getting the cat into Trina's hands took precedence. After pulling behind the café, he put the truck in PARK and left the engine running. "You stay in there," he told the cat, then slammed the door and headed to the café's back door. He spotted Trina at the dishwasher. Aunt Deborah was nowhere in sight.

Opening the door just enough to be seen, he called, "Can you come here?"

Without questioning him, Trina wiped her hands on her apron

and skipped to the door.

He crooked his finger at her. With a quick look over her shoulder, she followed him to the truck. The moment he peeled back the lid, the little cat shot straight in the air and into Trina's waiting arms.

"Oh!" Trina cradled the frightened cat. "You poor little thing. What happened to you?"

"It belongs to the Doug Ortmanns. They don't know what happened to it."

Andrew watched Trina put the cat in the crook of one arm and gingerly examine its eye with her free hand. To his surprise, the animal didn't fight to free itself, although it did try to turn its head away from her prying fingers.

"It looks like he's got an infected scratch," Trina said. "Probably from some sort of wire." Lifting the kitten beneath her chin, she let it nuzzle her. A purr sounded, and Trina laughed softly. "Oh, you're a sweetie." Smiling at Andrew, she said, "Thank you for bringing him to me. I'll clean out that sore and put some ointment on it. Hopefully his eye will be okay."

Andrew nodded, smiling, too. He enjoyed Trina's pleasure. Just then, the back door opened and a cranky voice interrupted.

"Trina! What are you doing?"

Trina sent Andrew a guilty look before facing her mother. "Andrew found a kitten with a sore eye."

Deborah stepped carefully across the muddy expanse to look at the kitten. "Well, I'd say it's sore." She shook her head, her arms folded. "You and these animals." Although her tone gave the impression of disgust, Andrew glimpsed sympathy in Aunt Deborah's eyes. "Where do you plan to keep it?"

Trina's brows went up in an innocent expression. "In the storage shed?"

Andrew glanced at the shed, which once had housed the original owner's buggy. The building had stood empty for years, and the wood had weathered to a dull gray, but it would make an acceptable home for an injured kitten.

"That's fine. Put it in there now, and you can see to it after the supper rush." Aunt Deborah headed back toward the café, calling, "And mind you wash well when you come back in! I don't want cat hair in any food!"

"Yes, Mama!" Trina reached with one arm to give Andrew a hug. "Thank you, Andrew. I'll take good care of him, I promise!" She headed to the storage shed, the kitten held against her shoulder.

Andrew paused for a moment, watching until she sealed herself inside with the cat. It gave his heart a lift to see Trina's happiness at the prospect of nursing the kitten. He'd managed to please one female today. Giving his shirt pocket a pat, he remembered he had a way to please Beth, too. He climbed back into his truck and drove behind the studio.

He found Beth just where he'd left her, leaning over the platform, arranging glass squares, diamonds, and triangles. The moment he closed the door, she pushed herself to her feet and released a huge yawn. But she broke into a smile when he offered the nails.

"Oh, good." She counted them, then twisted her lips into a funny pout. "I hope I'll have enough nails to hold things in place. It's a big window." Her gaze returned to the glass-scattered platform.

Andrew stepped forward, hands in pockets, and looked down at the unconstructed window, too. "You have a month," he reminded her, but he knew the amount of time it took to put the pieces together for a small work. This window was not a small work.

"A month. . ." Her voice quavered, mute evidence of her uncertainty. "And that lilac-and-cardinal piece still needs completion."

"I'll do the lilac-and-cardinal piece. I can follow the drawing as well as you. You keep going." Andrew wondered when he had finally let go of the idea of working on McCauley's window. He also wondered at the wisdom of making such a promise when Dad was pressuring him to be at the farm. Then an idea hit. An idea for striking a deal. But not with Beth—with Albert Braun, his father.

FIFTEEN

Sean held the digital camera over his head, hoping the angle would capture the entire platform. He prayed his face hadn't reflected the dismay he felt when he'd seen how little of the project was put together. For a few moments, he had considered not taking pictures at all, but Dad and Patrick expected to see evidence of Beth's work. Besides, he'd told Beth he would be taking pictures, so he felt trapped. He just hoped Dad's reaction wouldn't be negative.

He snapped twice, checked the screen, and sucked in a satisfied breath—he'd caught the whole thing. But a frown formed as he examined the image and anticipated his father's concern. Didn't Beth understand speed was as important as quality? McCauley Church Construction was known for keeping its schedule—late-arriving windows could slow construction and cast a bad light on the entire company.

"I know it doesn't look like much now because it's just the border. I started with that to be certain the dimensions would fit the window casing exactly." Beth's voice pulled his attention away from the camera. She wove her fingers together and pressed them to her stomach. "But it *will* come together."

"Oh, I know." Sean chose his words carefully. "I've seen your completed works, so I know you have the *ability* to finish this one." He forced a soft chuckle. "But I bet you didn't realize how time-consuming a piece of this size could be."

Her nod bounced her shining ponytail. "You're right. It is a major project." She drew a deep breath that raised her shoulders. "But I'll be done on time. I made a commitment—I'll keep it."

The fervency in her tone encouraged Sean and increased his admiration. Her determination to be successful must equal his. They were a perfect match in so many ways.

Placing his hand on her shoulder, he gave a slight squeeze. "I know you will. I trust you. But"—he felt her tense—"it does seem to be moving more slowly than we had expected."

Sean waited, giving her an opportunity to explain delays, but Beth remained silent, her lips clamped tightly together. He offered another squeeze of her shoulder before lowering his hand, pleased that she hadn't rattled off excuses.

"If you're going to need an extension, now is the time to ask so we can modify the construction schedule. That isn't something we do in the middle of a project, but it can be done before we send out a crew."

Beth shook her head. Her ponytail swung so hard it slapped her on the side of the neck. "No. Don't modify your schedule. I said I'd have it done, and I will."

The stubborn set to her jaw made Sean want to smile, but he swallowed and managed to maintain a businesslike demeanor. "Thank you for your diligent attitude. That's exactly what McCauley Church Construction desires." He paused, hoping his next words would be accepted in the manner intended. "And expects."

Beth looked at him, her brow puckering momentarily. Then she gave a small nod, biting down on her lower lip. "I understand. Don't worry."

Although he hated to admit it, Sean was worried. He knew the demands that would be placed on Beth should she end up being McCauley's designated designer. He also recognized his own desire to spend time with her, to get to know her as a woman rather than an employee. If she didn't meet this first deadline, his father wouldn't trust her with a second, and Sean's time with her would be over.

Mixed emotions warred inside of him as he said, "I'll try not to worry, but you try to pick up the pace a bit, huh? We want this to work out—for all of us."

"Then I'd better get busy." Turning her back on him, she knelt on the platform and picked up a piece of glass.

He watched for a few moments, intrigued by her focus despite the fact he stood behind her. It didn't take long for him to feel uncomfortable and neglected. He cleared his throat.

She looked over her shoulder, her ponytail cupping her cheek. "I'm sorry. Did you need something else?"

"Um, I guess not." He released one brief huff of laughter, then lifted his shoulders in a shrug. "And I am expected in Carlton in. . ." He glanced at this wristwatch. He had plenty of time, but he realized diverting her attention would only slow her work. "Soon." Backing toward the door, he held up the camera. "Thank you for the pictures. I'll be in touch."

A nod gave her only reply, and he stepped out the door. He knew he should appreciate her focus and dedication to the project. After all, he'd meant to convey the importance of meeting the deadline, and her actions only proved he'd succeeded. Yet a regret he didn't fully understand hovered over him the remainder of the day.

Thursday morning, Andrew's truck followed Beth into the parking area behind the studio. He swung out of his cab and jogged across the uneven ground to open her door for her.

"Good morning," she greeted. "Thanks." They walked side by side to the stoop where she unlocked the back door. "How did your day go in the fields yesterday?" She asked as they stepped into the studio.

Andrew didn't smile. "It went fine."

She shot him a curious look. "Wasn't your father pleased to have you back?"

Andrew chuckled, but it lacked his usual enthusiasm. He tugged at his smooth-shaven cheek with one finger. "Yes, but he's still grumbling about only having me two days a week."

Beth leaned against the worktable, crossing her arms. "I'm sorry working here has created so many problems for you." Henry had informed Beth that Andrew's father opposed his son dabbling in art. Andrew paid a price to be here, and she knew she didn't show him enough appreciation for his choice. Somehow she needed to rectify that.

Andrew crossed to the cabinet and removed goggles and gloves. "It isn't your fault. My dad and me. . .we haven't seen eye to eye on much since I was pretty young. He's always gotten along better with my brothers."

Beth considered his words. Oddly, some of Sean's comments from yesterday replayed through her mind. Both men hinted at difficult relationships with their fathers. Even so, she experienced a stab of envy. At least they each had a relationship with a father—something she'd never known.

She opened her mouth, intending to encourage him to try to work things out, but she realized if Andrew were to satisfy his father, it would mean the end of his working here. Confused over which choice was right, she chose silence.

Pushing off from the worktable, she crossed the floor to retrieve her own gloves. "Well, just wait until this window is finished and the contracts with McCauley come rolling in," she found herself saying. "Your father will be glad you had a part in that."

"That's what I'm counting on."

His growling tone gave Beth a chill. She shrugged it off and said with a forced nonchalance, "Well, let's get busy, huh?"

As Beth worked, meticulously fitting the pieces within their lead came framing, her mind tripped over Sean's visit yesterday and his obvious concerns about her ability to complete the project. She understood; she held the same concerns. Glancing up at the calendar on the wall, she felt her heart skip a beat. Even if she continued working Monday through Saturday, that left only twenty-two days to finish.

She looked back at the wooden platform. Its expanse seemed endless, emphasized by the colorful border of glass held in place with dull, silver horseshoe nails. *How will I get this done, Lord? Help me!* her heart begged. So many of her prayers recently had centered around this project. Her business. Gaining new contracts.

Fitting another wedge of glass into place, she defended that focus to herself. What else did she have besides her business? She didn't have a husband. Or children. Or even a church family like the rest of the community. Her studio was her life. God surely understood that and would honor her prayers to build it. After all, hadn't He given her this ability and paved the way for her to discover it? Surely He would now bless it with the means to keep it going, to build it, to be successful. Why else would He have brought Sean McCauley to her doorstep?

Sean McCauley. A picture of his face appeared in her memory. Not the image from yesterday, with worry creasing his brow, but the first time—the open, eager, interested expression that lit his blue-green eyes and brought a curving smile to his lips beneath the neat mustache.

Although their contact hadn't been excessive and had been largely limited to e-mails and telephone calls, she felt as though she knew him well. She recognized in him the same drive to succeed that existed in her own heart, and it both impressed and terrified her. What if his drive to succeed ending up forcing her off the road?

She sat up and rubbed her lower back, working loose the kinks that always formed from leaning over the platform. While she worked the tight muscles, her thoughts pressed on, constricting her chest. Would she ever be able to trust a man to have her interests at heart rather than his own?

Behind her, the scraping of the stool's legs against the concrete floor reminded her of Andrew's presence. Although he had been faithful in his commitment to helping her, she still couldn't fully trust that his diligence wasn't selfishly motivated.

She remembered his shining eyes when he'd explained the compromise he'd worked out with his father. Originally, he had only planned to work at her studio until it was time to cut the winter wheat. That was happening now all around Sommerfeld. But he had gained approval to work in the fields two days a week—Wednesday and Saturday—and continue in the studio the remaining weekdays. She frowned as she recalled his exact words when he had explained the details of his arrangement: *"But once you prove this studio can support us full-time, my father is willing to let me pursue art as my job instead of farming. So let's do it!"*

That seemed to prove that his desire to get her business up and going had more to do with his own desires to pursue art than with a genuine interest in seeing her dreams come true. And it also made her wonder if he would try to undermine her in order to become the artist rather than the employee.

Bolting to her feet, she spun to face him. "Andrew."

He jumped, dislodging the piece of glass he'd been placing. With a grunt, he slid the piece back where it belonged and then looked at her.

"I was counting the days I have left to meet the McCauley deadline."

Andrew's gaze drifted briefly to the calendar. He turned back to her and nodded.

"I'm not sure I can do it, even working Saturdays. I'm thinking about working Sundays, too—just the afternoons. I'd still go to the meetinghouse in the morning." Her mother would have choice words if Beth skipped Sunday services, and she also knew she shouldn't expect God to make time for her if she didn't carve out time for Him. "What do you think?"

"You would dishonor God's third commandment?"

Beth blinked twice. He both looked and sounded flabbergasted. "What do you mean?"

"We are commanded to keep the Sabbath day holy. That means following God's example to rest."

Suddenly Beth understood. He referred to one of the Ten Commandments Moses brought to the people—she had read about it in one of the earliest Old Testament books, although she couldn't remember if it was Genesis or Exodus. "So the people of Sommerfeld wouldn't take kindly to my working then, huh?"

Andrew shook his head, sadness in his eyes. "Beth, when I say *we*, I don't mean Mennonites only. I mean Christians. That includes you. Your God takes seriously His teachings. Rest is important. You wear down and get sick if you never rest. God knows this. That's why He gave us the instruction."

Well, her mind argued, *God understands I have a deadline hanging over my head!* But she didn't voice the thought. Andrew's serious expression held her too-often-flippant tongue. "Okay." She sighed. "I won't work on Sundays. I'll just work a few more hours every other day."

When Andrew's brows pinched, she laughed. "I know what you're thinking. I already look awful." She tipped her head and smirked. "Yes, I *do* look in the mirror on occasion."

His ears turned bright red, and she knew he remembered his uncomplimentary comment from Monday.

"But it won't be for much longer. Twenty-two more days, *excluding* Sundays, to be exact. Then, with contract in hand, I will advertise for two or three more employees. I will instruct you and those additional employees to put together stained-glass windows. And I will be the creative force behind the windows!" She threw her arms outward and exploded in an exaggerated laugh of glee. "And I will have it all!"

If she thought Andrew would join her in laughter, she was mistaken. Instead, when she looked at him, she found him wearing a smug, almost conniving grin that erased the momentary playfulness from her heart.

She recounted Andrew's response to her attempts at teasing that evening when she stopped by to see her mother and check on the progress of the addition. They stood in the second of the two bedrooms. The unpainted walls and ceiling and uncovered wooden floors gave the impression of standing in a tomb.

"I just wish," Beth said, her soft voice echoing in the empty space, "I could set aside my worries that Andrew is going to somehow take over or destroy what I'm trying to do."

Mom's arm slipped around Beth's shoulders. "I understand why you're worried, honey, after what you went through with Mitch. But you have to remember Mitch isn't a Christian. He doesn't have the same moral values that Andrew has. Don't you believe Andrew's

Christianity is important to him?"

Beth remembered his shocked response to her question about working on Sunday. She also recalled his devotion to a father who seemed bent on destroying his dreams. Yes, Andrew's Christianity was important to him. Still. . .

"Not only that," Mom continued, her eyes crinkling, "I happen to have it on good authority that Andrew likes you."

"And I don't know if that makes it better or worse!" Beth stepped away from her mother and stormed several feet away. Turning back, she said, "I like Andrew, too. He's one of my few friends around here. But liking him as more than a friend? I don't think I could ever do that."

Mom crossed her arms over her stomach, her fine eyebrows crunching together. "Because?"

Beth sighed. "Because he's Mennonite. And if I end up liking him as more than a friend, the only way our relationship could work is if he leaves the Mennonite faith or I join it."

"And you don't see that happening?"

Beth examined her mother's face. A hint of pain existed in her eyes, creating an ache in Beth's heart as she admitted, "I don't think so. At least not for me. I-I'm sorry if that hurts you."

Mom moved forward, her steps stiff. "No, Beth, I understand. You weren't raised in the faith of my family. For me, it was coming home. For you, it's something completely different. You only see the constraints, and it doesn't offer a feeling of security for you as much as a feeling of being stifled."

Beth nodded. Her mother had managed to put into words exactly the way Beth viewed the lifestyle "rules" of the Old Order Mennonite sect's teaching.

Mom continued. "It's enough for me to know you've accepted

Jesus as your Savior. Being a church member won't secure your place at His side in heaven, but asking Him into your heart did. That's what is important."

Beth nearly expelled a breath of relief. But then she shook her head. "Still, it doesn't solve my issues with Andrew. There just seems to be. . .something more. . .he wants from me. If it's a relationship, I can't give it. And if it's equal footing in my studio, I *won't* give it. But I don't know how to make that understood."

Mom's gaze suddenly jerked somewhere behind Beth. Her face turned white. Puzzled, Beth turned to look. Her heart fell to her stomach. Henry and Andrew stood right outside the door.

SIXTEEN

U ncle Henry moved into the bedroom, but Andrew's feet remained glued to the floor. Beth's comments rang in his head. She didn't want a relationship with him—either working or personal. He couldn't face her, so he stayed beside the unfinished door frame, staring at the toes of his boots.

"Andrew stopped by to offer his help in mudding, sanding, and painting the new rooms." Uncle Henry spoke softly, sympathy underscoring his tone.

Andrew held his breath, waiting for Beth's reply, explanation, or apology, but she said nothing. He jerked his chin up. "I meant to come by earlier this week, but I got busy with a cat." He realized how stupid his excuse sounded, but he didn't know what else to say.

Aunt Marie sent a weak smile in his direction. "That's kind of you. Henry will appreciate the help. Our time is running short, isn't it?"

Beth's time on the window was running short. And Andrew's time to convince her he was needed in all aspects of her life had apparently run out.

"Marie?" The concern in his uncle's tone caught Andrew's attention. "Is your stomach bothering you again?"

Andrew peered through the doorway in time to see Uncle Henry take his wife's chin and tip her face so their eyes could meet.

Aunt Marie laughed softly. "Now, you know an upset stomach isn't anything to worry about." The words were meant to appease fear, but even Andrew could see the white lines around Marie's mouth and the way she held herself in an odd position, as if standing straight was too painful.

"I'm not convinced it's your stomach." Henry put his arm around Marie's waist and guided her from the room.

Andrew stepped back to allow their passage, then followed them to the front room. He stood beside the couch where Marie sat on the edge of the cushion. Beth stood at his elbow, but he was careful not to look at her.

Marie peered up at the trio and shook her head. "It's nothing. Just a pulled muscle, probably, from carrying this extra weight. At my age, it's harder than it would have been twenty years ago."

Henry looked at Beth, his brows low. "She's been throwing up. Should a woman be throwing up at six months pregnant?"

Andrew flitted a glance at Beth's face. Her wide blue eyes blinked in confusion.

"I don't know. I've never had a baby. But it does seem odd. I always thought women just got sick in the first trimester."

"That's what I thought, too."

Andrew's ears felt hot, and he wanted to leave the personal conversation, but he didn't know how to gracefully walk away. So he clasped his hands behind his back and stared at the black ribbons dangling from his aunt's cap. They emphasized the pale pallor of her skin.

Marie caught Henry's hand. "Stop talking about me like I'm not here."

Henry bent down on one knee, still holding his wife's hand. "Marie, I'm worried."

Andrew caught Beth's eye. Despite the hurt she'd caused with her comments a few minutes earlier, he sensed her distress and wanted to help. Like he always wanted to help. She stared at him helplessly, and he reached out to brush her shoulder, just a light graze with his fingertips. A nothing touch. But she offered a small smile of thanks before facing her mother again.

"I'm fine, Henry. Really. Just old and tired." Marie released a light laugh, convincing Andrew there was no need to fear. "There are two of them in here." She cupped her stomach with both hands, shaking her head. "They're probably putting pressure on a nerve or something, which is why I hurt."

"I don't know. . ."

Marie shook her head, her expression tender. "Poor first-time daddy. You're overprotective, and I love you for it, but you don't need to fuss so. I'm sure it's nothing."

Henry rose, but his frown remained. "First it's pulled muscles, then pressure on nerves. And I don't like it."

Marie stretched her hand up, pressing it to her husband's chest. "Don't worry. In another few months they'll be here, and I'll be back to normal. Or"—another laugh sounded—"as normal as it can possibly get with two infants vying for my attention. Believe me, you may want to return to these days when my only complaint is a stitch in my side that upsets my stomach."

Andrew chuckled, and Beth echoed it. He looked at her again, but her gaze was on Marie.

"I'll come by and help with housework, Mom," Beth offered.

Marie shook her head. "Oh, no. You have a studio to run, and you need to concentrate on that. I'll be fine. But if you want to do something to help"—she raised her brows—"you could cut Andrew loose for a day or two so those rooms can be finished on the inside."

"I can do that." Beth's answer came quickly.

Too quickly. Andrew frowned. Did she see this as a way to get him out of her studio, to distance herself from him? "What about the cardinal piece?"

Beth barely glanced at him. "You're ahead of schedule on it. We can spare a few days off from that. Take tomorrow and Monday to work here, Andrew. It's fine."

"I'm ahead at the shop, too," Henry inserted. "With everyone working their fields, this is a good time for me to take a couple of days and finish those rooms."

Andrew looked from person to person. It appeared plans had been settled. He gave a brusque nod. "Okay. I'll be here tomorrow morning then, and I'll bring my own trowel."

"Dress in old clothes," Henry warned, a grin finally finding its way to his face. "It gets messy."

Andrew didn't need to be told that. He'd done more than his share of mudding when other community members had built extra rooms onto their houses. Since there seemed little to add, he inched toward the door. "I'll see you tomorrow then. Good night, Uncle Henry and Aunt Marie. . .Beth." He ducked out the door before anyone answered.

Since Uncle Henry was also a man of few words, Andrew and he worked mostly in silence Friday. Aunt Marie popped in periodically to check on their progress, but Uncle Henry always chased her out, scolding her about breathing in the fumes from the spackle. Her teasing replies made Andrew smile. Beth definitely inherited her spunk from her mother.

Each thought of Beth brought a stab of pain. Not since he had started working at the studio several months ago had he gone more than a day without seeing her. Now he was facing four days with only a brief contact at the meetinghouse Sunday. Days had never seemed so long.

At the same time, he welcomed the break. What he'd overheard her tell her mother was hard to swallow and even harder to digest. Maybe these days away would help him find his peace with her statement. But he doubted it. Uncle Henry had carried a torch for Marie more than two decades, and it had never flickered. People always told him he looked and acted like Henry. What if he proved to be like his uncle in that regard, too? What if he was never able to let go of his desire for Beth?

That question plagued Andrew over the next two days. It wiggled through his brain during Sunday service, stealing his attention from the minister. He was contemplating it again in the churchyard, when someone slapped him on the back and nearly startled him out of his hat.

Doug Ortmann stood beside Andrew. His daughter Livvy held on to his arm and peeked around his shoulder at Andrew. "Livvy said you came by when I was out. Did you find what you needed?"

Andrew nodded, centering his hat back over his ears. "Yes, sir. A couple dozen horseshoe nails."

"She said you also took a cat."

Andrew noticed Livvy's grin. He turned his gaze to Mr. Ortmann. "Yes, but I'll probably bring the cat back."

Trina bounced over, her white ribbons dancing beneath her chin. She caught Andrew's elbow and clung to him, much the way Livvy clung to her father. "Mr. Ortmann, the kitten's eye is looking better already. A thorough washing and application of ointment made a big difference. He could probably go home this afternoon, if you like."

Mr. Ortmann shrugged. "It doesn't really matter, Trina. I was about to tell Andrew that we have plenty of cats. He can just let it go somewhere as far as I'm concerned."

Trina's gasp made Andrew press his elbow to his ribs, giving her fingers a comforting squeeze. "I think Trina's gotten attached to it," he said, "so maybe you could let her keep it?"

Ortmann smiled. "Sure. And if you need any more of those nails, just come on out." He gave Andrew another hearty clap on the back and strode away. Livvy waved over her shoulder as they moved to speak with someone else.

Trina beamed up at him. "Thank you, Andrew! How could anyone just abandon a poor little kitten that way?" Her face clouded. "But Daddy will never let me keep it. He doesn't mind my nursing hurt animals, but he always says no when I ask if we can have a pet."

Andrew scratched his chin, thinking. Out of the corner of his eye, he saw Beth with her mother and her aunt Joanna Dick. Beth's straight brown skirt and fuzzy sweater, although much more conservative than her normal tight-fitting jeans and bright T-shirts, still marked her as non-Mennonite. His heart ached as he remembered her saying she could never be Mennonite.

"Andrew?"

Trina's plaintive voice reminded him he'd drifted away again. Looking back at his cousin, he gave her hand on his arm a light pat. "Don't worry. I'll help you find a home for it. I rescued him, remember?"

Her smile returned, lighting her freckled face. Stretching up on her tiptoes, she planted a quick kiss on his cheek. "Thank you, Andrew. You're the best!"

She scampered off, and Andrew stood alone, thinking. Who would take a small cat with one damaged eye? Someone who could use the company. . .

One person came to mind. The same person he'd been trying to forget. But maybe a little gift like a pet would help her look at him differently. It was worth a try.

Beth said good-bye to Aunt Joanna and her mother and turned toward her car. Her gaze swept across the churchyard and landed on Andrew, who stood alone in the middle of a patch of brown grass. He seemed lonely. The past two days, she'd been lonely, working by herself in the studio. She'd discovered she missed his company, and for a moment she considered lifting her hand in a wave.

But she reminded herself that part of the reason she'd insisted he work at Henry's was to give them some time apart, to reevaluate their relationship. Waving would only encourage him. She stuck her hand into her purse and fished for her car keys while she crossed quickly to her car. Her sporty red car with its shiny silver bumpers and white pinstripes, even though it was several years old, stood out among the Mennonites' plain black or blue sedans. It looked especially modern next to the few horse-drawn buggies on the edge of the parking area.

Once more, she was reminded of her ill fit in this community, and she felt the urge to hurry from the churchyard. Aunt Joanna had invited her to join her family for lunch, but she had declined. Despite Andrew's warning, she had considered sneaking to the studio, but the more she thought about a day of rest, the better it sounded.

A nap. A long nap. A refreshing nap. That's all she wanted right now. She'd eat a quick sandwich and jump into bed for the afternoon. The decision made, she drove home. After dressing in her pajamas, she leaned against the kitchen counter and ate a peanut butter sandwich. The sandwich, followed by a glass of milk, filled her, and she headed for the bedroom. Snuggled beneath the covers, she closed her eyes and was drifting off when her telephone rang.

Her eyes popped open. For a moment she considered letting it ring itself out, but concerned it might be her mother or Henry, she threw back the covers and dashed to the kitchen. Snatching up the receiver, she said, "Hello? Beth here."

"Beth."

The masculine voice—not Henry's—threw her for a moment. She rubbed her eyes. "Sean?"

"Yes. I'm sorry to bother you on Sunday."

"Oh, that's all right." She stifled a yawn. "What did you need?"

"I'm going to be out of town for the next ten days. I'm flying to Denver and then driving into the mountains to finalize the building plans with a committee in Blue River."

Beth didn't reply, uncertain why he found it necessary to share his plans with her.

"Sometimes at that elevation my cell phone doesn't work, and I'm not sure if I'll have Internet access, so I wanted to let you know if you couldn't reach me, you could call the home office and leave a message with the receptionist. She'll forward it on to me eventually."

For what reason would she need to contact him? Her fuzzy brain tried to process the reason for this unexpected update on his itinerary. She had only called him once. Every other conversation had been initiated by him.

"I'll let you get back to what you were doing—"

She yawned again, slumping against the wall.

"And I'll talk to you when I get back, if not before."

"Okay. Have a good trip." She put the receiver on the cradle and stumbled back to bed. She dropped across the mattress, but when her head hit the pillow, she came fully awake. Popping back up, she blinked in rapid succession, her mouth open in surprise.

Sean wanted her to know where he would be.

He wanted her to know she didn't need to worry.

He wanted her to be able to contact him.

Flopping backward with her arms out to the side, she stared at the ceiling. That was not a business call. That was personal. Very personal.

She couldn't decide if she found the realization flattering. . .or troubling.

Seventeen

Beth marked an X in the calendar box, then stood back and frowned. She had hoped having a visual reminder of the days left to complete the McCauley window might motivate her. All it managed to do was scare her.

Flipping the pencil around, she forcefully applied the eraser to remove the X. Despite herself, she felt a chuckle building. The last time she had marked Xs on a calendar, she had been counting down the days before she would be allowed to leave Sommerfeld. When Great-Aunt Lisbeth had left her the house and café, it hadn't come without its stipulation—live on the property for three months before dispensing of it. Who would have thought she'd end up living permanently in this little, religiously based community?

Beth tipped her head, staring at the remnants of the X, and considered her aunt's motivation for the requirement. Great-Aunt Lisbeth had wanted Beth to stay, to become a part of Sommerfeld and the Koeppler family. And she had. But not completely. She lived here. She worked here. She even worshipped here. But still. . .underneath. . . she didn't belong here.

"And I hate always being reminded of that!"

She nearly shouted the words, slapping the wall beside the calendar and spinning away from it. Her gaze landed on the platform. The window awaited her attention. This was her last day to work alone—Andrew would return tomorrow—so she might as well make good use of the lack of distraction.

Kneeling beside the platform, she reached for the glass pieces. Not even Sean would bother her today since he was on his way to Denver. A full day of uninterrupted work. "So, how much do I think I can accomplish?" she murmured, then shook her head. Was she going to resort to talking to *herself?* How ridiculous would that be!

Her tongue between her teeth, she leaned forward and carefully fitted a red diamond into place. An odd noise—not a knock, but more of a muffled scratch—came from outside the door. Puzzled, Beth turned her head in that direction. Had she imagined it? But no, there it came again.

Curiosity drove her to her feet. She opened the door slowly, peering out left and right. No one was there. The scratching sound came again, louder, and she looked down. A box with a line of Sunshine ketchup bottles printed on the side sat on the stoop. The scratching came from inside the box.

"What's this?" Beth crouched down and stuck her fingers between the folded-down flaps. Something furry batted her hand. She jerked back for a moment, startled, then grabbed the flap again and pulled it open.

A gray and white whiskered face with round yellow eyes peered at her. It seemed to wink with one eye.

"A cat!" Beth laughed, delighted when the little thing raised one paw toward her as if to shake hands. "Where did you come from?"

Of course, she got no answer, but it leaped from the box and ran past her directly into the studio.

"Hey!" Beth jumped to her feet and followed. She watched the little cat walk around the periphery of the studio, stopping to examine anything that remotely resembled a threat. Threats included the legs of the display bench and Beth's shoes, which she'd kicked off and left beside the door. She chuckled softly at the little thing's ruffled fur, twitching tail, and lowered ears.

Its survey apparently complete, it stuck its tail straight in the air and dashed to her. Rubbing against her legs, it sent out a loud purr.

Beth knelt down. "Well, you are a nice. . ." She peeked. "Boy. Do you have a name?"

The kitten placed one paw on her knee and stretched the other toward her face, his whiskers twitching.

"No? Well, if you're going to stick around, you'll need a name." She offered her hand, and the cat rubbed his chin against her fingers, his motor increasing in volume. He continued to hold his left eye at half-mast, as if caught in the middle of a wink. She chuckled again. "Maybe I'll call you Winky, since you seem to enjoy doing it."

At closer examination, Beth could see the winking eye had recently sustained some kind of injury. A scab, partially hidden by his fur, showed beneath the eye. Her heart stirred with sympathy. "You poor little guy." She scooped him up and was delighted when he allowed her to hold him. He bumped his head on the underside of her chin and kneaded her shoulder with his little paws.

"I've never had a pet before, besides goldfish. And I have to admit, they weren't nearly as friendly as you," she informed the cat, "but I've always lived in apartments. I have my own house now, and I get to make the rules. So I suppose it's okay if you stay."

The telephone rang, and Beth got to her feet without relinquishing the cat. He grabbed the receiver with both front paws and bit it when she pressed it to her head. "Good morning, Quinn's Stained-Glass Art Studio."

"Good morning, honey." Mom's voice came through in a cheerful tone. "I called the house, but you must have left early."

Beth lifted her chin, trying to avoid Winky's swinging paws. "Yes. I've got to make use of every available hour these days."

"I understand. Henry and Andrew are painting today, and they promise me the rooms will be ready for inspection by suppertime."

"Really?" Winky caught her ponytail and chewed on the strands, his motor rising several decibels. She put him on the floor, where he wove around her feet, his tail whipping the air. "They've made good progress then."

"Oh, yes." Mom's light chuckle sounded. "And they demand a celebration. So I'm fixing pot roast, potatoes, carrots. . .the whole shebang. Want to join us?"

"Why me? I didn't have anything to do with it."

"Yes, you did. You let Andrew have a couple days off so he could work here. So you're included."

Beth chewed her lower lip and watched Winky attack a piece of string he found under the display bench. Did she want to spend an evening with Andrew? It might give him ideas. Then again, it might give her an opportunity to ease back into their working relationship. Thinking about being alone with him tomorrow gave her an uneasy feeling in the pit of her stomach. But an evening with Mom and Henry in attendance might provide a nice transition to once again being alone with Andrew.

"That sounds fine. Want me to bring something?"

"Well, if the café were open, I'd call Deborah and ask her to set aside some rolls and dessert, maybe a coconut cream pie. Henry loves it. But since it's Monday, we can't do that."

Beth swallowed a hoot of laughter as Winky rolled onto his back, holding the string between his front paws and kicking at it with his back ones. *He must think it's a vicious string.*

"Beth? Are you there?"

Beth gave a start and turned her back on the cat so she could focus on what her mother was saying. "Yes. Sorry. How 'bout I pick up some rolls and a prebaked pie at the grocer? They won't be as good as Deborah's, but they'll be better than anything I could cook."

Mom's laughter sounded. "Okay, that sounds fine. Be here by six. We'll tour the bedrooms first and then eat."

Beth nodded. Perfect. After dinner she could return to the studio for a couple more hours of work if need be. "Okay. Thanks, Mom. See you then."

After hanging up the receiver, she put her hands on her hips and shook her head at the cat. "You are entirely too cute, Mr. Winky. I don't know how you got here, but I think I'm going to enjoy having you around."

Andrew prolonged the last few sips of his coffee as he listened to the one-sided telephone conversation. His heart thumped. Had Beth opened the back door and found the cat yet? Her early arrival had spoiled his initial plan of having the box waiting for her when she got to the studio. He'd had to be extra quiet placing the box on the stoop and sneaking away.

But now worries struck. What if the cat managed to escape and all she found was an empty box? Should he have stuck around and made sure the cat made it safely into the studio?

He wanted to ask Aunt Marie, yet he wanted to keep the surprise gift a secret. He wished she'd say something to give him some clue about whether or not Beth had found the cat.

Marie moved to the stove with a swaying gait and picked up the coffeepot. She sent a smile in his direction as she held out the pot. "More?"

Andrew swallowed the last drops and shook his head. "No. I better get my paint roller out. Uncle Henry's already hard at it. Did Beth"—he searched for a question that might lead Aunt Marie to offer what he sought—"say anything. . .about. . . ?"

Aunt Marie raised one brow. "About coming to dinner? Yes, she'll be here. And I promised her a tour before we eat."

Her smile encouraged Andrew to go get busy. He gave a nod. "It'll be ready."

Midmorning, Beth took a break and walked to her uncle Art's place of business, Koeppler Feed and Seed. Although he dealt mostly in farm implements, she knew a small selection of pet supplies was stored in the back corner of the store. She hoped she'd be able to find cat litter and one of those scooper things in addition to food and perhaps a collar with a little bell on it. She smiled. Winky was a sneaky beast—her feet had been attacked numerous times in their short time together. If a bell signaled his presence, maybe she wouldn't be caught off guard anymore.

Entering the shop, she headed straight to the counter, where an old-fashioned cash register took up one full corner. No digital readouts or computers in Sommerfeld. This store, like so many others in town, still held the feel of its early 1920s beginning. The wide planked floor and simple shelving, lit by bare bulbs hanging from twisted wire from the stamped tin ceiling, gave Beth the impression of stepping back in time. The smells—leather and sawdust and grain—added to that sensation.

Art's wife, Doris, stood behind the counter, shifting items around in a box. She looked up and, probably without even realizing it, swept her gaze from Beth's head to her feet and up again. The seconds-long examination complete, a small smile formed on her lips.

"Why, hello, Beth."

"Good morning," Beth greeted, forcing a cheerful tone. Doris's perusal and the hesitant warmth in her eyes once more reminded Beth of her worldly—in the town's opinion—appearance. She tugged at the tails of her flannel shirt and fidgeted.

"What brings you here this morning? Surely you don't need a plow."

"Oh, no." Beth gave the expected laugh. "But I do need some cat food, a collar with a bell, if you have one, and a litter box."

Doris's eyebrows shot high. "Marie didn't mention you were planning to get a kitten."

Beth shrugged. "She didn't know." Beth didn't bother to mention she herself hadn't known.

"Well, we do have clay litter. Lots of our farmers use it to absorb oil spills from their farm equipment." The rubber soles of Doris's sensible oxfords squeaked against the wood-planked floor as she stepped from behind the counter. "But we don't carry litter boxes." She led Beth past aisles of knotty pine shelves holding tools, boxes of boots, and stacks of work pants to the area where pet supplies were kept. "However, you could probably go next door to the variety store and buy a dishpan. It would work just as well."

"Thanks. I'll do that."

Doris returned to the counter while Beth looked at the small selection of cat collars. She chose a pale blue one with felt underlining. Its little bell sent out a low-toned jingle. "That'll keep you from creeping up on me," she mumbled. And, she decided, Winky would look quite jaunty with the blue collar against his gray fur.

She looped the collar over her wrist, then scooped up a ten-pound bag of litter and a five-pound bag of cat food and waddled to the counter. For a moment, she wished she'd brought her car; the three-block walk to the studio might seem longer carrying her burden.

Doris punched the amounts into the register and gave a blunt total. When she put the collar in a little bag, she commented, "This is a ten-inch. Are you sure you don't want a nine-inch?"

Beth frowned. "What's the difference?"

"A ten-inch might not stay around a kitten's neck; it could be too long."

"Well, he's not quite a cat, but he's not a kitten anymore." She smiled at Doris's puzzled expression. "I'm guessing he's halfway to grown up."

"Oh." Doris rolled the bag closed. "Then this will probably be okay if you hook it on the inside notch. Getting the bell is a good idea. It will keep him from catching birds." She grimaced. "Nasty thing to do."

Beth agreed. But she intended to make Winky a studio cat, and the only birds he could chase in there were ones formed from bits of colored glass. She thanked Doris once more, then headed out. As she aimed her feet toward the variety store, she released a chuckle. It wouldn't be long before the entire town knew she was the proud owner of a half-grown cat. Word spread amazingly fast in this little town.

Winky seemed pleased to scratch around in his dishpan-turned-litter box, which relieved Beth mightily. He also gave no indication of being offended by the plastic cereal bowls that held his food and water since she'd been unable to find an official pet dish at the variety store. However, he turned into a real stinker when she tried to fasten the collar around his neck.

"Now, behave yourself," she scolded as he backed up between her legs, eluding her grasp. "This is for your own good!" She spent at least five minutes chasing him around the studio before she finally conceded defeat. Smacking the collar onto the worktable, she warned, "You've got to sleep sometime, and I'll get you then."

From across the room, Winky washed one paw and fixed her with a heavy-lidded stare. She laughed. "Whoever left you on my doorstep is going to get the biggest thank-you. You really are precious." She sighed. "But now I've got to get back to work. Leave my feet alone, huh?"

Winky simply winked.

EIGHTEEN

And there it was, right on my doorstep." Beth buttered another roll and took a bite of it. "But unlike the movies where there's always a note attached saying, 'Take care of my baby,' there was no communication."

"Hmm. . ." Henry stabbed a forkful of green beans. "A cat, you say?" He sent a speculative look across the table to Marie. "Didn't Trina say something Sunday evening about needing to find a home for a cat?"

Andrew cleared his throat loudly and pointed to the saltshaker. "Could someone pass the salt, please?"

Henry obliged, and Andrew grabbed it with a mumbled "Thank you." Beth hoped her mother wasn't insulted. In her opinion, everything tasted great, but judging by Andrew's zealous application, the food was flavorless.

"You said Trina?" Beth chewed thoughtfully. Yes, she could see Trina giving her a kitten. But she couldn't imagine why the girl would be so secretive about it.

"Yes." Mom sat back, most of her plate untouched. "Something about it having been hurt, but—"

"This is all really good, Aunt Marie."

Andrew's ears turned as red as the plum jelly in the middle of the table as everyone stopped eating and stared at him. Gesturing with his fork, he added, "All of it. Really good."

Mom offered a slow nod. "Thank you." Her tone indicated puzzlement.

"Yes." He cleared his throat again. "Did you. . .use any special kind of seasonings on the meat?"

Henry burst out laughing. "Don't tell me you're collecting recipes."

Beth didn't think Andrew's ears could get any redder. But he was only embarrassing himself by butting in and inserting topics that were clearly outside of his area of interest. What was he. . . ? Her thoughts were interrupted by the theme song from *Looney Tunes* coming from her purse. She leaped from the table.

"Sorry," she said as she snatched it from the floor beside the door, "but I'm expecting a call from the owner of the Salina mall about my commission check from the craft fair." She flipped open the phone and looked at the number. Her brows pinched. She didn't recognize it. After clicking the TALK button, she held the phone to her ear. "Hello?"

"Hello, Beth. It's Sean."

"Sean! Are you in Denver?" Eating came to a standstill at the table. Three faces aimed in her direction. She pointed to the hallway and mouthed, "I won't be long." Then she moved around the corner, out of sight of her parents and Andrew.

"Yes. I'm calling from the hotel. I wanted to give you the number."

Beth shook her head. "Thanks, but if I needed something, I could've just contacted the office."

"I know, but. . .I wanted you to have it."

"Oka-a-ay." Beth drew out the word, uncertain how to respond.

"That way," his soft voice continued, "I can stay up-to-date on your progress, and you can check on mine."

A self-conscious giggle spilled out. "Why do I need to check on yours?"

"Because if this committee signs with McCauley, they've already indicated they want seventeen stained-glass windows. A large one of a rainbow with a dove behind the lectern; and eight on each side of the sanctuary, nine representing the different fruits of the Spirit and the remaining seven showing symbols of Christianity. That should challenge your artistic side."

Beth leaned against the wall. "S–seventeen? The fruits of the Spirit?"

Sean's chuckle sounded. She pictured his crinkled eyes, his warm smile. Funny how given the few times they'd been face-to-face he could appear so easily in her memory. "Yes. That should keep you busy, I'd think."

"Oh, yes, I'd think. . ."

Another chuckle. "So get that one finished and out of the way so we can get moving on these fruits."

Already her mind was spinning. "Yes." Fruits of the Spirit: gentleness, mercy. . .what else? "I will. Well, the number of the hotel will be in my phone's memory bank, so I've got it."

"Oh. Good. Then. . .I'll let you go. I've got an early meeting tomorrow."

"Thanks for calling." She snapped the phone shut and dashed around the corner.

"Mom! Guess what!"

Andrew lowered his fork and looked up, his heart leaping at Beth's glowing face.

"What?" Marie asked, tipping her head.

"That was Sean—Sean McCauley—and he says their next project includes seventeen stained-glass windows. Seventeen!" She nearly danced to the table, her fingers in her hair. "They want each to be a depiction of a Christian symbol or one of the fruits of the Spirit."

Marie's jaw dropped. "W-what?"

Henry leaned his elbows on the table. "That sounds like quite the challenge."

"I know." Beth shook her head, her eyes wide. She faced Andrew and clasped her hands beneath her chin. "Andrew, I know I've said you need to work on other things and let me do the McCauley window, but I've changed my mind. You know, woman's prerogative and all that. . ." Her giggle filled the room. "Starting tomorrow, you're going to work with me. I want to finish early—beat the deadline."

Andrew put down his fork. "But what about the Fox Gallery? You have a deadline there, too."

"I know, but it's commissioned; there's no set customer waiting for that one, so a delay won't really hurt anything. This McCauley project is absolute top priority."

The way she emphasized the last words set Andrew's teeth on edge. Although all along he'd wanted to help with the window, now resentment smacked hard. Since when should McCauley be the only customer who mattered?

"Why?" He nearly barked the word, startling himself as much as Beth.

She moved slowly to the table and put her hands on the back of her chair. "Why?" She crunched her mouth into a scowl. "I should think it would be obvious. I want the chance to design those windows."

Suddenly the room faded away. All that existed for Andrew was he and Beth facing off. He folded his paint-speckled arms across his chest. "I understand you want to win the contract. But that can be done without setting everything else aside if you keep up the pace you've been doing lately. Are you sure it's only the contract you're after?"

Beth's scowl deepened as her fingers curled tight on the chair's top rail. "What is that supposed to mean?"

"Are you sure you're not trying to win"—Andrew's bravado briefly flickered, but a jealous wave drove the final word from his heart— "Sean?"

Beth yanked out the chair and plunked into it, her jaw dropping. "I can't believe you just said that."

Andrew couldn't either. But he was glad he had. The way she'd lit up when she realized who was on the telephone. Her willingness to set aside everything—everything!—to please that man. Her defensiveness now. In his eyes, it all pointed to one thing: Beth liked Sean. And even though he recognized it, he wouldn't say it aloud and give it credence.

"Honestly, Andrew, you're just out of line." Beth angled her head with her chin jutting to the side. "I thought we'd come to the understanding that you are my employee, not a co-boss. It isn't your business to presume on my motives. You're just to do what you're told. So plan on helping with the McCauley window starting tomorrow morning."

"Whatever you say, *boss*." What was he doing? He'd never spoken to Beth this way before. In the back of his mind, the biblical reminder to be angry yet sin not raised a flag, but he refused to acknowledge it. He clamped his jaw, holding back the apology for which she was certainly waiting. She could just wait, the stubborn, bossy girl!

They sat glaring at each other across the table for long seconds until a strangled sound—not quite a snort, not quite a cough—came from Henry's side of the table. Andrew shifted his gaze to his uncle. Uncle Henry's lips were pursed as if trying to hold something back, and his eyes were watering. Had something gone down the wrong pipe? Andrew lifted his hand to give his uncle a whack on the back, but before he could do it, Henry's mouth popped open, and a loud burst of laughter broke out.

"Henry. . ." Aunt Marie's voice held a warning, but a sparkle lit her eyes, as well.

Uncle Henry covered his mouth with his fist and coughed, bringing himself under control. "I apologize. I really do. But if you two could see yourselves." Another guffaw blasted, and Aunt Marie followed it with a giggle muffled by her hand.

"I don't see anything funny," Beth inserted, her blue eyes sparking dangerously.

Neither did Andrew. Conflict held no humor for him, even when it was necessary. And this time it was necessary.

Uncle Henry held up both hands in defeat. "As I said, I apologize. But after just having talked about Beth getting a cat, it was like watching two tomcats square off for battle."

Aunt Marie added, "Or watching siblings squabble."

Andrew jerked his gaze in her direction. Siblings? He nibbled the inside of his cheek. The only other people with whom he'd ever openly argued were his brothers. He'd never felt comfortable enough to be boldly forceful with anyone else. Yet right then, he'd held nothing back from Beth.

But surely he didn't look at Beth the way he looked at his brothers. That was ridiculous! He faced her again, taking in her jutted chin with its delicate cleft, her narrowed eyes still snapping fire, and her tightly crossed arms. He'd manage to rile her as much as he'd ever riled his brothers. And he wasn't any sorrier about it than he'd ever been when he'd argued with either Ted or Joe. Confused, he looked down at his empty plate.

A lengthy silence hung over the table, broken by Aunt Marie clearing her throat.

"Well, I believe I'm ready for dessert. How about you?"

The bright note in her voice did little to ease Andrew's discomfort, but he lifted his gaze and nodded. "Sure. Sounds good." He glanced at Beth. Would she be willing to set aside her aggravation and try to end the evening pleasantly?

She unfolded her arms and placed her hands in her lap. Her lips curved up in a tight smile. "Just a small piece, please. Thanks." Her tone was light, giving no indication of lingering anger, but when Andrew met her gaze, the spark in her eyes let him know they'd address this topic again. Soon.

Well, he decided, maintaining eye contact and lifting his brows, that was fine with him. Maybe it was time he and Beth defined their relationship. This time, though, it would be defined to his satisfaction. Maybe it was time to stop letting Miss Beth Quinn have the upper hand in everything.

Beth opened the plastic sack of goodies she'd gathered from the house and grinned down at Winky, who stood at her feet with his whiskers and tail tip twitching in synchronization. "Yes, I brought you some entertainment. You need something besides my feet to play with around here."

The kitten stretched up on his back feet and pawed her leg, releasing a mournful meow.

"Don't be so impatient," she scolded with a light laugh. "Just like a male. Wants everything right now."

Even though she had made the determination to keep her mind on finishing the window and not allowing thoughts of either Sean or Andrew to distract her, her own comment immediately had the opposite effect.

Sean wanted the window done *right now*.

Andrew wanted to be in the middle of everything *right now*.

And she didn't know what she wanted.

With a sigh, she pulled a mateless sock—with every trip to the Laundromat, she seemed to lose one half of a pair—from the bag and began rolling it at the toe. "Let me turn it into a ball for you. It'll be more fun."

But Winky jumped up, eager to explore this new item. With a chuckle, Beth dropped the sock across the kitten's back. He leaped in a circle, dislodging the sock, then dove on it. She watched him scoop the sock between his front paws and give it a thorough kicking with his back claws while emitting dangerous growls.

"You are something else." She emptied the remainder of the bag onto the worktable. When he tired of the sock, she'd offer a new toy—a ball of tinfoil, a shoestring, or an empty matchbox. Anything to keep him occupied so she could work.

She glanced at the wall clock, her chest constricting. Andrew would be arriving soon. They needed to have their chat concerning yesterday's dinner fiasco. For some odd reason, she felt hesitant to reopen the discussion. Maybe, she acknowledged, because she feared there might be some truth to what he'd said.

Why else had her heart fired into her throat when she realized Sean was on the other end of the telephone connection?

She shoved that thought aside. It didn't matter if Andrew's comment had merit. What mattered is that she needed him to focus on work instead of her personal life. And if that meant fighting like siblings or—she glanced at Winky, who crouched in preparation for a mighty pounce on the unwitting sock—two tomcats, then so be it.

The back door opened, startling Winky from completing his intended attack. Instead, he scuttled across the room and cowered behind the platform, peering out with round, yellow eyes.

Beth knelt down and stretched her hand toward the kitten, grateful for the opportunity to avoid eye contact with Andrew for a few minutes. "Hey, it's okay. Come back here."

Although she didn't look, she knew from the silence he remained by the door rather than stepping into the room. Obviously, he was as uncertain about how to proceed as she was.

"So that's the cat, huh?"

She didn't turn around, but she nodded and picked up the sock, jiggling it to entice the kitten out of hiding.

"What did you name him?"

The cat's tail waved above the platform like a flag. Beth snickered. "Winky."

"That'll make sense until his eye heals. But he probably won't wink so much after that."

Beth slowly straightened to her feet, the sock forgotten in her hand. "How did you know he had a bad eye?"

Andrew stared at her for a moment; then he scratched his head and shrugged. "Uncle Henry said it last night."

Beth replayed the conversation concerning the kitten that had taken place at the dinner table. "No, he didn't. Mom said if it was the same kitten Trina had, it had been hurt somehow, but nothing was said about a hurt eye."

As she'd come to expect in moments of uncertainty, Andrew's ears changed to a rosy hue. Suddenly she remembered another comment he'd made about being busy with a cat. She pointed at him. "You."

He looked at her and gulped—one mighty up and down of his

Adam's apple. He jabbed his thumb against his chest, his eyebrows high.

"*You* gave me Winky!" The deepening color in his ears was the only confirmation she needed. "But why?"

Nineteen

Andrew watched the cat dash from behind the platform and leap at the sock that dangled from Beth's hand. The moment the furry streak smacked the sock with his paw, Beth released it, and cat and sock tumbled in a tangle at her feet.

"I love the cat," she said softly. At the tenderness in her expression, he felt as though his heart tumbled in his chest as erratically as the cat tumbled on the floor with its toy.

"Good," he managed.

Tipping her head, she lowered her brows in puzzlement. "But why leave it on the doorstep? Why not just give him to me?"

Even though his motivation for gifting her with the kitten had been to gain favor, he hadn't anticipated her finding out so soon. He found himself at a loss for words, so he simply stood stupidly in front of the door with enough heat in his ears to replace the furnace.

Beth's face fell. "You meant it to be a secret, didn't you? I'm sorry I guessed."

Andrew had heard an apology from Beth only once before, and that time she'd followed it up with a *but*. This time, no excuse or explanation followed. His lips wobbled into a smile. "That's okay. I'm surprised you didn't figure it out last night when I kept pouring salt on my food to get Uncle Henry to stop talking about it."

Beth giggled. "How could you even eat after emptying the salt-shaker on it? Mom has always seasoned her food well enough. It must have tasted awful!"

He rubbed the underside of his chin, grimacing. "It was pretty bad. I drank lots of water after I went home."

They laughed together. When the laughter faded, Beth crouched down and petted the cat, which had finally given up its fight with the sock and lay washing its feet.

"Andrew, about last night. . .and my reaction to your comment about Sean. . ."

Andrew took a deep breath and moved forward several feet. He bent down, too, his elbows on his bent knees. "I might have been out of line, but I'm not going to say I'm sorry. Because that would be lying."

Her forehead creased. A warning sign.

He continued. "I do have some concerns."

To his surprise, rather than bristling, she sat on the floor with her legs criss-crossed. She tugged the cat into her lap and scratched his chin. His purr rumbled. "Okay. What?"

"Okay. . ." He paused, organizing his thoughts. Beth had so often insinuated he couldn't separate business from personal, he wanted to be sure he kept this conversation on a business level. Personal could wait. "First of all, this idea of asking for an extension on the consigned piece so we can finish the McCauley window early. I don't think that makes good sense."

Her fingers continued stroking the cat's neck, but her gaze didn't waver. "Go ahead."

"I thought your goal was to have your own gallery, make pieces of art available to the public, *and* work for McCauley." His knees complained, so he shifted, moving to sit on the edge of the platform. Beth's eyes followed him. "But if you forgo everything and just focus on McCauley, you risk running off the very people who can bring in business to the gallery or online."

Beth surprised him by smirking.

"What?"

"You said 'online.' "

Andrew frowned. "What's wrong with that?"

She shrugged. "Nothing, I guess. It's just you're the first Mennonite I've heard use a word that referenced the Internet."

Andrew snorted. "We might not use it, but we're aware of it, Beth."

"Don't get defensive," she said, but her tone remained friendly, open. The kitten had fallen asleep. She planted her palms on the floor behind her and leaned back. "How can focusing on McCauley run off other business?"

Her return to the topic caught Andrew by surprise, and it took a moment to get his thoughts back together. "Think about it. What if Uncle Henry, when a particular person came into his shop with a mechanical problem, set everyone else's needs aside and took care of that person exclusively? How would those who had tractors or cars waiting feel, being treated as though their vehicle didn't matter as much?"

Beth's shoulders rose and fell in a slow-motion shrug. "They probably wouldn't like it."

"Do you think they'd bring their business to Uncle Henry again, or go elsewhere?"

The impish smirk returned. "Well, seeing how there's only one mechanic in the whole town of Sommerfeld, they'd probably grumble and wait their turn."

Andrew refused to be caught up in teasing. "And that works as long as you're the only one providing the service. But you aren't the only stained-glass artist in the state, are you? The Fox Gallery can go elsewhere. Customers can go elsewhere. You have more to lose."

Even as he spoke, he recognized Beth had a rare talent, something that set her apart from other stained-glass artists. He waited for her to point out her unique ability to create depth. To argue that her work was worth waiting for. But she surprised him again.

"Maybe you're right. Maybe I shouldn't put one ahead of the other but recognize that each client, each project, has equal value. But. . ." Her brows pinched; her tongue sneaked out to lick her lips. "But if I don't get the McCauley contract, so many of my other desires won't be fulfilled. I need the money from the McCauley contract to expand the studio, buy equipment, hire more—"

"If you want it all, you have to do it all." Andrew leaned forward, increasing his volume and fervor. "You can't let anything slide. You've got to satisfy Fox, you've got to satisfy McCauley, and you've got to prepare for the customers who will be coming to your door."

She had to listen to him. Only if everything she had planned—the showroom, the Web site, the church windows—came to pass could she hope to support more than one person with this studio. He couldn't let her drop one for the other. She needed them all to see her dream come true. *He* needed them all for *his* dreams to come true. He wouldn't let her back off now.

Beth sat staring at him, her lips clenched together, for several long seconds. Finally, she drew in a breath through her nose, her gaze narrowing. "Andrew, will you answer one question for me as honestly as you can?"

Although he knew he might set himself up for an uncomfortable situation, he could do little else but nod.

"Are you sure you don't want me putting everything else except the McCauley project aside to keep me from having a long-term relationship with Sean McCauley?"

Andrew stifled a groan. He'd agreed to answer, but now he wasn't sure he could form one. Yes, he was jealous of the attention she paid Sean McCauley. Yes, he wished she would pay more attention to him—and not as an employee. That was why he'd given her the cat, which she clearly loved. But never having said anything remotely personal to a girl before, he had no words. He stared at his linked hands in his lap.

After a few silent seconds, Beth released a sigh. "It's okay. You don't have to answer. It's enough that you think about it and realize that if this studio is to take off, Sean McCauley is going to be a part of the picture around here. You'll need to accept it eventually. And sooner would be better than later."

After their lengthy talk that morning, Beth had put conversation on hold so she could concentrate on the window. Despite Andrew's arguments, she had instructed him to stop working on the second cardinal piece after lunch and help with the McCauley project instead. He'd scowled but followed her instruction, working in from the opposite corner of the platform.

The work was painstakingly slow, each piece requiring a tight fit with no gaps if the window was to hold its shape without buckling when lifted to a vertical position. Twice Beth had stopped and applied the carborundum stone to small bumps on the edge of a piece to insure a better fit. The meticulous task, while satisfying, was also stress-inducing, given the need for accuracy.

Winky did his best to add moments of levity by pouncing on their feet or leaping onto the platform to curl into a ball and turn on his motor. He always managed to land right where she needed to place the next piece of glass, bringing a laugh that eased her taut muscles and refreshed her.

As suppertime approached, Beth found herself glancing at the clock at closer intervals, eager for the excuse to stop, stretch her legs, and rest her eyes and fingers. She suspected Andrew felt the same way by the number of times he sat straight up on his knees and twisted his back. She understood. Leaning over the platform was much more difficult than leaning over the worktable. The angle was different, putting more pressure on the lower spine, and one had to avoid the horseshoe nails that kept the project square on the wooden base. But if he was going to be working on other big projects, he might as well become accustomed to using the platform.

She was scooping the cat out of the way for the umpteenth time when the telephone on the wall jangled. "I'll get it," she said as Andrew started to stand. Lifting the receiver, she offered her standard, "Quinn's Stained-Glass Art Studio. May I help you?"

"Hello, Beth. I hope you're ready to design like crazy."

Sean's greeting made her heart double its tempo. "They signed?"

"They signed."

Her smile stretched across her tired cheeks. "Congratulations!"

"To you, too. The stained-glass windows are part of the contract."

"Yes, if I meet your stipulation for this first one." Beth looked at the partially completed window, which would determine whether or not the stained-glass windows for the Colorado church would truly be her projects. Her stomach turned a somersault. She still had so much to do! And those windows in Denver wouldn't be hers if this one wasn't completed.

"So how are you coming along over there?"

Beth clenched her teeth for a moment, holding back the grunt of frustration. "It's coming," she said. "I've got Andrew working on it, too."

Andrew glanced up, meeting her eyes. She smiled and pointed at the platform—a silent reminder to keep working. His brows tipped together briefly, but he picked up another piece of glass.

"Well, good. He needs to learn how to do the larger pieces."

"That's what I thought." Beth smiled when the distinct sound of a yawn met her ear. "I didn't realize meetings were such exhausting work."

At his laughter, her smile grew. "I think it's the elevation. Whenever I get up in the mountains, I feel sleepy."

Beth couldn't confirm that. She'd never spent time in the mountains. She'd done little traveling, although she'd always wanted to. But Mom's limited income hadn't allowed for long vacations in faraway places. Now her focus was on getting her studio running. She frowned. If the studio became the success she hoped, would there be time for travel in her future?

A brief wave of panic struck. Did she want her work to be *everything*?

"Well," Sean's voice carried through the line, "I know you're hard at it, so I'll let you go. I just wanted to share the good news. By the end of the week I'll have dimensions for the windows and a construction schedule. You'll need that information before you can proceed, but be thinking about the designs and how you can bring in that wonderful depth."

Beth swallowed. "Yes. Yes, I will. 'Bye, Sean. Thanks for calling. And congratulations again." She hung up and looked at Andrew, who settled back on his haunches and pressed his hands to his knees. "You ready for a break?"

He answered with a shrug.

"Let's walk next door, work some kinks out. I need to. . ." She paused. Did she want to involve Andrew in her worries? If she shared her concerns with him, she would be leaning on him. More than she already was in letting him help with the window. Mitch's face appeared in her memory—his smiling, beguiling, devious face—followed by the remembered pain of his betrayal.

Waiting beside the platform, Andrew prompted, "You need to. . . ?"

"Walk." She gave a single, empathic nod. "I need to walk. And I'm hungry for one of Deborah's greasy burgers. So let's go."

They slid in on opposite sides of an open booth, where they could look out on the peaceful street. Since it wasn't the weekend, not many tourists were around, but Beth easily recognized the patrons who were not citizens of Sommerfeld.

The two tables closest to the booth she and Andrew shared were each occupied by a young family—mother, father, and preschool-age child. Beth's gaze flicked back and forth between the tables, her mind unconsciously recording the similarities and disparities.

One family was Old Order Mennonite—the man's closely trimmed hair, the woman's cap, and the little girl's tiny braids serving as calling cards. The second family was obviously not. Even their daughter, who couldn't be more than four, had pierced ears and designer-brand blue jeans.

At each table conversation took place, the adults leaning forward now and then to speak in lowered tones, the mothers occasionally pausing to offer instruction to use the napkin or be careful with the cup of milk.

Beth examined their faces, searching for evidence that one family might be happier, more contented, more complete than the other. But she couldn't make a determination. They both seemed like normal, involved, satisfied families. Her heart begged for an answer to the question plaguing her mind: In which of those families—Old Order or worldly—would *she* have the best chance to find fulfillment and contentment?

Swinging her gaze away from the families, she found Andrew openly examining her. Heat rose from her neck to her cheeks as she got the distinct impression he knew what she had been trying to discover.

TWENTY

Leaning her elbows on the table, Beth brought her face closer to Andrew's. "Are you happy here?"

Andrew raised one brow.

"In Sommerfeld, in the fellowship. Do you ever wonder what it's like 'out there'?"

Andrew glanced out the window, then at the worldly couple seated nearby. His lips twitched, and he rubbed his hand over his mouth. "I guess all of us wonder. Outsiders come in driving fancy cars and wearing their fancy clothes and talking about the things they do. So, yes, I've wondered."

She nodded. "I can see why. Everything here is so. . .regimented. Controlled." With a grimace, she added, "I don't know how you stand it."

Sorrow filled Andrew's eyes. "I don't just *stand* it, Beth. I embrace it."

The word *embrace* wrapped around Beth's chest in a breath-stealing hold. "How?" The word came out in a strangled whisper. She gestured to the café. "What is it that you find so. . .desirable here? I see the smiles, the contentment, the acceptance of the simplicity, but I don't understand. Help me understand, Andrew." *So I can find out whether or not it can one day be mine.*

Andrew's brow furrowed, and for long moments he looked out the window. His jaw worked back and forth, letting Beth know how deeply he sought the right answer to her question. Although impatience tugged at her like Winky at her pant leg, she managed to stay silent and allow him the opportunity to collect his thoughts.

Finally, he looked at her, and his eyes held a variety of emotions she couldn't define. "There's security, Beth, in knowing what applied to my parents' world at my age also applied to my grandparents and great-grandparents and now applies to me. The history, the generations-long tradition, feels stable in a world that—out there—isn't always stable. There's security in having a firm boundary around me, a fence that keeps me safe."

She opened her mouth to protest, but he held up his hand.

"I know you see it as hemming you in and holding you back. But I see it as keeping potentially dangerous things away and giving me freedom within the boundaries of my beliefs."

Beth leaned back, sucking in her lips as she processed his answer. The words sounded good in theory, but there was a problem. "Then why are you bucking so hard to break free of your father's plans for you?"

He jerked as if her words had impaled him.

"Your family's history is farming, right? Your father, your brothers, probably your grandfathers, too—all farmers. But you? You're trying to be something else."

His ears filled with the familiar red. Although his mouth opened, no words came out.

She nodded. "See? You don't like the boundaries, either, or you'd just farm and not say anything." Sitting forward, she allowed a small smile to form on her lips. "But I have to tell you, Andrew, I admire you for going after what you want. I might get aggravated with you sometimes because I feel like you're stepping on my toes, but I still admire you." Lowering her eyes, she fought a feeling of sadness. "At least you know what you want."

"You know, too." The fervency brought Beth's head up. "You know. You want success." He pointed to the table beside them where the worldly family prepared to leave the café—the mother helping the little girl into her pink denim jacket and the father digging in his wallet for a tip. "I saw the look on your face when you were watching the families. You think being a wife and mother will hold you back. That's why you don't want to be Mennonite. A Mennonite wife wouldn't spend all her day in an art studio. You don't think you can fit the role."

He gave the saddest smile Beth had ever seen. "I heard you when you told your mother you could never be Mennonite. I tried not to hear, but I heard. And I've been thinking about it."

Beth wasn't sure she wanted to know what he thought, but she couldn't deny a fierce interest in hearing his opinion. In the past days, a side of Andrew—a strong, confident, openly knowledgeable side—had come into view, piquing her interest as much as it surprised her. It gave a new, attractive dimension to him worthy of further exploration.

"So what do you think?" Her breath came in little puffs as her heart pounded, waiting, hoping for some nugget of insight that might help her find her place in this community.

Andrew squared his shoulders. "I think you were raised in the world, and that's where you belong. You found God here, and maybe that's what you came for, to become part of His family. But what you told your mom is right. You'll never be a Mennonite. It isn't who you are." His back slumped as if his honesty had cost him his strength.

"And maybe, since you'll never fit unless you are Mennonite, you'd be better off somewhere else."

"You'd be better off somewhere else."

Andrew's words haunted Beth the remainder of the week. Each morning as she opened her Bible for her devotions, those words tried to steal her focus and interfered with her ability to pray.

Hadn't Sean told her she should relocate her studio away from this quiet town? And now Andrew had indicated the same thing.

"You'd be better off somewhere else."

Fear held her captive. These two men, in whom she needed to be able to place her confidence and trust to build her studio and fulfill her dreams, each seemed to have agendas that would benefit themselves if she followed their advice.

Sean suggested Kansas City, closer to his home, where undoubtedly he could keep a close eye on her projects and have some control. Could his increased, more personal contacts be a means of drawing her closer?

And Andrew suggesting she go somewhere else would leave an empty studio in Sommerfeld for someone else's use. His use? Is that why he said she would never be happy here?

God, please help me set the fears aside! she begged each time the worry rose, yet it continued. Each glimpse of Andrew across the platform increased the feelings of uncertainty, and finally on Friday morning, she sent him back to the cardinal piece with the instruction to see it through to completion and then work on suncatchers.

"I'll need a stash ready for when I get the Internet store up and running," she said in response to his questioning look. To her relief, he didn't argue. But sending him away from the platform didn't solve the problem. Just having him in the room was a constant reminder, and she came close to telling him to go work in the fields.

When he left for the noon break, the telephone rang. Wearily, Beth answered it to find Sean on the other end. He would be back in Kansas by Saturday, and he had a final meeting with the Carlton church committee next week on Wednesday. He asked if could swing by the studio, take another peek at the window, and perhaps treat her to supper to celebrate the Colorado contract.

"No." The word burst out much more forcefully than she intended.

Sean's shocked silence on the other end filled Beth with embarrassed shame, and she struggled to explain herself.

"I mean, I'd like that, and you can certainly stop in if you want to, but"—her gaze fell on the wall calendar, the few squares remaining in the month sending a new jolt of panic through her chest—"I really can't afford to be away from the studio right now. I have less than three weeks to finish this project."

"And you and Andrew can't get it done?" He sounded more puzzled than worried.

"Yes, I can if I stay here and see it through!" Once more, against her will, her tone reflected her anxiety.

"Beth. . ." Sean's voice lowered, and she pictured him pressing the receiver closer to his face. "If this window is too much for you, then maybe—"

No more suggestions! "It's not too much for me," she insisted, forcing a levity to her voice she didn't feel, "I just prefer to commit my time to work right now. When the work is done, there will be time for play."

But not much time, she realized, since two more churches were already lined up and waiting for Beth Quinn stained-glass windows. She felt dizzy and slid down the wall to sit on the floor.

"Okay then." Sean sounded resigned. "I'll pop in on my way back from my meeting at Carlton. It will be late afternoon or early evening, so hopefully I won't disrupt your routine too much. I look forward to seeing. . .your progress."

Beth was certain he had intended to say he looked forward to seeing her and had changed it at the last minute. The thought brought mingled emotions of relief and regret.

"Wednesday then. Thanks, Sean. Have a safe trip home." She hung up before he could create more conflict in her heart.

Winky pranced over and batted her pant leg in his typical bid for attention. She scooped him into her arms and rubbed her chin on his head. His purr expressed his appreciation. She petted him for a few minutes, letting the cat's soft fur and gentle motor soothe the frayed edges of her nerves.

"You are quite the gift," she whispered, giving him a kiss between his ears and setting him back on the floor. "Thank you for your sweet attention. At least I don't have to second-guess your motives."

Winky padded beside her as she returned to the platform and picked up a green triangle. "Okay, now, no pouncing. I have to focus," she warned the kitten. He licked one paw and stared at her with an innocent expression she had learned never to trust. Maybe she should locate one of his toys to keep him occupied.

He shifted positions, holding down his tail with one paw and beginning a thorough wash of the tip. She smiled. The cat was too cute for his own good. Convinced he was duly occupied, she turned her attention to the window.

Leaning forward between two horseshoe nails, she rested her weight on one hand and positioned the triangle on the wooden surface, centered below two red diamonds. She held her breath, prepared to slip the triangle into its location, when four paws hit smack between her shoulder blades.

With a yelp of surprise, she jerked forward, cramming the point of the triangle into the existing design and banging her knee on a horseshoe nail. The worn denim tore. Pain shot up her leg as the head of the nail gouged her flesh.

"Winky!"

The cat shot away from the platform, his fur on end. He huddled beneath the display bench, his wide eyes peering back at her in fear.

Stumbling to her feet, Beth stretched the slit in her jeans to examine the cut. It bled freely—a good thing, she thought, considering what caused it. She limped to the supply cabinet and opened a bottom drawer, withdrawing a small first-aid kit. Winky watched her progress with interest, his tail twitching. She glared at the cat as she rummaged for a Band-Aid.

"Didn't I tell you to leave me alone? What was that all about? Do you think you're a mountain lion or something? Really!" Still grumbling, she applied the bandage, wincing as the pad came in contact with the cut. "I'll have to leave you at the house instead of bringing you here with me if you can't behave."

The cat tipped his head sideways as if to question the sincerity of her threat.

"Yeah, yeah, you know I couldn't do that," she muttered, shaking her head. As aggravated as she felt at the moment, she knew she wouldn't leave the kitten alone all day. It would be too lonely for him. And, she admitted, she would miss him too much. Shaking her finger at him, she added firmly, "But no more jumping on me!"

She took a minute to locate the empty matchbox he enjoyed batting across the floor and skidded it under the bench with him. He slapped his paw on it, tail swishing back and forth, then rolled onto his side and closed his eyes.

"*Now* you nap." Beth sighed, shaking her head. Her knee stung as she walked back to the platform, and she sucked air through her teeth when she knelt down.

But the real pain struck when she looked at the window. "Oh, no!" She ran her fingers along the border, which no longer formed a straight line. Apparently when she had kicked the nail loose, she had also bumped the squares forming the boundary of the project. Her panic increased when she picked up the green triangle and realized she'd nicked its tip when she'd shoved it across the platform.

She sank onto her bottom, her knee throbbing with each pounding beat of her heart. "I don't have time to redo anything," she moaned aloud. "Oh, why did this have to happen now?"

A furry head bumped her hip, and she lifted the cat into her arms, cradling him against her shoulder. "Winky, you naughty cat. Look what you made me do." His purr offered an apology, but it didn't fix the problem.

Pressing her face to the cat's neck, Beth dissolved into tears.

Twenty-one

"Trina." Andrew waved his cousin over.

"Ready for your check?" She removed the little order pad from her pocket.

"I'm done, but I think I want to take a sandwich over for Beth." He fidgeted under Trina's speculative look. "She didn't take a lunch break, but she needs something to eat."

"That's nice of you," Trina mused, one eyebrow rising higher than the other. "What's her favorite?"

"Turkey on wheat with lettuce, tomato, and honey mustard." The answer came so promptly, even Andrew had to laugh. Trina grinned and scampered off, disappearing into the kitchen.

Yes, he'd gotten to know his boss pretty well. And most of it came from observation, because even though she wasn't one to mince words, most of her spouting had little to do with Beth-the-Person. Beth-the-Person tried to remain aloof. But Andrew had finally peeked beneath the surface.

This had been a rough week. He'd seen it in the tense set of her shoulders, the creases in her forehead, and the tightness of her voice. The only smiles had been aimed at the cat, and at times Andrew had felt envious of the furry critter. At the same time, he felt grateful she had something in her life that seemed to bring her happiness.

It had pained him to be so honest with her last Tuesday when they'd come to the café for supper. But knowing Beth, seeing how she fought against the dictates of the fellowship and the community, he couldn't imagine her making Sommerfeld her permanent home. Thinking of her leaving brought pain on a different level, but not so much as he would have expected a few weeks ago.

Maybe, he mused, accepting the unlikelihood of her becoming Mennonite had begun the process of releasing his fascination with her. He still admired her, still was intrigued by her, but he was beginning to understand their backgrounds would never mesh. What he wanted in a wife, Beth surely wouldn't give. How could he be happy with that?

And she would never be happy living in a box. That's how she viewed the simple rules of the Mennonite community. Beth was a free spirit, an untamed wind. Even—he nodded to himself—a rebel. It suited her. But a Mennonite? No, she would never be that.

He glanced up and spotted Trina trotting toward him with a paper bag in her hand. He stood and tugged his money clip from his pocket.

"There you go, and Mama put in some chips and a pickle, too." Trina took his money. "I'll get your change."

"Keep it," he said, picking up the sack.

With a grin, she returned to work, and he headed out the door. He weaved between the café and the studio so he could enter through the back door. Pushing it open, he called, "Beth, I brought you a—"

His voice died when he spotted her sitting on the floor with the cat in her arms. The sound of her sobs filled the air.

Dropping the sack, he rushed to her and bent on one knee, touching her shoulder. "Beth, what is it?"

She lifted her tearstained face. "I ruined the window."

He scowled, shifting his gaze to the window. At first glance, everything appeared fine. But when he looked closer, he noticed a slight bend along the closest edge. Though not more than two or three centimeters, it was enough to guarantee the window wouldn't fit the intended frame unless repair work took place.

"What happened?"

"Winky." At the mention of his name, the cat pushed against Beth's shoulder with his front paws. She released him, and he dashed away with his ears back. "He was playing, and he startled me. I. . .I fell onto the platform. I cut myself"—she pointed to a tear in her jeans, which exposed a Band-Aid on the side of her knee—"and messed up the window."

Andrew puffed his cheeks and blew out a noisy breath. "I should have known we needed more nails to hold something this big. And I shouldn't have brought that kitten here."

She sat sniffling. He settled back on his haunches and scratched his head. "Well, I can go out to Ortmanns', buy some more nails, and we can press this back into position. Hopefully, with no further than it's been moved, it'll go back without affecting the strength of the joints. We'll double up the nails so there won't be the chance to move it again."

Without a word, she held up a thick green triangle.

Even without taking it, Andrew could see the shattered tip. It wouldn't fit tightly that way. He pulled his lips to the side in a pucker. "Do you have more green?"

Her shoulders slumped dismally. "Scraps. I didn't order much excess because of the cost."

He gave her back a pat and pushed to his feet. He located a piece in the scrap box just large enough to replace the chipped triangle.

Showing it to her, he said, "I'll have to be extra careful when I cut it, but I think this will work."

Beth took both pieces of glass and lay the triangle on top of the odd-shaped scrap. She nodded. "Yes, it's big enough, barely. I like to have more space around the cut to insure a crisp corner."

"Me, too," Andrew said, "but beggars can't be choosers. We don't have time to wait for an order of a new sheet."

She held her hand to him, and he gave a tug that brought her to her feet. When she grimaced, his heart gave a lurch.

"Are you sure that leg is okay?"

"It's fine," she insisted. Still holding the glass in one hand, she said, "Go on out to Ortmanns' and get those nails. While you're gone, I'll score this glass and get it cut."

Andrew swallowed a grin. She sounded like the old bossy Beth again. "Do you want me take the cat with me and leave him at the farm?"

Her gaze flitted sideways, and a soft smile grew on her face when she found the kitten lying on his side with both front paws over his eyes. "No. That was his first major offense. I think I can forgive him. Besides. . ." She turned back with a chuckle. "I'll get even when I start the grinder. I'm sure his nap will be seriously disturbed."

Andrew grinned. He turned toward the door and spotted the discarded lunch sack. After picking it up, he dumped its contents onto the worktable. "Here. Deborah made you a sandwich—your favorite. Eat it. It'll help you feel better."

It gave his heart a lift to see her smile of thanks. He took the empty bag with him and drove as quickly as possible to Ortmanns'. Dust rolled behind his pickup and sneaked between window cracks, making him sneeze. When he reached the farm, he pulled his pickup right up to the barn. Since Mr. Ortmann had told him he was welcome to as many nails as he needed, he let himself into the tack room and loaded the paper bag with several handfuls of pewter-colored nails, not even bothering to count. He'd count them as he used them and make sure he reported it later.

His mission complete, he returned to the pickup. Just as he opened the door to the cab, someone called his name. He looked over his shoulder and saw Livvy Ortmann stepping off the back stoop. She balanced a basket of wet clothes on her hip.

Andrew held up the bag. "I came for more nails. I'll settle with your dad later."

"That's fine," she said, a smile tipping up the corners of her lips. "I heard Beth might be doing even more of those big windows."

Andrew chuckled. Beth often complained about everyone knowing her business. But this time he hadn't told, so she couldn't blame him for blabbing.

"I bet it's fun, putting the pieces together. Like working on a big puzzle." Livvy's voice sounded wistful.

"Yes, it's fun," Andrew confirmed, "but it's also work. And I'd better get back to it. We have a lot to do."

Livvy stepped forward, prolonging his leave-taking. "How many windows do you have to do?"

Andrew pulled himself into the cab. "None, if she can't finish this first one on time." Then, realizing he probably shouldn't be sharing something so personal, he stammered, "B–but I'm sure she will."

Livvy's smile drooped. "Well, I won't keep you. But maybe. . . maybe I could come by the studio and see how the pieces go together sometime?"

"Sure, Livvy. Sometime." Eager to return to the studio and help Beth set things to right, Andrew slammed the door. He put the pickup in REVERSE, made a quick turnaround, and headed out of the Ortmann yard with a wave of his hand. When he reached the end of the drive, he glanced in his rearview mirror.

Oddly, Livvy still stood where he'd left her, staring after the truck.

Sean turned off the engine and sat, staring at the front of Beth's simple, metal-sided studio. For reasons he couldn't fully explain, he hesitated approaching the front door. He was impatient to see her—he'd missed her more than he understood. Yet given their last stilted conversation, he felt as though his friendship with Beth had faded before it had had a chance to bloom.

He snorted in derision. Hadn't he made fun, not too long ago, of a man from the recreation center where he worked out who'd met some woman online and fallen head over heels after a few brief e-mail messages? He'd thought it ridiculous, the man desperate to feel such intense emotion for someone he hardly knew. Yet sitting here, staring at the studio and trying to summon up the courage to go in, he understood that man's feelings.

After only a few face-to-face meetings, a mere dozen less-than-meaningful conversations, and a spattering of e-mail communications, he was. . .smitten.

Another snort blasted. Since when did he use old-fashioned words like *smitten*? He shook his head, grasping the door handle. It must be the simple setting that inspired the use of a word from time past. But the truth remained. Sean was attracted to Beth.

Taking in a great breath, he opened the door and stepped out. A mild breeze tousled his hair as he followed the smooth white sidewalk to the front door. Since his last visit, the grass had started to green up, showing the promise of spring around the corner.

Spring meant new life in so many ways. In nature, of course, but also in business. Most new contracts came in the spring, when people were ready to build. And this year, it seemed that spring had opened his heart to the idea of leaving his bachelor days behind.

He stopped in the middle of the sidewalk, the bold thought taking him by surprise. *Marriage?* His dad would certainly tell him it was premature to be thinking marriage. Yet in his twenty-five years of life, Sean couldn't remember ever coming close to coupling the M word with any other female.

"Smitten for sure," he mumbled, and he raised his hand to knock on the door.

Beth herself opened it, and he felt his shoulders tense as if she could read on his face what he had been thinking only moments before. Well, he decided, if she was able to ascertain his thoughts, she didn't find them repulsive, because she offered a smile.

"Come on in. Is it good to be back in Kansas?"

Sean closed the door behind him and unzipped his light jacket. "It's always good to be home." He faltered, seeking a topic of conversation that hadn't been covered in their brief telephone conversations and didn't relate to the window. Suddenly one was provided without warning.

A gray and white furball zipped across the floor and dove on the shoelaces of his right shoe.

"Hey! What's this?" The cat rolled on its back, all four feet in the air, batting at the loop that formed the bow.

Beth chuckled and picked up the cat. "This is Winky, the newest addition to Quinn's Stained-Glass Art Studio. He thinks he owns the place, so don't tell him otherwise."

Sean scratched behind the cat's ear. "Winky, huh? He's pretty cute."

The cat allowed Sean to make one more sweep with his fingers before it struggled in Beth's arms, and she put him down. Straightening, she shrugged. "I guess it's silly to have an animal running loose in here, but he's good entertainment."

"Not silly at all." Sean watched the kitten crouch, its tail sweeping madly, before bouncing on a splash of sunshine on the concrete floor. "I bet he's good company, too."

"That he is."

Sean looked around. "Speaking of company. . ." He glanced at his watch. "Has Andrew gone home already?"

Beth turned and moved toward the platform. "Our schedule has changed a bit. I don't have Andrew on Wednesdays or Saturdays anymore. He works for his dad then."

"Oh?" Sean trailed Beth, his gaze on the colorful array of glass on the wooden platform. "Is he easing back into farming?"

Beth released a short, humorless laugh. "No, actually he's trying to ease *out* of farming." She slipped her hands into the pockets of her apron and looked at Sean. "He's worked a deal with his dad that if the studio picks up the contracts from your company, which means it can support a full-time staff of workers, he'll be an artist instead of a farmer. So. . ." She raised her brows and quirked her lips.

Sean completed her thought. "A lot rests on this project."

"It always has."

Her voice sounded tight, and for a moment Sean regretted the pressure he'd put on her to meet this initial obligation. He knew the time had been short, yet he and his father had needed to see how well she stood up to pressure. The construction business was one requiring speed and accuracy. If Beth was going to be part of the team, they had to know she could meet the requirements.

"Well, let's see how it's going." He tempered the words with a grin, then stepped beside her and made no pretense of doing anything but thoroughly examining every minute inch of the design.

He whistled through his teeth. The completed sections were amazing. The play of color, the illusion of some sections standing out from others, the perfect balance of lights and darks. . .it was a work of art, there was no doubt.

"It looked great on paper, but in reality. . .wow."

Beth shot him a worried look. "But it isn't done."

"No, but I can see how much progress you've made since I was here last." He pulled a camera from his jacket pocket. "I'll take a couple of updated shots. Dad will want to see this."

Beth stood back and allowed him to take the pictures. In the last one, her cat leaped onto the platform at the last minute. He put the camera away, laughing. "So he's entertainment, company, and a nuisance."

"He can be," she agreed, shooing the cat from the platform.

Sean noticed something. "You've really barricaded this thing in with tacks." He pointed to the line of nails surrounding the project. "Afraid it's going to fall off or something?"

Beth grimaced. "No, just wanting to make sure it stays square. I want it to fit the opening you've got waiting for it."

He sensed there was another reason for the number of nails. It looked as though she and Andrew had built a miniature picket fence around the window. Shaking his head, he shrugged. "It certainly looks secure."

"Good." Beth now sounded grim. "If it's secure, then my future is secure."

TWENTY-TWO

Sean, his meetings completed and a signed contract tucked securely in his leather portfolio, turned his car onto the highway and headed west. He would have rather gone south, back to Sommerfeld, to spend a pleasant evening with Beth. But she'd made it clear she needed to work.

Dad would be thrilled. Her dedication to the task was exactly what Evan McCauley wanted in employees. Sean had always seconded Dad's opinion on that and had adopted the work ethic for himself. Even though his office was in his own home with no time card to punch or boss close by to check up on him, he'd kept the same working hours as any other businessman, even spending many Saturdays and Sunday afternoons in his office, as well. With no family of his own demanding his time, Sean's sole focus had been McCauley Church Construction. Just like it was for Dad.

And now, it seemed, pleasing McCauley Church Construction was Beth's focus, too. Yes, that would certainly please Dad. Sean realized he should also feel pleased. But something other than *pleased* flitted through his mind when he considered Beth's response to his invitation to dinner.

The midafternoon sun glared off the hood of his car, causing him to squint. Frowning, he groped for his sunglasses in the pocket on the side of the door, slipped them into place, and rested his arm on the window ledge. He drove past a wheat field, where a plainly dressed man with a beard used a tractor with metal wheels to pull an implement that looked like it came straight from an antique store. Yet the outdated equipment seemed to be getting the job done, as the wheat fell in a neat swath.

The sight of the farmer—although Sean was sure this man was Amish rather than Mennonite, judging by the beard—reminded him of Beth's comment about Andrew trying to ease out of farming. What an awkward position for the man—answering to a woman in a workplace. Sean couldn't imagine that being the norm in the Old Order community.

Although he hadn't spent a great deal of time in Sommerfeld, he surmised the religious group would discourage women from being in positions of leadership over men. Yet there was Andrew, contentedly following Beth's instructions in the hopes of never planting another crop.

Or was there a deeper hope existing in the tall man's heart?

Sean snorted. No sense in creating problems where none existed. Even though Sean suspected Andrew's protectiveness of Beth went beyond mere employee to employer, he knew Beth held no interest in Andrew outside of his assistance in the studio. Neither her words nor her actions even hinted at a personal interest in Andrew. Sean had no competition there.

Competition. Shaking his head, he hit the button to roll down the window and let the rushing air cool his warm face. He'd be better off focusing on the competitors for his business. Although McCauley held its own in the world of construction, it still took considerable time and attention to stay in the game. Juggling three projects while planning six more was Dad's goal, and that took time. Sean didn't have time to be dwelling on a relationship with a pretty artist. Especially when the relationship must be handled long-distance.

Still, thoughts of Beth—wisps of hair slipping free of her ever-present ponytail to frame her heart-shaped face, the little cleft in her delicate chin, and the determination in her bright blue eyes—teased him all the way home.

"Amen."

Beth cupped her hand beneath her mother's elbow and helped her rise from a kneeling position. Although she'd gotten over the initial embarrassment of kneeling in a room full of people for the closing prayer at service, she wished they would set aside the tradition for the sake of her mother. As Mom's pregnancy progressed, she could hardly get back to her feet. And since Henry sat on the opposite side of the church in the men's section, it was up to Beth to assist her.

Beth's aunt Joanna offered help on the other side, and between the two of them, they helped Mom settle on the bench.

"Whew," Mom huffed, as if she'd done the work alone. "It's a good thing the end is in sight, because I don't know how many more times I'll be able to do this."

Joanna sat down and took her sister's hand, giving it several pats. "How many more weeks?"

"Seven weeks and two days," Mom answered promptly, "but who's counting?"

The two women laughed.

"I'm counting." Beth made the firm assertion. "I have enough to worry about at the studio without worrying about Mom's swollen feet and stomachaches."

Joanna tipped her head back and stared at Beth in surprise. "Why, you don't need to worry about those things, Beth. Those are very typical for expectant mothers." Her smile didn't quite convince Beth. "You'll see when you get married and carry your first child. It's all just part of the price we pay for the privilege of creating new life."

Beth arched one brow. "Maybe. . ."

"No 'maybe' about it," Mom insisted as she planted her hands against the backless bench and pushed to her feet. "These babies are worth every bit of trouble." She cupped her expanded girth, chuckling softly. "And truthfully? They are probably less trouble in here than they will be after they're born."

She and Joanna shared more smiles. Beth had little to offer in the way of experience. But like her mother, she was ready to see the pregnancy over and these babies born so things could settle down.

Henry wove his way through little clusters of congregants who gathered to talk before heading home for a good dinner. He stopped beside Beth and put his hand on her shoulder. Although the touch was not inappropriate and although there were times Beth longed for a closer relationship, she still squirmed a bit under the familiar gesture. When would her prayers to finally feel completely at ease with her stepfather be answered?

"Did you invite Beth to dinner?" Henry asked.

"She knows she has a standing invitation," Mom replied, sending Beth a quick grin. "I invited my parents today, so it would be nice if you would join us."

It had taken a long time for Beth to develop a relationship with the grandfather who had refused to acknowledge her existence for the first two decades of her life. But both Grandpa and Grandma Koeppler had gone overboard in the past year to make up for their earlier neglect. In fact, Grandpa Koeppler was convinced her talent in art came from him since he enjoyed creating works of art from wood. He had been her biggest supporter when the studio was constructed.

It had been awhile, though—since the McCauley project started, to be exact—since she'd spent an afternoon with her grandparents. So she eagerly accepted her mother's invitation.

"I'll come on one condition." Beth shook her finger at her mother. "You let me serve and clean up afterward."

Mom laughed lightly, but she nodded. "I'll take you up on that, honey. Thank you."

Mom had put pork chops with cranberry sauce, sliced onions, and green peppers in the oven to slow bake. Henry insisted Mom sit with Grandpa Koeppler in the front room while Grandma sliced home-baked bread, Beth boiled water for instant rice, and he placed the plates and silverware on the table.

The smells teased Beth's senses, and her stomach growled, reminding her how her eating schedule had gone haywire in the past weeks. She could hardly wait until they sat down to eat. With five chairs around the kitchen's round table, their elbows touched, but no one seemed to mind. Grandpa asked the blessing, and they chatted as they enjoyed the meal.

Well, Beth acknowledged with a small stab of discomfort, Mom and Grandma chatted, and Henry and Grandpa chatted, but she ended up being left out of most of the conversation. It wasn't intentional—she knew that—but the odd number simply left her without a conversation partner. For a brief moment, she wished her parents had asked someone—Andrew? Trina?—to join them so she wouldn't feel so. . .ignored. Then Grandpa accidentally bumped her elbow, and she realized that even if they had asked someone else, there wouldn't be room for another person at this table.

In fact, she thought as her scowling gaze swept around the periphery of the table, once those twins were born, there wouldn't really be room for her here. The thought ruined what was left of her appetite, and she put down her fork.

Mom glanced over at the *clink* of the silverware against the plate. "Are you finished?"

Beth glanced at her plate. She hated to waste food, especially food that had only moments ago given her taste buds great pleasure. But she knew she wouldn't be able to swallow another bite. "Yes." She pushed away from the table. "Do you want me to cut the pie and put it on dessert plates?"

Mom started to rise, too. "Let me get the ice cream out of—"

"I'll do it," Beth said, rising quickly. "You stay put."

She listened to the continued conversation as she sliced the apple pie purchased at Deborah's café. Once each slice had been topped with a healthy scoop of vanilla ice cream, she carried the plates to the table and refilled the coffee cups for her grandparents and stepfather. Mom had sworn off coffee for the duration of her pregnancy, claiming the caffeine created water retention. Beth didn't think Mom could possible retain any more fluid than she already had.

Even though she didn't cut a piece of pie for herself, she did sit down and sip coffee while the others ate.

Grandpa slurped at his cup, then gave her a speculative look, his bushy gray brows high. "So I hear you have lots of windows to build."

Beth resisted shaking her head. Word sure got around if it made it all the way out to Grandpa's farm! "Yes, they're waiting for me. But I have to finish the first project McCauley gave me to their satisfaction before they'll trust me with anything else."

"Well, that Andrew is helping you, isn't he? At least, his dad was fussing that the boy is always at your studio." Grandpa's voice held a note of teasing.

Beth chose to ignore the insinuation that Andrew hung around the studio for reasons other than working. "He's there quite a bit, but he's helping his dad, too. I know he wants to work at the studio full-time, though."

Grandma nodded slowly. "He's always been different from his brothers, not interested in farming and such. It's good there's something he likes to do that is close by."

"He's a big help to me at the studio." Beth drew a thoughtful sip of the hot liquid before continuing. "But even with his help, we've had some trouble finishing this *one* large project. I'm pushing mighty close to that deadline. It makes me a little nervous, thinking about the big windows waiting for me."

"Maybe I can come in and help," Grandpa said.

Beth imagined her elderly grandfather bending over the high worktable or on his knees beside the platform. Neither picture would gel. But she wouldn't tell him that. "If you want to spend a day at the studio, you're more than welcome, Grandpa."

He nudged her with his elbow and grinned, his lips twitching. "I build things, too, you know. In my woodshop. It's pretty much the same thing." Suddenly his face lit. "Say, I have an idea. We could work together. I could build cabinets, and you could make stained-glass windows to put in the door panels."

Without intending to, Beth groaned.

Grandpa reared back, his forehead creasing. "You don't like the idea?"

"Oh, no, it's a great idea. I love it, actually!" She touched his arm. "It would be an honor, considering the furniture making that's been done in the family throughout generations. Then I'd have a part in that, too." She sighed. "No, it's just the idea of one more project. Right now it's a little overwhelming."

"So hire workers," Henry said. He pushed his empty pie plate aside and draped his arm across the back of Mom's chair. "You know McCauley plans to use you. You've seen a contract to know how much they will pay, so we could sit down and figure out the hourly wage you could offer."

"Workers? Plural?" Beth propped her elbows on the table.

"Certainly plural." Henry's fingers drew a circle on Mom's shoulder—Beth was certain he wasn't even aware he was doing it. "You've had Andrew with you for several months now, and sometimes it's still hard to keep up. If your workload is going to increase, it makes sense to add a few more employees to the studio. They could start with the little things—the suncatchers—and work up to the larger projects, just as Andrew has. On-the-job training."

Beth considered what it would be like to have more than one person in the studio. She frowned. "I like the idea of extra hands, but right now with just Andrew and me, it can feel crowded. I don't know how we'd fit more people in there."

"So expand." The enthusiasm in Henry's voice stirred excitement in Beth's chest. "You've got enough land to build on three of the four sides if you need to. Start interviewing people now who would like to learn stained-glass art. Then, when it's time to start working on those multiwindow contracts, you'll have people in place ready to go."

"But how will I pay for a bigger studio?" Beth threw her hands outward. "I don't have any money from these contracts yet."

"Take out a small-business loan," Henry said.

"A loan?" Grandma sounded horrified.

"An investment," Henry countered, his tone gentle. "If Beth is going to build her business, a loan may be necessary."

"No loans. I don't trust banks." Grandpa shook his head adamantly and wrapped his hand around Beth's forearm. "You don't go to any bank. If you want to expand the business, I'll give you your portion of your inheritance early."

Grandma immediately sat up straight, her face lighting. "Yes! Much better."

"In-inheritance?" Beth looked from one grandparent to the other. "But I already got an inheritance from Aunt Lisbeth. Her café and house. That's enough." It was much more than she could have anticipated, having grown up far away from this community and her mother's relatives.

"That was from Lisbeth," Grandpa said. "But I always planned to divide my holdings between my children and grandchildren. Already one of Art's boys claimed his portion when he took a wife and needed to purchase land for a house. Now you can do the same. There should be enough to add on to your studio."

Beth's heart raced. "If I add workers, I'll need more equipment, too."

"If the community puts up the building for you, like they did last time, you'll have money for equipment."

Beth stared at her grandfather. "You'd really let me do that? Take my inheritance early?"

Grandpa looked steadily into her eyes. "Do you believe this studio is what God planned for your future?"

The seriousness in his expression and tone made Beth think carefully before she answered. She had prayed about the studio, and she did believe she'd been given the talent and desire by God to create beauty with stained glass. She nodded. "I do believe it's what He intended for me."

"Then I will give you the money. Tomorrow."

TWENTY-THREE

G randpa Koeppler is quite the go-getter." Beth and Andrew sat on opposite sides of the worktable and sipped lemonade from tall paper cups. There wasn't anything from Deborah's café that Beth didn't like. The sweet, cool liquid revived her after a long day. Her work had been interrupted several times to confer with her grandfather on the addition to the studio. "He's done more in one day than most people would accomplish in a full week."

"Because he wants to see you happy," Andrew said, his smile crinkling his eyes. "And he knows the studio makes you happy."

"Well. . ." Beth bit down on her lower lip for a moment. "I'm wondering how you feel about all of this. The expansion is moving pretty fast." Grandpa had already placed the order for materials to build toward the alley. Tomorrow a small crew of men would pour the concrete foundation so it would be dry and ready for construction when the steel beams and siding arrived by truck next week. Beth's head spun with the idea that by the beginning of April she could have a staff of three under her supervision!

"You need to expand if the studio is to be all you've envisioned." Andrew raised his broad shoulders in a shrug. "Your success is my success, so I'm not arguing."

Beth could have reminded him of his comment that she shouldn't stay in Sommerfeld, that she didn't belong. But she chose instead to ask a question. "Since we'll have the space for a full crew in here, do you have any suggestions for employees? I have no real preference for male or female, but I do think I'd like the workers to be at least eighteen years old."

It wasn't uncommon for youth as young as fourteen to begin working full-time, whether on their own family farms or in other positions in and around Sommerfeld. But given the potential danger of some of the equipment used in the studio, Beth preferred workers with a little more maturity than the normal fourteen-year-old.

"Hmm. . ." Andrew's furrowed brow and thoughtful tap of his finger against his lips told Beth he took her question seriously. "If you want to hire young people from here in town, I would start with your uncle Ben Koeppler's older girl, Catherine. She is eighteen but not yet married, and I heard she was looking to be hired at the big discount store in McPherson. Her parents would rather she wasn't driving."

Beth nodded. She'd met Catherine at family gatherings. She was a sweet, quiet girl who would likely prefer staying close to home. "Anybody else?"

"Maybe. . ." Suddenly Andrew's ears began filling with pink. "She's another of your relatives, although not so close—a cousin from your maternal grandmother's side. Doug Ortmann's daughter Livvy asked me not long ago if she could come by and see what we do. Maybe she would be interested."

Beth, observing his flaming ears, resisted making a teasing remark. "I had thought about Trina. She'll be eighteen next month, right? And I know she's said she'd rather not work at the restaurant."

"Working here would be the same as working there to Trina."

Andrew's voice held a touch of sadness. "She wouldn't be any happier. And asking her would only create problems with her mother."

Beth agreed with that. Although she didn't find Deborah as intimidating as she first had when she'd come to Sommerfeld, she still tried to keep her distance from the forceful woman. The last thing she wanted was to cause conflict in Trina's relationship with her mother.

"Okay, then. My cousin Catherine and. . .Livvy, you said?" At his nod, he shifted his gaze to the side. A curious reaction. Beth pressed her lips together to keep from grinning. "Well, here's what I suggest. We might as well find out now whether they're interested. That way, if they aren't, we can look for someone else. We also need to know if they can learn the process. Do you suppose they could come in tomorrow and watch you make a suncatcher from start to finish? Maybe even start one themselves."

Andrew's head whipped around. "Tomorrow?"

Beth flipped her hands outward. "Why not? If they get some training, they'll be ready to step into full-time slots when the addition is finished. I can't pay them a wage until they actually start working, so I'd need to make that clear, but if they're interested and can prove their ability, I could put them on the payroll when they start constructing projects."

"Or maybe pay them per project to get started?"

"Not a bad idea. . ." Beth leaned her chin on her hand, thinking out loud. "To start with, I had thought of paying minimum wage. But I kind of like the idea of paying per project. Then, as their skills grow and they work on the bigger projects, the pay could increase. I'll probably also start them out part-time—maybe just mornings. Ease into it. What do you think?"

Andrew's lips curved into a lopsided grin. His brown eyes glowed. "I think we are going to have a real art studio right here in Sommerfeld."

He released a hoot that surprised Beth. She'd never seen him so animated. He reached across the table and gave her hand one quick squeeze. "It's going to happen, isn't it?"

Beth couldn't stop her own smile from growing. "It's going to happen." She looked over at the platform. The kaleidoscope of color sparkled beneath the overhead lights, and her heart rate increased as her gaze skimmed around the circle of glistening shapes. "And to think it all rests on one window. . . ."

"Both Ben Koeppler and Doug Ortmann have telephones. Do you want to call the girls' fathers now and make arrangements for them to come in tomorrow morning?"

Beth jerked to face Andrew, blinking in confusion. "Ask their fathers?"

"Well, of course. The girls still reside beneath the roof of their fathers' homes. They must have permission for the job."

Beth hadn't considered having to ask permission for employees to join her workforce. Her stomach churned. She was still considered an outsider. Even though the men were related to her, they could say no.

"You know them better than I do." She clasped her hands in her lap, almost holding her breath. "Would you mind making the calls? You'll be pretty much in charge of their training anyway, as my top assistant."

Andrew sat up straighter, his smile wide. "I can do that. Should I call now?"

"Please do." Beth slipped from the stool. "And I'll get busy on the McCauley window. The last thing we want to do now is miss the deadline!"

Beth listened with half an ear as Andrew made telephone calls. In both cases, the men were working away from the house, but he elicited promises for them to call him at the studio when they returned home for the evening. It occurred to her as she listened to the calm surety in Andrew's voice how much he had changed in the months at the studio. His self-confidence had grown by leaps and bounds, and she realized with a small rush of pride that she had shared in his growth.

A warmth spread through her middle, and she lifted her face to send him a smile of approval. When he smiled back, his ears didn't even turn red.

By ten o'clock Tuesday morning, Beth wished she had a pair of headphones to block out the noise that stole her concentration, yet she didn't complain. She would show nothing but appreciation for the four men who'd graciously come to block and pour the floor for her addition no matter how raucous their laughter and noisy their hammers.

Inside the studio wasn't much better with Andrew running the cutting wheel to ready pieces for two pink butterfly suncatchers. Beth glanced up and swallowed the giggle that tried to form. Both Livvy and Catherine in their dresses, white caps, and neat anklets seemed so unsuited to this setting. Yet they stood side by side, aprons and goggles in place, and watched each step of the process with concentration. The hammering and voices from behind the studio didn't seem to distract them at all, and for a moment, Beth envied them their complete attentiveness to their task.

If only she could be so single-minded today! Last night she'd lain awake, her mind refusing to shut down. So many things to think about. If she hired workers, she needed to file paperwork with the Social Security Administration, be sure she talked to an accountant about tax laws, and update the record-keeping system in her computer so if she was ever audited, she'd be prepared. She needed to browse catalogs for the best prices in new equipment—another cutting wheel;

more gloves and pliers and nippers; and an oven for staining and firing her own glass.

Her heart tripped at the idea of coloring glass. Creating her own hues and shades rather than relying on a little block of color from an online store or paper catalog to match the hue and shade in her imagination. Her dreams were rapidly becoming reality, and Beth alternated between wanting to dance and shout and sing. . .and wishing she could hide and cower and cry.

Lord, thank You for the progress being made, for the people willing to help me. Let my studio be a reflection of what You have planted in me—let these projects bring glory to You.

The prayer formed effortlessly, and the fear shrank. Surely, as she'd told her grandfather, this studio was God's plan for her life. "If God is for me, who can be against me?" She murmured the words, paraphrasing a verse she'd encountered in her devotional reading. The thought washed her in peace, the fear melting away. It would be fine. Everything would be fine.

Andrew and his two observers moved to the worktable, where he demonstrated and then allowed each of them to snap the glass. Soon the three of them each held a carborundum stone and applied it to the edges of the wedges of pink glass. Beth, watching out of the corner of her eye, developed an even greater admiration for Andrew. He would be a wonderful foreman.

She sat upright, wondering when she'd finally released her worry over depending on him too much. God must be working on her, too. Humming to herself, she bent back over the platform.

With all the hammering outside, she almost missed the sound of the telephone ringing. Andrew stepped away from the worktable to answer it, then held it out to Beth. "It's Sean McCauley."

Beth rose, brushed off her knees, and took the phone. She plugged her opposite ear with her finger. "Good morning, Sean."

"Good morning. It's noisy over there!" His chuckle softened the complaint.

"I know." Beth paused, suddenly unwilling to divulge everything taking place. She couldn't explain why, but she didn't want Sean to know about all of the changes. . .yet. She sought a way to tell the truth without divulging specifics. "There's some construction nearby. It gets loud."

"I guess so." He seemed to accept her explanation. "Listen, I won't keep you because I know you're busy, but I needed to let you know Dad will be accompanying me to Sommerfeld next Wednesday. Although he's stayed up on the progress of the window through my reports and has seen pictures, he wants to meet you in person and see the window himself before we finalize McCauley's working relationship with you. Will that work?"

Beth's heart set up a patter. One more week, and everything would be final! "That sounds fine."

"And Dad would like to take you to dinner. We'll discuss all the details while we eat."

Beth frowned. "Well, the café here in town closes early on Wednesday since that's Bible study night, so we'll have to drive in to one of the bigger towns."

Sean's laughter came through the line, giving Beth a lift. "Not a problem, although one of these days I do want to sample the cooking at that café. I've heard good things about it."

"Someday," Beth promised, then fell silent. How many times would she and Sean meet face-to-face once her employment was set? Wouldn't they just communicate through e-mail, fax, and phone calls? The thought depressed her. She shook her head, throwing off the sadness. "Do you know what time you'll get here Wednesday?"

"We'll probably leave K.C. at noon. It generally takes me a little over three hours, so look for us around three, three thirty. Is that okay?"

Beth licked her lips. "Sure. That'll leave me most of the day to finish things up."

"Sounds good." A pause, and then his voice returned, lower, husky. "I'm looking forward to seeing you again."

Beth's mouth went dry. "Me—" She swallowed. "Me, too, Sean. See you then." She hung up the phone before anything else could be said.

As she returned to the platform, she glanced at Andrew. He smirked and winked. Heat rose in her face, and she turned away to get busy.

Sean pushed the disconnect button on his telephone, then released it and punched in his father's number. When he heard his father answer, he spoke without preamble. "Next Wednesday afternoon will be fine. Do you want me to swing by and pick you up?"

"I'll pick you up. I want to drive."

"Okay. Noon then. Anything else you want me to do in preparation for the final contract?"

"No." Dad's authoritative voice boomed through the line. "You've done the legwork. I'll do the paperwork. But do bring all the dimensions for the windows for that Denver church, as well as the one in Carlton. Even though we'd have time to get that to her later, given the construction schedule, I'd prefer she have them so she can fit the planning into her schedule."

Sean fingered the neat paper on his desk. It already bore the dimensions of each window and its location in the finished buildings. "Not a problem."

"Does she plan to continue doing her own work, as well?"

Sean frowned. "I'm not sure. I know initially she hoped to, but I'm not sure how she could handle all we're throwing at her plus her own stuff." For a moment Sean felt guilt press at him. He hoped Beth wasn't setting her own dreams aside for the sake of fulfilling McCauley contracts.

"Where there's a will, there's a way," his father stated emphatically. "Let her work it out. What matters is being able to brand that young lady as the McCauley stained-glass window artist. No other churches will sport windows with the kind of design we can offer. It'll give us yet another edge in the construction world. So how are the mock-ups for that annex in South Carolina coming?"

It took Sean a moment to catch up with Dad's abrupt change of topic, but he answered several questions about the potential recreational facility on the East Coast. They discussed the project in Mexico, which was nearing its completion, and argued about the best supplier for cross beams before hanging up.

As Sean put the phone back in the cradle, he felt as though something had been lacking in their conversation. He pressed his mind, and when the answer came, it surprised him. Because it had nothing to do with business.

When, he wondered, was the last time he and Dad had talked about anything that didn't directly involve McCauley Church Construction? He couldn't remember. But why did that bother him?

TWENTY-FOUR

Beth whistled, enjoying the quiet inside the studio. She'd come early to beat the crew, who planned to pour concrete into the frame they'd constructed yesterday. Mixing and pouring concrete was much less noisy, yet knowing they were out there might still provide too much of a distraction. She hoped that by getting a jumpstart, she'd be so focused she wouldn't even notice when the men arrived.

Knowing she'd be the only one inside the studio since Andrew spent Wednesdays with his father, she had told the two girls to come back on Thursday. She came close to taking Winky with her. She'd left him home yesterday out of worry the confusion outside would frighten him. In the end, though, she'd decided a day of no distractions also meant a day of no Winky. As much as she loved the kitten, he did tend to demand attention.

He was also turning into a real jumper. His back legs must have springs in them. In the middle of the night, a mighty crash had signaled his naughtiness. She hadn't been too happy when she'd discovered her answering machine on the floor instead of on the corner of her desk where it belonged. That had finalized her decision to leave the kitten at home. She intended to make full use of this totally-to-herself day and finish the McCauley window before the deadline.

Taking stock of the remaining unfinished area, Beth calculated how many more hours would be needed before she could solder and glaze the entire panel. The last step would be soldering metal crossbars in place to give the window additional strength—the last thing she wanted was to have this window buckle! But attaching crossbars would be the simplest task of the entire project. If she worked hard today and there were no more errors—unlikely, she chuckled, with the pouncing Winky at home—she should be able to finish just under deadline.

Oh, please, Lord! I want this studio to be everything You planned it to be!

She organized the next section of glass on the floor, then knelt down and picked up the first piece and slid it into the left-hand side of the H formed by lead came. Just as she wiggled it firmly against the lead border, the back door opened. Assuming it was one of the men ready to start pouring concrete, she kept her eyes on her work and called, "I'll be right with you."

"Beth."

Andrew's voice—and the serious note held in the single word—brought Beth's head up. When she saw his face, her heart fired into her throat. The piece of glass forgotten, she pushed to her feet. "What is it? What's wrong?"

"You haven't answered your phone." Andrew took a step forward. He twisted his hands at his waist, the nervous gesture heightening Beth's worry with each passing moment.

"It hasn't rung this morning."

"Last night, Henry tried to call."

"H–Henry?" Beth stumbled around the platform. Why wouldn't she have heard the phone? Then she remembered. She'd had a headache, probably from the additional activity at the studio, so she'd turned off her cell phone and the ringer on her home phone. She had been in such a hurry this morning to get to the studio, she hadn't bothered to turn either of them back on.

Grabbing Andrew's hand, she begged, "What did Henry need?"

Andrew shook his head, his eyes sorrowful. "Last night, a little after midnight, Aunt Marie woke up and felt as though something was wrong. She woke Uncle Henry, and he took her to the McPherson hospital. They transferred her by ambulance to Wichita."

Beth's heart pounded so hard her ears rang. "Mom? Is she okay? The. . .the babies?" A cold chill broke out over her body. She tugged Andrew's hands. "Tell me! What happened?"

Andrew shrugged. "That's all I know. My folks followed Uncle Henry to McPherson, then followed the ambulance to Wichita. Your grandparents went, too. But I haven't heard anything this morning. Uncle Henry asked me to let you know what was going on."

Beth dashed to the door. "Which hospital?"

"Wesley Medical Center." Andrew stepped toward her, his hand outstretched. "Uncle Henry would have called if something. . .bad. . . happened. I think you can assume no news is good news."

Beth pushed that comment aside. "I've only been to Wichita a couple of times since I moved to Kansas. I'm not sure I can find the hospital on my own. Do you know where it is?"

Andrew nodded slowly, his delayed reactions infuriating Beth. "Yes. My grandpa had surgery there once."

"Good. Then you can take me. Let's go." She pushed the door wide and started to step through. But a glance at Andrew's face stopped her. "What's wrong?"

"I can't go. Dad needs me to work today, especially since he isn't here." He shifted his gaze toward the platform. "And you have the window to finish."

She stared at him, her jaw hanging open. How could he even

suggest she work on the window while her mother lay in a hospital bed, and the babies. . .

Beth couldn't complete the thought.

He turned back to face her. "Will you be able to meet the deadline if you don't work today?"

The full impact of his question nearly buckled her knees. If she missed the deadline, she wouldn't have the contract for more windows. If she didn't have the contract, how many people would be affected? She ticked them off one by one.

The McCauleys, who were planning on her meeting their needs for windows.

Andrew, Catherine, and Livvy, who were planning on the studio providing jobs for them.

Her grandfather, who had willingly given her the money to expand the studio.

Even the men who were now arriving, preparing to pour concrete. They had postponed their own work in order to help her. Would they resent the time spent away from their own pursuits if she didn't follow through on the expansion?

Beth's head spun, and she clutched the door frame. How could she let all of those people down? But how could she stay here, knowing her mother or her unborn brother and sister might at this very moment be slipping away? Tears spurted into her eyes.

"Andrew, I have to go!"

Andrew's brows formed a fierce V. "But what about the studio? All the plans?"

Suddenly Beth knew the answer. "If the studio is God's will, it will happen with or without the McCauley contract."

Andrew gestured toward the platform. "And what if the McCauley contract is God's way of making everything available to you, and you throw it away? What will God think?"

"What will God think if I turn my back on my mother for some. . . some window?" Even she knew that was a simplification—the window was merely the representation of the whole of her dreams. Still, she shook her head wildly, her ponytail slapping her shoulder. "If you think God can't make it happen without my help, without that window, then you're underestimating Him." She smacked the doorframe with her open palm, creating a sharp sting that shot to her fingers. She grimaced, coiling the hand into a fist. "There's no way I'm staying here today, Andrew. I'm going to Wichita."

She didn't wait for him to respond. Charging out of the building and past the two men who stood, silent and watchful, at the edge of the wooden frame for the footing, she called, "Thank you for coming today. You can work without me here, right?" They each gave a nod, and she headed straight to the café. She bolted through the dining area to the kitchen, where she found Deborah at the stove.

"Deborah, can you tell me how to get to Wesley Medical Center?"

Deborah put down the spatula to offer a quick, brusque hug. "Of course I can. Trina, get something to write on and a pencil so I can put down directions for Beth." She scribbled a coarse map on a strip of paper towel, then handed it to Beth. "Tell Henry I'm praying for him, for all of you."

"I will, Deborah. Thank you." Beth forced the words past a lump in her throat. She accepted a hug from Trina before racing back through the café and out the door. The mumble of voices from the patrons told her everyone knew of the situation. She hoped they, like Deborah, were praying.

Oh, Father—Beth added her pleas as she slammed herself into her car and revved the engine—*please don't let anything happen to Mom or the babies! They're all I have.*

Andrew watched from the window of the studio as Beth zipped down the alley, creating a mighty cloud of dust that drifted across the frame awaiting concrete. The men began working, their movements automatic, but no banter was heard. Apparently they, too, knew of Uncle Henry and Aunt Marie's midnight run to the hospital.

Stepping away from the window, Andrew crossed to the platform and looked down at the stained-glass project. So close. They were so close. He knew what his dad would say if the contract didn't come through.

"Art isn't something you can count on. People will always need bread, so wheat is a secure future. I tried to tell you, didn't I?"

Andrew resisted putting his hands over his ears, knowing he wouldn't be able to stop the voice in his head with such a childish action. But his father didn't always have to be right, did he? The dream was here, right within reach, and it could be realized if this single project was finished on time.

Temptation teased. He had the pattern, the materials, the know-how. He could work on the window. Finish it, if need be. But Beth hadn't given him permission to work on it. Being a man who followed the rules, as much as he twitched to pick up the next piece of glass and get busy, he couldn't bring himself to do it. Not without her approval.

Besides, Dad had given him instructions for today. Since he and Mom were in Wichita with Uncle Henry, Andrew was expected to fill Dad's spot in the fields. If he didn't go, Dad would be furious. With a sigh, he locked the studio. He spent a moment visiting with the men and apologizing for not being able to help them; then he climbed into his truck.

As he aimed his vehicle toward the farm, he wondered what was happening in the hospital at Wichita. Belatedly, he remembered to offer a prayer.

Following Deborah's map, Beth managed to locate the medical center. After circling the campus and reading the names on the buildings, she pulled into the parking area off of Murdoch, next to the Birth Care Center. She jogged across the parking lot and entered the building, searching for someone—anyone—who could direct her.

A blue-haired lady sat at a desk with a little placard reading INFORMATION hanging over her head. Breathlessly, Beth dashed to the desk.

"Marie Koeppler," she said shortly.

The woman consulted her computer screen, her face crunched into a scowl. "Mrs. Koeppler is in High Risk Obstetrics, which is on the third floor of Building Three."

Beth stared at her in confusion. The woman must have read her expression.

"Here." She picked up a piece of paper, drew a zigzagging line, circled something, then handed it to Beth.

Beth looked at it, a campus map. "Thank you." Paper in hand, she exited the Birth Care Center, jogged through a parking garage, and entered Building Three. She located an elevator, punched the UP button, and bounced in place until a beep signaled a car's arrival. A jab of her finger on the three brought the doors closed, and she continued her anxious bouncing during the brief ride.

Once in the hallway, she wheeled around a corner and glanced through a plate-glass window. She spotted an elderly couple side by side, the man's gray head close to the white cap covering the woman's equally white hair, their hands linked. Her heart leaped in her chest.

"Grandpa! Grandma!" She dashed to them, dropping her purse on the way. Leaning forward, she shared a three-way hug, then sank to her haunches in front of them. "How is Mom? Where's Henry?"

Grandma's faded eyes looked glazed from the presence of tears. "He and Al and Maura walked down to the garden. . .to pray."

Beth realized Grandma hadn't addressed the first question. Fearful, she squeezed her grandmother's hand. "And Mom?"

"All we know is she has HELLP." Grandpa's voice, usually so strong, came out soft and broken.

Beth frowned, confused. "Yes, of course she has help. But what's wrong with her?"

Grandpa shook his head. "No. She has some condition called HELLP syndrome: H-E-L-L-P. I forget what it stands for. Her blood pressure is too high. And the babies. . ." Grandpa's chin quivered. "This morning. . ."

Beth thought her chest might pound clear out of her chest. She wrapped her arms around her grandfather's neck. "It's okay, Grandpa. It's okay."

The sound of footsteps intruded, and Grandpa gently pushed her away to wipe at his eyes with his sleeve. He leaned into Grandma as Beth rose and turned. Henry, followed by Andrew's parents, entered the room.

When Henry spotted her, he stopped and simply held out his arms. She raced across the floor and threw herself against his chest. Immediately, his arms closed around her, and she pressed her cheek to his collarbone. Never had a hug felt as good as the one she now experienced. She tightened her arms around Henry's middle, tears stinging her closed eyes, as she wondered why it had taken something so extreme to finally lead her to this moment with her stepfather.

Somewhere behind her, she heard Al quietly telling her grandparents the surgeon had located Henry. His voice dropped to a mumble, and she couldn't understand what he was saying. Then Henry spoke, covering Al's voice.

"You came."

She heard relief and wonder in his tone. "I came," she reiterated unnecessarily. Where else would she be? Her throat constricted with the realization that she had surprised Henry by coming. How out of touch with the family had she become that he would think she would stay away?

"I'm so sorry you couldn't reach me last night. I. . .I turned off my phone because I had a headache. If I'd known—"

"Shh." Henry rocked her gently back and forth. "Your knowing wouldn't have changed anything. The doctor said this condition, this HELLP, has been bothering your mother for several weeks. We didn't pay enough attention because we didn't know. But don't blame yourself for anything, Beth. You're here now. That's all that matters."

She felt him rest his cheek on her head. His rough hand caught in her ponytail as he stroked its length. His tender words, his sensitive attention to her needs touched Beth on a deeper level than anything she'd known with any other person besides her mother. *This then*, she thought, *is what it is to have a father.* She allowed herself a few minutes of comfort, safe within the circle of Henry's arms. Eventually, the questions that had plagued her all the way from Sommerfeld to Wichita pressed upward again.

Swallowing her tears, she pulled back enough to study his face. He looked as though he'd aged ten years since last Sunday's dinner. Although she feared the answer, she had to know.

"Henry, the babies—are they. . . ?"

"The babies were delivered early this morning. They did it

surgically, a cesarean section. They had to, to save them. Both were in distress—their heart rates dropping too low. So the doctors took them from your mother's womb."

She searched his face. A gentle smile curved his lips.

"A boy and a girl, just as the ultrasound predicted. Both not much bigger than my hand." He held up one hand and examined it.

Beth looked at it, too, trying to imagine her little brother and sister near the size of the broad hand only inches from her face.

With a disbelieving shake of his head, Henry added, "Such tiny miracles."

Beth zipped her gaze back to his face. "Then they're. . .alive?" She whispered the last word.

"Alive." Henry swallowed, cupping her cheek. "But critical. We won't know for several hours, maybe days, whether they will be. . . healthy."

Beth read a great deal into the simple statement. She would worry about the babies later. Right now she needed to know something else. "And. . .and Mom?"

Henry's face crumpled, and he crushed Beth to his chest. She clung, her hands convulsing on his back as she felt him shudder. *Oh, no, God. Please, no. Not my mother.*

TWENTY-FIVE

A s if in answer to her silent prayer, Beth heard Henry's rasping voice whisper, "She lives. Praise our Lord, your mother lives."

The relief was so great, Beth nearly collapsed. Henry guided her, with a firm arm around her waist, to the row of plastic chairs. She sank into the one next to Maura, and Andrew's mother put a steadying hand on her knee. Beth clasped it, drawing strength from the simple touch.

"Can I see her?"

Henry shook his head. "No. The surgeon just now said we have to wait until she's stabilized. She lost a lot of blood in the surgery to deliver the babies. The doctor said this HELLP made it so her blood won't clot. They're keeping her sedated so she won't move around and start the bleeding again. He explained to me that the high blood pressure can cause damage to her liver and other organs."

Beth gasped, but Henry offered a reassuring squeeze on her shoulder. "They're running tests to make sure everything is all right. Her body needs a chance to recuperate." A small, hopeful smile played on the corners of his lips. "We can go peek at the babies, though, one at a time, as long as we stay quiet and don't try to touch them yet."

"Why not?" Beth looked at the other two women in the room. "Isn't it harmful to just leave babies without any contact? Doesn't someone need to. . .to *bond* with them?"

Maura squeezed Beth's knee. "Honey, these babies are fragile. It's more important not to cause any distress. Touching them could overexcite them, which would do more harm than good. We need to let them rest and gain strength. Then we can all stroke their little backs and sing lullabies to them."

Beth wasn't sure she agreed, but she decided arguing would only cause more stress for Henry. "When are you going to go see them?"

Henry glanced at his wristwatch. "The surgeon said we could start visiting the special nursery at one o'clock. So. . ." He held out his hands in a helpless gesture. "Until then, we wait."

Over the remainder of the morning, more people arrived, turning the waiting room into a somber family reunion. The room rapidly filled with Henry's brothers and their wives, each of Beth's aunts and uncles, and many of her cousins. Even Deborah, her husband, and their children showed up unexpectedly shortly before one.

When Henry sent Deborah a questioning look, she snapped, "Yes, I closed the café." Her voice broke as she added, "Don't you know you, Marie, and those babies are more important than any café could be?" Then she spun toward Beth, held out her arms, and said, "I see you made it. Come here and thank me for that map."

Without exception, the new arrivals greeted Beth first, offering hugs and words of support, before giving the same to Henry or to Beth's grandparents. Beth thought her chest might burst from the warmth of their acceptance. How could she have waited so long to embrace these people as her family? Looking back, she realized she had held them at arm's length, distancing herself from gatherings out of fear of rejection. Now her fears seemed foolish.

Trina sat close, her capped head on Beth's shoulder, and a thought struck Beth. She was not a member of their church, but she was a member of their family. Apparently in their opinion, she *did* belong. Their actions today clearly expressed that. Now it was up to her to accept it. Beth felt as though she matured at least five years in those moments of reckoning.

The instant the clock on the wall read one o'clock, Henry bounded for the door. Before leaving the room, he paused and looked back at Beth. "You'll be next," he promised. Then he clipped past the window and disappeared.

Trina lifted her head and smiled at Beth. "Are you excited?"

Beth released a short, humorless laugh. "I'm more nervous than anything. I've never been around babies. And for them to be born so early, and to be sick. . ." Tears stung again.

"They'll be okay," Trina said with such certainty Beth almost believed it. "Wait and see."

"I'd feel better if I could see them for myself." Beth looked longingly toward the door. But Henry had only been gone a few minutes. She shouldn't be selfish and hurry him back with her thoughts.

Trina touched her arm. "Beth? Was it hard for you to come, knowing you have work to do?"

Beth looked at the younger woman. Trina's spattering of freckles stood out like copper pennies in her pale face. She seemed to hold her breath as she waited for Beth's reply, but Beth couldn't imagine why it held such importance.

"It wasn't hard at all," Beth answered honestly.

Trina's eyes widened. "Really?"

"Really. Suddenly the studio, the artwork—all of it—seemed secondary." Shaking her head, she gave a soft, rueful chuckle. She glanced around the room at the gathered family members. "This is first: family." With a sigh, she admitted, "The studio is still there. It might take me longer to do all the things I've planned—the expansion, the new equipment, the big projects—but I believe God led me to open the studio, so I'll just trust Him to open the door to me when the time is right. Apparently the time wasn't right yet."

Trina shook her head, the white ribbons of her cap swaying gently with the movement. "Oh, yes, Beth. The right time. Thank you."

Beth wanted to discover the reason behind Trina's reaction, but Henry returned.

"Beth? Come on. I'll walk you down."

Beth eagerly joined her stepfather.

Sean hung up the phone, an unexplained concern weighting his chest. He glanced at his wristwatch. Where could she be? She'd said she would be working at the studio, yet she didn't answer the phone there. Nor did she answer her cell phone, and last night when he'd called her home phone, it had also gone unanswered.

Dad was waiting for a reply to his questions concerning the weight of the glass she'd chosen for the window they'd assigned. Sean assumed she had used tempered glass, which was thicker and more durable, but he couldn't remember her ever stating that for sure. He wanted to verify it before reporting to his father.

But he couldn't do that if he couldn't reach her. He picked up the phone and dialed again, then allowed the telephone to ring a dozen times before hanging up again.

He pressed his memory. He knew she'd had an answering machine at one time, yet no recording message had invited him to leave a call-back number. Maybe she'd turned off the machine, although he couldn't imagine why she would choose to do that. He had no idea if

Sommerfeld offered caller ID. But if she had it, could she possibly be choosing not to answer his calls?

He didn't like that thought. If Beth wasn't answering the telephone, there had to be a logical reason. She was straightforward enough to simply tell him she didn't have time to talk; she'd done it before. He chuckled. Beth was honest. Sometimes painfully so. But that honesty was something he'd come to appreciate, even it meant being put off. At least she didn't play games.

Sean's computer beeped, indicating the arrival of an e-mail. He gave his office chair a push that slid him to the computer. A click of the mouse brought his mailbox into view. His heart sank. The message wasn't from Beth. But it was from a pastor in Texas, asking questions about the electrician they had subcontracted to wire the new Sunday school classrooms McCauley Church Construction had added to their existing church. It took a few minutes to address the concerns.

The moment he hit SEND, his fingers itched to write another e-mail. This one to Beth. If he couldn't get through via the telephone lines, perhaps e-mail would reach her. He brought up a message box and quickly typed his father's question. He finished the brief message with, "Give me a call, if you would, please. I'm concerned that I haven't been able to reach you."

He reread the last line, his heart thudding. Should he leave it or not? It didn't sound like something a business associate would say. It sounded more like a friend. After a few moments of contemplation, he decided a friendly comment wasn't inappropriate. His finger trembled slightly as he connected with the SEND button, but he didn't reverse his decision.

Once more he glanced at his wristwatch. One fifteen in the afternoon. She could possibly have run home for a late lunch. He'd try her house again. *Ring. . .ring. . .ring. . .*

Holding the receiver to his ear, he leaned back in his chair and ran his fingers through his hair. "C'mon, Beth, where are you? Answer, huh? You're starting to scare me."

Monitors emitting soft beeps and flashing dots of light stood sentinel over the clear Plexiglas boxes where Beth's new baby brother and sister lay. The enclosed beds were necessary to maintain their oxygen levels and body temperature, the nurse had said, but it made her sad to see them separated after they'd shared a single womb. She wondered if they felt lonely being apart from each other. Standing between the two Isolettes, Beth fought tears as she looked back and forth at the tiny babies. Completely naked on stark white sheets, they looked so helpless and vulnerable.

On the way to the neonatal intensive care unit, Henry had done his best to prepare Beth for the myriad tubes inserted in each baby's arms, nose, and stomach, but seeing it was still a shock. He explained the babies had IVs to receive fluids, withdraw blood, and administer antibiotics. The little boy had a tube that appeared to be inserted through his throat—a gentle *whoosh* indicated it sent oxygen to his lungs. Beth cringed at the sight of the tiny wrinkled neck with the crisscross of tape holding the tube in place. She bit back a sob. Poor little guy. . .

Both babies required feeding tubes since they were born too early to have developed the ability to suck. Looking at the green tubes in the impossibly small nostrils, Beth felt another stab of sadness. Mom had so looked forward to breastfeeding the babies. Would that be possible later, when they were bigger?

Before sending her in, Henry had shared, "Their names are Theodore and Dorothea. Both names mean 'gift from God.' That's what they are, Beth—gifts. Children are His, only loaned to us for a time."

Beth hadn't been sure if he was preparing her for the possibility of God taking them back or was sharing the Mennonite viewpoint. Either way, she hadn't questioned him but had merely nodded and repeated the names, trying them out: "Theodore and Dorothea."

Now, examining the miniscule infants, she thought the names were far too big for such tiny babes. She leaned over Dorothea's Isolette and whispered, "I'm your sister Lisbeth, but everyone calls me Beth. I'll have to come up with a nickname to call you. I'm sure I'll think of something special for you, little girl."

Turning toward the baby's twin, she added, "You, too. Theodore is for someone big and brawny, and you will be, someday. But for now, I need something that fits you better." She smiled as the baby curled fingers no bigger than a pigeon's toes into a pearl-sized fist. "How about Teddy, huh? Do you like that?"

She got no response, but it didn't matter. Just looking down at the baby, taking in the downy tufts of hair on his perfectly shaped head and the pucker of his sweet mouth was enough for now. There would be time for Teddy to respond to her later. She'd be around.

Turning back to her sister's Isolette, she continued in a voice as soft as a sigh. "And you, Dorothea, maybe I'll just call you Dori. I had a friend in kindergarten named Dori. She was sweet. She shared her raisins with me at snack time. We'll have time to share things, too, little girl. Maybe not makeup tips or clothing styles, but secrets. Lots of secrets, the way sisters do."

Little Dorothea shifted her fuzzy head slightly, and tears spurted into Beth's eyes. The baby's tiny chin had a clearly discernible cleft. Just like Mom's. Just like Beth's.

A rush of emotion swept over Beth, a love so intense it nearly toppled her. She put her hand on the top of each Isolette and closed her eyes for a moment, willing what she felt to somehow transfer through the plastic case to the babies inside.

"Miss Quinn?"

Beth opened her eyes and blinked, clearing her tears. A nurse wearing a scrub shirt printed with pink and blue hippos stood nearby.

"I'm sorry, but it's time to change the babies' IV fluids. I'll have to ask you to return to the waiting room."

Although Beth considered begging to be allowed to stay, she remembered Maura saying the babies were fragile and shouldn't suffer undue disruptions. Doing what was best for the babies took precedence over her own desires. She nodded. But she took one more second to place her fingers against her lips and then press a kiss on the top of each plastic box.

"I'll be back, Teddy and Dori. Sister loves you."

TWENTY-SIX

Sean clinked the ice cubes in his glass and stared at the clock ticking above the sink in the kitchen. Raising the glass, he tipped a cube into his mouth and chewed, his gaze never wavering from the clock and its slow-moving second hand.

Six thirty-one. Six thirty-two. Six thirty-three. . . . Would he stand here forever, waiting for the telephone to ring?

Plunking the glass onto the counter, he whirled back down the hallway to his office and slumped into his desk chair, his chin in his hand. Another minute-measurer in the lower right-hand corner of his computer screen captured his attention. He watched three more minutes click by before releasing a sigh.

She was working late. That's why she hadn't answered his e-mail. It didn't explain why the telephone rang unheeded in the shop, unless she was so focused on her work she chose to ignore it. It didn't explain why her cell phone went unanswered. He'd stopped calling it, embarrassed by the number of times she'd be greeted with "missed call" when she finally picked it up.

He wished he could avoid picking up his telephone. Dad had called three times today, and his impatience at having his question unaddressed was creating a knot of tension between Sean's shoulder blades.

He lowered his head and closed his eyes for a moment, offering a silent prayer. *Dear Lord, is everything okay over there in Sommerfeld?* The nervous twinge in the center of his chest made him want to suspect something was wrong, but he also wondered if it was just his imagination running wild. In this day of increased communication, he wasn't accustomed to waiting to reach someone. It could be his own impatience causing this feeling of dread.

He looked at the little clock on his computer screen again. Six forty-four.

C'mon, Beth, where are you?

Beth looked up as Henry slapped his knees and rose, his gaze sweeping the room.

"It's past suppertime. Would anyone like to walk to the hospital cafeteria and get something to eat?"

Although Beth wasn't hungry—the weight of worry sufficiently filled her stomach—she knew Henry could use the company. She offered a nod. "I'd eat a little something." She looked at Grandpa and Grandma, who sat close to her in the corner. "Do you want to come along, or would you rather I bring you something back?"

Grandpa answered. "Someone should stay here in case the surgeon comes to tell us about our Marie. You go ahead. Bring us a sandwich." He looked at his wife. "A sandwich, Mother?"

Grandma gave a halfhearted shrug.

Grandpa touched Beth's hand. "See if they have ham. Your grandmother likes ham."

Beth nodded and looked at the others. "Anyone else?"

Al, Maura, and Deborah got up and joined Henry in the doorway. The others said they would eat when they went home, which they planned to do as soon as they received word on Marie's condition. Henry turned toward the hallway with Al at his side, and Maura and Deborah fell in step with Beth as they followed the two men.

There was a slump to Henry's shoulders that told of his fatigue, yet not once had he complained. Beth's respect for her stepfather raised another notch as she thought of his steadfast positive attitude and calm assurances to everyone else over the course of the long day. Without conscious thought, she skipped forward two steps and slipped her arm around Henry's waist.

Surprise registered on his face, but he quickly replaced it with a warm smile and a tired wink. He draped his arm over her shoulders, and they made their way down the elevator to the first floor, then through long hallways, their feet in step with one another as if they'd done this dozens of times.

The cafeteria smells greeted them before they turned the final corner. Although the food odors were much more pleasant than the antiseptic odor that had filled Beth's nostrils since she had arrived, her stomach still churned. Henry's hand slipped away as he gestured for her to enter the cafeteria first.

Deborah, Maura, and Al followed Beth, with Henry at the rear, and they loaded a tray with sandwiches, fruit, plastic-wrapped cookies, and small cartons of milk and juice. When they reached the register, Henry withdrew his wallet, but Al stepped forward.

"No, Henry. I'll take care of this."

Henry hesitated, his fingers already grasping a few bills. But when Deborah touched his arm and shook her head, he said, "Thank you, Al," and slipped the wallet back in his pocket.

The cashier put everything in two brown paper bags, and the little group made its way back to the waiting room, this time with Henry and Beth in front and Al walking with the other two women. The moment they stepped back into the room, Henry asked, "Has anyone come about Marie?"

"Not yet, Henry," Deborah's husband, Troy, answered.

Henry released a sigh, rubbing the back of his neck. "When will they come?"

Beth wrapped both hands around his upper arm and gave a comforting squeeze. "Surely it won't be much longer. Sit down, eat something. You'll feel better."

He gave her a dubious look.

She forced a light chuckle. "Okay, then, it'll make the time pass more quickly."

His smile thanked her, and he sat down and took the sandwich and cookie offered by Deborah.

The group ate in silence, each pair of eyes flitting to the clock on the wall periodically. At seven thirty, people began leaving. One by one, they gave Henry and Beth hugs, whispered words of encouragement, and promised to continue to pray for Marie and the babies. Eventually only Henry, Beth, Al and Maura, and Beth's grandparents remained.

Al turned to Grandpa, who sat slumped forward so far his chin nearly touched his chest. "JD, how about Maura and I take you and Erma home?"

Grandpa sat up, his jaw jutting forward. "I don't want to go until I've seen Marie."

"I can tell you're tired." Al spoke softly yet evenly, more matter-of-fact than persuasive. "It's been a long day"—he yawned—"for all of us. I'm ready to go."

"I'm not."

Al sent Henry a look that communicated he needed assistance.

Henry leaned forward and put his hand over Grandpa's knee. "JD, there's no sense in waiting here. It could be hours. Go ahead and go home. Sleep in your own bed. As soon as I hear something, I'll call."

Grandpa shot Henry a sharp look. "I don't have a telephone."

"But I do," Al inserted, "and I'll drive out and share the news with you as soon as Henry calls me. Come on." He stood up, looking expectantly at Grandpa. "Let's go on home and get some rest. We can all come back tomorrow."

Grandpa and Grandma exchanged a long, silent look, during which Beth was certain they expressed their thoughts clearly to the other without the need for words. Observing them, Beth felt the prick of tears behind her eyelids.

Grandma sighed and gave a tired nod. "We'll go. Thank you."

Both of her grandparents took the time to embrace Beth, Grandpa planting a kiss on the top of her head and Grandma kissing both of her cheeks before talking quietly with Henry and hugging him, too. When they left with Al and Maura leading the way, Beth and Henry were alone.

The first time she'd ever been completely alone with her stepfather.

Although she would have expected the situation to be uncomfortable, it wasn't. Despite the location, despite the worry that must still be pressing on him as much as it pressed on her, she discovered she was glad she was there. Glad that she could offer a bit of support to Henry during this time of mixed emotions.

She watched as he paced the periphery of the room, his hands in his pockets and his head low as if measuring his steps. He stopped in the center of the room and looked at the wall clock. Sighed. Paced the room in the opposite direction.

Beth started to suggest they turn on the television but remembered in time the inappropriateness of the idea. She sat back in the two-person settee she'd occupied earlier with her grandmother and picked up the magazine from the small table tucked in the corner.

Just as she placed the magazine in her lap, Henry spun and faced her. "I'm tired of sitting. Do you want to take a walk?"

Beth set the magazine aside, rising. "What if the doctor comes looking for us?"

Henry chewed the inside of his lower lip for a moment. "We can stop by the nurses' station and tell someone we're out in the garden area. I could use some fresh air." He pinched his nose, his dark eyes twinkling.

Beth couldn't help it. She laughed. "I couldn't agree more."

Her purse strap looped over her shoulder, she walked with Henry to the nurses' station, and he informed the woman on duty where they could be located. Then, his wide palm resting gently between her shoulder blades, he guided her to the elevator and, once on the first floor, to glass doors that led into a grassy area surrounded by towering buildings.

A concrete bench invited one to relax, but Henry passed it, instead ushering Beth along the sidewalk. Although dusk had fallen, the area was well lit with light from the buildings' windows, as well as lampposts standing sentinel all along the sidewalk. Beth inhaled deeply, enjoying the tangy scent of freshly cut grass. The antiseptic taste that had lingered on the back of her tongue all day washed away, and she sighed, lifting her face to the brief expanse of pinkish sky glimpsed overhead between the towers.

"I'm glad you came." Henry's deep, quiet voice fit the peacefulness of the surroundings.

"Me, too." Beth looked at her feet, matching her stride to his. "The babies. . .wow. They're amazing. So small but so perfect." She looked into Henry's face. "Dori even has little stubby eyelashes already. I think she's going to be a beauty."

Henry's lips curved into a lopsided, questioning grin. "Dori?"

Heat filled Beth's face, but she didn't look away. "Yes. Dorothea. . . well, it's pretty, but it's too much name right now. So I've been thinking of her as Dori."

"I see."

They reached the turn in the sidewalk, and Beth slowed her steps so Henry could make the outside curve without leaving her side. She searched his face for any sign of disapproval. "Do you mind?"

"Of course not. I kind of like it." He clasped his hands behind his back and pursed his lips as if in deep thought. "What about Theodore? Did you shorten his name, too?"

"Mmm-hmm. Teddy."

"Teddy?"

Beth laughed at his doubtful expression. "Yes, Teddy. Someone small and cuddly and warm."

Henry tipped his head to the side. "I suppose that's okay. For now. But it's not something I'd want attached to him at, say, sixteen."

"I agree. But Theodore. . .it's pretty stuffy for an infant."

Henry chuckled. "Point taken."

They walked on in silence until they'd made a full circle. Henry paused, looking toward the double doors that led back inside.

Beth, sensing his thoughts, said, "I'm not ready to go back in. Want to make another loop?"

Henry's smile expressed his answer, and once more they set out. Beth glanced over her shoulder at the doors and blew out a noisy breath. "I keep wishing somebody would chase us down and tell us something."

"I know." Henry raised his hand to grip her shoulder for a moment.

"But your mother is in good hands. We have to trust." He lowered his hand and sent her a worried look. "But you probably need to get back. You have that window to finish."

Several faces paraded through Beth's mind: Sean's, Andrew's, Catherine's and Livvy's, her grandfather's, the workers', people who depended on her to follow through on her plans. Plans that depended on the signing of the contract with McCauley. Without intending to, she grimaced. She came to a stop.

"Henry, I'm torn. I want to be here with you and Mom and the babies, but I'm worried about what will happen if I don't get the McCauley window done. I don't want to let anyone down."

"If you need to go, your mother will understand. She knows how much the studio means to you," Henry said, his voice warm and assuring.

Beth knew Mom would understand. Mom had always put Beth first. And Beth had always allowed Mom to take second place, never considering her mother might have needs and wants that weren't addressed. But over the past year and half, Beth had tried to change her selfish mind-set. Right now, however, she didn't know which was less selfish: allowing the contract to slip away, which meant hurting a number of people she'd come to care about, or honoring the deadline, which meant leaving Henry to handle this heartache without her support.

She opened her mouth, prepared to ask Henry what he would do if it were his decision. A siren blasted, making conversation impossible. Even before the siren faded into the distance, a man and woman charged from one of the other buildings and immediately broke into a fierce argument about who would get Milt's matching sofa and loveseat.

Henry swallowed and glanced down at Beth, his brows raised in silent query. She gave a brisk nod, and the two of them crossed the center of the courtyard, right across the grass, and ducked back into Building Three.

Beth decided she'd go back to the little waiting room that had been assigned to the family and talk to Henry there, where they'd have more privacy. They rode the elevator to the third floor without speaking. The silver doors slid open, and Henry gestured her through. As they turned toward the waiting room, a nurse hurried up to them.

"Mr. Braun, Dr. Mulligan needs to see you."

Henry stopped, and his hand reached outward, as if in need of support. Beth clasped it. He squeezed her fingers as he asked in a surprisingly calm tone, "Whom does it concern: my wife or my children?"

The nurse spun around, beckoning them to follow with a glance over her shoulder. "Your wife."

TWENTY-SEVEN

Andrew heard the back door open, and he set aside the book he'd been reading and rose. His parents' voices pulled him to the kitchen, where he found them beside the door engaged in quiet conversation.

"How is Aunt Marie?" He interrupted them to ask the question, but he'd been waiting for hours for word. Courtesy didn't seem as important as being informed.

His father turned to him, slipping off his hat. "Has your uncle called?"

Andrew shook his head. "No one's called. What's going on?"

Briefly, his father recounted the details of Marie's surgery to deliver the babies, the possible consequences of the syndrome that created the need for early delivery, and what they knew of the babies' conditions.

Andrew drew in a slow breath. "Will they be okay?"

"We don't know yet." His mother bore dark circles beneath her eyes. "But Henry said he would call with any news. So we'll have to wait."

Andrew followed his parents as they moved toward their bedroom.

"What about Beth? Did she come back, too?"

"She was still at the hospital when we left." His father paused at the bedroom door, while his mother went on in and sat on the bed, her shoulders slumped. "I think she plans to stay there with Henry."

"For how long?" Andrew's heart caught. If it were only for tonight—if she planned to be back midday tomorrow, or even the morning after that—then if they worked together, maybe they could still finish the window.

Dad shrugged, his face twisting in a displeased scowl. "I don't know, Andrew. She didn't say."

Andrew wanted to ask other questions, but his father's foul mood stifled them. "Get some rest," he said, "and I'll listen for the telephone."

"Thank you," his mother called.

Dad closed the door.

Andrew moved slowly back to the front room, sat down with his elbows on his knees, and stared unseeingly at the patch of carpet between his feet. Surely she would come back. They were so close to being finished. Surely she wouldn't let the opportunity go when only a few dozen shapes of glass stood between a successful launch of a fully operating studio, or continuing to do craft fairs until another opportunity came along. *If* it ever came along.

"Andrew?"

He jumped and sat up.

Dad stood in the opening of the hallway. "Your mother is worried about Beth's cat. It hasn't been attended to all day."

Rising, Andrew said, "She keeps a key under the mat on the back porch, just like her great-aunt always did. I could go over and check on it."

Dad released a grunt of frustration. "Please do. Your mother won't rest until she knows the poor animal is all right."

Andrew was already moving toward the back door. "Tell Mom not to worry. I'll take care of Winky." As he passed his father, he added, "Get some sleep. You look like you need it."

Dad nodded, rubbing his hand over his whiskery cheek. "Yes. Thanks, son."

Andrew headed out the back door. Less than ten minutes later, he let himself into the utility porch of Beth's bungalow. Winky wrapped himself around his ankles before he could get the back door closed. The cat's yowls pierced Andrew's eardrums.

"Hey, hey," he chided, slapping the light switch and scooping up the cat in one smooth motion, "stop yelling. I'm here now."

Winky continued to emit strangled mewls between loud purrs as he bumped his head on the underside of Andrew's chin and worked his paws against Andrew's shirt front.

"You sure know how to make a guy feel welcome." Andrew held the cat for several minutes, stroking his fur. Finally, the little critter struggled to get down.

Winky headed for the kitchen, his tail straight in the air, yelping out a series of meows Andrew interpreted as a command to follow. He found the cat weaving back and forth between the stove and his empty pet dish, which had been turned onto its side.

"Sure, I'll feed you," he said, picking up the dish. "But where does Beth keep your food?" He spent a few frustrating minutes opening every cupboard door in the kitchen, all without success. Winky's meows became more insistent, and Andrew muttered soothing words while he considered where else cat food might be kept.

Suddenly he slapped his forehead. "Oh, the basement!"

Winky trotted along as he headed back through the utility porch to the basement door. Just inside the door, on the second step, waited a half-full bag of dry cat food. Andrew grabbed it and had to high step his way back to the kitchen to avoid Winky, who darted in and out between his feet in eagerness.

Andrew filled the dish on the counter, thinking it would keep Winky out of his way, but to his surprise the cat leaped up beside the bowl and stuck his head under the flow of small brown squares, sending a flurry of cat food across the countertop and floor.

"Winky!" He pushed the cat to the floor, but before he could even take a breath, Winky was back on the counter, in his way again. Finally, out of desperation, he closed the cat in the bathroom while he finished filling the food dish and cleaned up the mess on the floor. Winky's indignant yowls spurred him to work quickly. Once released, the cat pattered right to the bowl and buried his face in Kitty Krunchies.

While Winky ate, Andrew wandered to the front room, scanning for any messes the cat might have made while Beth was away. Other than a rug all askew by the front door and a tennis shoe dragged beneath the dining room table, it appeared the cat had behaved pretty well. As he turned to head back to the kitchen, his gaze fell on Beth's cell phone, which lay on the desk in the corner of the dining room.

A little red light next to the stubby antenna flashed on and off. Curious, he moved to the desk and touched the slim silver phone with one finger. What did the flashing light mean—that the phone was going dead or that someone was calling? Uncertain what to do, he simply stared, watching the repeated blinks until he realized he was becoming mesmerized.

Shifting his gaze, he encountered the desk telephone. A small red button beneath the word "ringer" glowed as brightly as the flashing light on the cell phone. He touched the button and the color changed to green. He raised his eyebrows, realizing he must have turned it on. He reached to punch it back to off when, *ri-i-ing!* He jumped, jerking his hand away from the offending noise.

Ri–i–ing!

Should he answer it? It might be Henry. But no, Beth was with Henry. He had no need to call her.

Ri–i–ing!

Maybe it was Dad, calling to find out what was keeping him. He'd better hurry on home.

Ri–i–ing!

He came to a halt. Dad would probably worry more if Andrew didn't answer, since he'd said this was where he would be.

Ri–i–ing!

No, he should just ignore it and go home. Andrew took two steps toward the kitchen, but then he whirled back and snatched the receiver from the cradle. "Hello?"

A dial tone greeted him. He'd waited too long. With a muffled groan, he slammed the receiver back in place. A glance in the kitchen showed Winky still hunkered over his food dish. Obviously the cat would need attention again in the morning, but for now Andrew had better go home.

While the cat was occupied, he slipped out the back door.

Sean whirled his chair away from the desk and rose, heading for the hallway. If he remained in his office, he'd only continue trying to call Beth. And she obviously wasn't able—or willing—to answer.

He stopped in the kitchen to remove a bottle of carbonated water from the refrigerator, then passed into the small family room that had been added on to the back of the house. Settling into his recliner, he propped up the footrest and pointed the remote at the large-screen television that filled the middle of the entertainment center on the opposite wall. A detective show of some kind exploded onto the screen. He sipped his fizzy water and watched.

Having come in midway through the program, much of the storyline didn't make sense, but it filled the time. He remained in the recliner until the water bottle was empty, the backyard was fully dark, and the ten o'clock news came on. Only then did he shut off the TV, slam down the footrest, and head for his bedroom.

As he passed his office, he felt the urge to go in and try Beth's number one more time. But unwilling to face another series of unanswered rings, he pushed himself past the door.

He lay beneath the solid blue sheet on his bed and stared at the shadowed ceiling, trying not to envision unpleasant scenarios that would keep Beth from having access to her telephone. Closing his eyes, he prayed for God to shut down the images that only created needless worry. He prayed for Beth to be safe, wherever she was. And he asked, pleaded, that he would be able to reach her tomorrow.

Beth, her legs feeling like rubber, made it to the corner to the chair she'd occupied earlier, and collapsed. She covered her face with her hands, determined to keep dammed the tears that pressed behind her lids. All through the doctor's explanation, the visit to her mother's room, and the long walk down the hallway, she had maintained a calm facade. But now in the privacy of the waiting room, her resolve faded. With a broken sob, the tears broke loose in a torrent that doubled her forward and convulsed her shoulders in uncontrolled heaves.

In moments, strong arms surrounded her, pulling her firmly against a solid shoulder. Henry. For a moment, she clung, welcoming the consoling embrace, but then she realized how selfish she was being. She shouldn't expect him to offer comfort when he was so in need of it himself. She pushed against his chest even as she continued to sob, and his arms loosened, allowing her to pull free.

Crunching into the corner of the vinyl-covered settee, she tried, unsuccessfully, to bring her weeping under control.

"Beth, Beth, shh now. . ." The low-toned voice filtered through Beth's sobs. "Come here. Let's pray together. You'll feel better."

"I. . .I can't!" Beth heard the recalcitrant note in her own voice, but she couldn't seem to stop it. How could she possibly find a way to convey the depth of her concern and worry? Her prayers would be senseless groaning.

"Beth, please, you're breaking my heart."

The words sounded strangled, and Beth shifted to meet Henry's gaze. His eyes, shimmering with empathetic tears, brought another rush of tears to her own. With a little cry, she forgot her resolve not to be selfish and threw herself into his arms. Her face buried against his chest, she choked out, "I'm just s-so scared, Henry. Mom's. . .Mom's all I've got. W-what if. . ."

His chin pressed against her head, the day's growth of whiskers catching her hair. "Your mother will be fine. The doctor didn't say we would lose her, did he?"

Snuffling, she admitted, "No, but. . .but he said she was w-weak from the babies' delivery, and that a second surgery could b-be risky." Beth pictured her mother on the hospital bed, her face nearly as white as the pillowcase beneath her head. The tousled curls scattered across the pillow took Beth by surprise. How long had it been since she'd seen Mom's hair free of her cap? Mom had looked young, fragile, defenseless.

"Risky, yes." His sigh stirred the fine strands of hair that had slipped loose of her ponytail. "But I trust she'll come through the surgery. She's a strong woman, and she's in good hands—the best hands, the nurse said, in all of Kansas. We must trust, Beth."

"It-it's so *hard*." She whispered the words against Henry's front, wishing they weren't true.

His soft chuckle vibrated against her ear. "Ah, Beth, if trust were easy, it wouldn't be worth having." Gently, he pushed her away and handed her a handkerchief from his shirt pocket. While she dried her eyes, he added, "And something else. Don't ever think your mother is all you have."

He paused for a moment, pulling his upper lip between his teeth and looking steadily into her eyes. She sensed he was gathering courage, and she held her breath, wondering what he might say.

Finally he spoke, his voice low and gravelly with emotion. "I've never said it because I didn't want to presume that you. . .you would accept me for something more than your mother's husband. But I love your mother, Beth, and you are a part of her. I love you, too."

Beth's breaths came in little spurts as she fought the need to weep again but not from anguish. No, not from anguish.

"You're a young woman already, and I know you don't need a dad, but—"

"Yes, I do." She blurted out the words, then lowered her gaze, abashed by the admission. She did need a dad—she'd always needed a dad. Her hands convulsed on the soggy handkerchief. Her words tumbled out in a harsh whisper. "But Mom got pregnant, and she has Dori and Teddy now, and you. . .you're. . ."

She didn't complete the thought. Right now, in an operating room, the surgeon was cutting into her mother, taking away the chance for her to ever bear another child. He'd said they had to, to stop her from bleeding. But the thought knifed through Beth's chest, stealing her words. How could she express a jealousy for the two tiny infants lying in Isolettes, knowing they would be Henry's only children? How could she expect him to want her—flesh of another man—when he had them?

"Yes," Henry said, his voice as tender as she'd ever heard it, and Henry was the most tender man she had ever known. "Your mother *and I* have Dori and Teddy. . .and *we* also have you."

She jerked her chin up to meet Henry's gaze. The subtly emphasized words delivered a message that reached Beth's heart and expanded it in a way she hadn't expected.

"Having Theodore and Dorothea doesn't change anything for your mother. You will always be her child. And just because I now have Dorothea and Theodore doesn't mean I won't have time for you. If you need a dad, I'm here. If you don't want me as a dad, I accept that, too. We're friends, aren't we?"

He waited, and she gave a slight nod. Yes, they were friends. Henry had never betrayed her, never hurt her, never ignored her, even though she had held him at bay. He had always shown her unconditional acceptance. . .and love.

He went on softly, his hand resting on her clasped fists. "Whatever you choose for our future relationship, Beth—whether a friendship or a father-daughter relationship—just know you are loved, by your mother *and* me. You can trust that."

Overwhelmed by emotion, Beth couldn't find her voice. For long minutes she sat looking into Henry's face, absorbing the sincerity reflected in his eyes. A part of her wanted very much to say, "Thank you." To say, "Thank you, Dad." But the words caught in her throat. The time wasn't appropriate, not in this needy moment. It would be as though she only wanted him for what he could give.

The time to call him by the name she now accepted in her heart would come later, when Mom was well, the twins were home, and they were all together under Henry's roof like a family. She could wait. Looking into his unwavering, accepting eyes, she knew he could wait, too.

She pushed her lips into a quavering smile.

"Are you ready to pray now?"

Beth gave an eager nod and closed her eyes. Henry petitioned God, speaking to the heavenly Father as easily and comfortably as he would speak to a friend. He thanked God for the precious gift of life in his children; he expressed gratitude for the care his wife was receiving and asked for divine help for the surgeon now operating; and he asked God to calm Beth's fears and remind her of His presence.

Beth swallowed hard at those words. Only a dad would think of her before he thought of himself.

He concluded the prayer by telling God he trusted Him for the outcome, whatever it would be. When Beth opened her eyes and met Henry's gaze, the calm peace she saw in his face gave her peace, too. Her mother would be okay. She trusted that implicitly.

Henry slapped his knees and pushed to his feet. "Now, the doctor said it would be morning before we'd be able to see your mother. I'm going to go call Al and have him share what's happening with those in Sommerfeld. Then I'll stop by the nurses' station to ask for pillows and blankets. Do you think you can get comfortable on this little thing?"

Beth gave the settee a pat. "I've always liked a firm mattress."

"Good girl." Henry gave her cheek a quick caress; then he headed out of the room.

TWENTY-EIGHT

"Beth? Beth, wake up."

The soft voice, the gentle hand on her shoulder drew Beth from a deep, dreamless sleep. She opened her eyes in increments, blinking against the glare of fluorescent lights, and finally focused on a face only inches from hers.

Henry's face, darkly shadowed by whiskers.

Frowning, she sat up, grimacing as her back complained. It took a moment for her to remember why she was folded into a small settee in an unfamiliar room. But then memories from yesterday—Andrew's announcement, her mad dash to Wichita, the visits to the nursery, and her mother's second surgery—rushed over her, and she jerked stiffly upright and grasped Henry's hand.

"Mom? Is she okay?"

Henry's tired smile gave the answer before he spoke. "Your mother rested well last night. The worry about bleeding is over. We'll be able to see her after breakfast."

Beth felt as though someone had taken the air out of her. She collapsed against the back of the settee and peered up at Henry. "Thank the Lord."

His eyes crinkled. "I already did."

With a yawn, Beth pushed to her feet.

Henry pressed a clear resealable bag into her hand. "The nurse said we could use the shower in the bathrooms on the lower level. She gave us these."

Beth looked into the bag. A toothbrush, comb, and sample-sized containers of toothpaste, soap, shampoo, conditioner, and deodorant awaited her use. "That sounds like a great idea." Looking down the length of her wrinkled clothes, she made a face.

Yesterday she'd been too concerned about Mom to worry about her clothes. But now she realized how slovenly she must look in her normal work attire of faded jeans, T-shirt, and oversized flannel shirt.

"I wish they had some clothes in here, too." She gave her armpit a sniff, wrinkled her nose, and said with a rueful chuckle, "I could use a change."

Henry shook his head, his eyes twinkling. "You'll be fine. People understand. Why don't you go down first? I'll stay here in case someone needs us. When you get back, I'll go clean up, and then we'll visit your new brother and sister before we see your mother."

Beth admitted it felt wonderful to be clean even if she did have to put on clothes that were wrinkly and slightly musty from yesterday's wearing. Her wet hair pulled up in a ponytail, she returned to the waiting room to find Henry finishing a simple breakfast of cereal and fruit. On the tray, a second box of cornflakes, a banana, and small carton of milk were untouched.

He pointed. "Look here. If you open the box on these dotted lines, you can pour the milk right inside and use the box like a cereal bowl."

His boyish amazement at using the box for a bowl tickled Beth, and she couldn't stop a giggle from forming. But when Henry sent her a questioning look, she said simply, "Pretty ingenious," and sat down.

He left for his shower. She turned on the television and watched a morning talk show while she ate her breakfast. Surprisingly, she was hungry. The food tasted better than she would have thought.

When Henry returned, she clicked off the TV, loaded the remains of their breakfast onto the tray, and stood up, tray in hand.

"The nurse said to leave it on the table there. A janitor will pick it up." He ran his hand over his smooth chin. "I think I'm presentable enough now to peek at the babies. Let's go."

As they walked toward the NICU, Beth said, "I wish I'd remembered to grab my cell phone yesterday. It would make calling people easier."

"The nurse said we could use the telephone downstairs as much as we need to."

"I know, but"—Beth sent him a sheepish look—"I need to call Sean McCauley and let him know the project has been delayed, and I don't have the number memorized. It's in my cell phone's memory bank."

Henry slowed his steps, his expression thoughtful. "Can't you ask an operator for help?"

Beth came to a halt and slapped her forehead. "Oh, duh! Information. . ."

Henry laughed. Throwing his arm around her shoulders, he got her moving again. "You can make your call after we've had our visits."

This time when Beth entered the nursery set aside for the babies in need of critical care, she didn't look at her brother or sister. She watched Henry. Frequently she had to blink to clear her vision as the man leaned over one Isolette, then the other, his broad hand pressed to the clear cover, his nose mere inches from the Plexiglas top that kept him from being able to touch his children.

The tenderness in his eyes, the gentle curve on his lips, the deep breaths he took while his eyes slid closed—Beth was sure in those moments he prayed—created a rise of emotion in her breast that was nearly impossible to contain. If she had hand-selected a father, she wouldn't have been able to find a better one. For the babies, or for herself.

Henry straightened and looked at her. "They look good, don't they?" He kept his voice whisper-soft so as not to disturb any of the tiny patients. "Small, yes. So small. . . But good. Strong." His gaze dropped to Teddy's bed. "Look at Theodore there, making those fists. He's a fighter." Turning to the second bed, his smile gentled. "And Dorothea. . .with that little dent in her chin. . .how much she looks like her mother."

Henry looked toward Beth. "All of my girls have dented chins."

Beth shook her head, emitting a quiet laugh. "That dent is called a cleft."

He shrugged, his face creased with a grin. "Okay. Clefted chins." He looked back at the sleeping baby. "I like it."

In those moments, Beth liked it more than she ever had before. She allowed Henry several more minutes of silent examination as she crouched between the two beds and prayed for each baby in turn. When she straightened to her feet, Henry took her hand.

"Come. I've memorized their faces so I can share. Let's go see your mother now."

It occurred to Beth as she and Henry headed toward the surgical ICU where her mother recovered that Mom had yet to see or hold her babies. Beth's heart twisted in sympathy. If she itched to reach through that Plexiglas and cradle Dori and Teddy, how much more must Mom's heart ache with desire to have them in her arms.

She and Henry stopped at the station briefly to make sure it was okay for them to go into Mom's room, and with the nurse's approval, Henry ushered Beth in. To her surprise, Mom was propped up on pillows rather than lying flat. A tray with a half-eaten piece of dry toast and a plastic tumbler with a bent straw sticking out of it sat on a tall cart beside the bed.

When Mom spotted them, she offered a weak smile and held out the arm that had no tubes running from it. Beth hesitated, but Henry gave her a gentle nudge, and she dashed forward to press her cheek to her mother's—a full hug would probably hurt her.

"Good morning." Mom's voice sounded dry and raspy. "You were here all night?"

Tears pricked Beth's eyes again at her mother's obvious surprise. Maybe it was a blessing she wouldn't get that McCauley contract. She had obviously spent far too much time being Beth, business owner, instead of Beth, daughter. Closing her eyes for a moment, she made a silent vow of doing a better job of balancing her priorities—and moving family higher on her list.

"Yes. All night. And I probably smell as bad as I look."

Mom laughed softly, shaking her head. "You look fine, honey." She turned to Henry. "Have you held the babies yet?"

Beth watched Henry lean forward to place a kiss on his wife's lips. "Not yet. But I've seen them, and they're beautiful. Perfect."

Sensing her parents' need to have some time alone, Beth inched toward the door. "I'll be back a little later. I need to go make some phone calls."

Henry sat gingerly on the edge of the bed and took his wife's hand. "All right. I plan to stay here until they kick me out."

Beth nodded. "I understand. I'll see you soon. I love you." When she spoke the words, she looked at her mother, but then allowed her gaze to flit over Henry, too.

His smile followed her from the room. A request from Information garnered the telephone number for McCauley Church Construction. Beth pressed her finger against the telephone's number pad. After only one ring, a friendly female voice chirped, "McCauley Church Construction. How may I direct your call?"

Beth licked her lips. "I need to speak to Sean McCauley, please."

"Mr. Sean McCauley is at a different location. This is the main office."

Beth sucked in her breath. Of course, she should have asked specifically for Sean's number rather than the construction company's.

"But," the voice went on, "Mr. Evan McCauley is in. Would you like to speak to him?"

Beth pressed her memory. Was Evan the father or the brother? She supposed it didn't matter. She just needed to let someone know she would be unable to meet the deadline. "Evan McCauley is fine."

"Your name, please?"

"Beth Quinn of Quinn's Stained-Glass Art Studio."

There was a brief, startled silence, then, "Oh! Miss Quinn—yes. Mr. McCauley has been trying to contact you. I'll put you right through. Please hold."

Beth tapped her fingers against the desktop while she waited. Seconds later a deep, almost brusque voice came on.

"Evan McCauley here."

"Mr. McCauley, this is—"

"Beth Quinn. The *elusive* Beth Quinn."

Although the words could be construed as teasing, Beth couldn't determine by his tone whether he intended to tease or berate.

"My son," he continued without giving her a chance to speak, "tried several times yesterday to reach you."

This time she was sure she heard a hint of accusation in his tone.

She chose her reply carefully. "Yes, sir. I apologize for being unavailable. You see, my mother was rushed to the hospital early yesterday morning. I left in such a hurry, I neglected to carry my cell phone with me. I'm sorry if I caused Sean worry." Picturing Sean repeatedly dialing her number, getting no response, created a tightness in her chest. She realized she truly did regret any concern she may have caused.

"And how is your mother?" The man's tone didn't gentle at all, but the lowered volume let Beth know the question was sincere.

"She had complications from a pregnancy and required an emergency C-section, followed by a second surgery late last night. She came through both surgeries well, and she's recovering. But it will be several days before she's released. Longer still"—she swallowed—"for my premature brother and sister. But we trust they'll be fine, too." When had she decided to simply trust? Of its own volition, a smile formed on her face. "However, it does create a problem for me. . .and you."

When he made no response, she continued. "I would like to stay at the hospital with my stepfather until my mother is released. Which means I'm not in my studio. I'm afraid, with these delays, the window I'm constructing for you won't be completed by April 1."

"You realize your failure to meet that deadline results in a termination of our agreement." It wasn't a question. Beth wasn't sure she would classify it as a statement, either. It sounded almost like a threat.

She licked her dry lips and formed a calm response. "Yes, sir, I am aware of that."

A lengthy pause followed, during which time Beth could feel the prickle of tension from nearly three hundred miles away. "Very well, Miss Quinn. I appreciate your honesty. Sean and I will pursue another artist for our company. My best wishes to your mother and her babies. Take care." The line went dead.

Beth slowly placed the receiver on the hook. She waited for regret, sorrow, self-recrimination to strike. But they didn't. Yes, there was a slight hollowness in her chest, a realization that a dream would go unfulfilled. She supposed eventually she would need to mourn that loss. But for now, she only felt a sense of calm, a realization that she'd done the right thing for her family and for herself.

Closing her eyes, she offered a silent prayer. *Thank You, Lord, for putting me where I should be for Mom right now. I said I trusted that she and the babies would be fine, and I meant it. I also trust that, somehow, things will work out for the best for the people involved in my studio.*

Heading back toward the maternity wing, Beth heaved a sigh. She might be at peace with her decision, but that peace may be shattered when she shared the loss of the contract with Andrew.

TWENTY-NINE

She declined the contract?" Sean's knees turned to rubber. He sank into the chair facing his father's massive oak desk. "I can't believe she'd do that."

"Yes." Dad drummed his fingers on the desktop, his lips twitching. "I was surprised, too. And it certainly leaves us in a lurch."

Sean wasn't as concerned about their "lurch" at the moment as he was about Beth. Knowing how many plans she had for the studio, he couldn't imagine her turning down the very means to seeing those plans through. "But why? Did she give a reason?"

Dad nodded. "Apparently, her mother had a complicated delivery and required surgery. She is staying at the hospital until her mother recovers. That equates to not meeting the deadline, so. . ." Dad raised one brow. "No contract."

Sean leaned forward, his heart pounding with alarm. "Did she say whether her mother was all right?" Beth adored her mother. She would be devastated if anything happened to her.

"She indicated her mother was recovering nicely. I waited for her to make the determination that, with her mother being cared for, she should return to her obligations, but she chose to stay at the hospital.

So that's that." Dad lifted a file from the corner of his desk, opened it, and began to peruse its contents.

Sean stared in amazement for several stunned seconds. "That's it?"

Dad didn't even look up. "Yes. She made her choice. The contract must not have been that important to her. If she isn't able to make honoring contracts a priority, then it's best we know that now. Obviously the girl isn't as dependable as we'd hoped she would be."

He flicked a quick glance at Sean. "Why don't you look up the number for the stained-glass studio we used for the Cincinnati project? See if they're available." He clicked his tongue, shaking his graying head. "Their work doesn't have the depth I hoped we'd be able to corner, but—"

"Is that all you can think about? The *depth*?" The only time he'd heard regret enter his father's tone was concerning what he'd wanted and couldn't have. What had happened to his Christian compassion? Didn't Beth and her family's difficulty make an impact at all?

Dad's brows lowered into a fierce scowl. "Watch your tone with me, Sean. You may be an adult and copartner of this business, but I am still your father and your boss, and—"

"And you're being a fool."

"What?" The word was growled.

Sean faced his father squarely and repeated in the same firm yet respectful tone, "You're being a fool. You're allowing an emergency that is completely out of Beth's control to dictate your assessment of whether or not she's dependable. It's hardly a fair measuring tool."

Slapping the file closed, his father roared, "She chose not to finish the window!"

"No, Dad. She chose to be with her mother in a time of need." Leaning forward, Sean lowered his voice. "What if Mom were in the hospital, recovering, and a church team was waiting for final blueprints on a project? Whose needs would you meet—your wife's or the team's?"

Dad scowled. "Sean, you're treading on dangerous ground."

"Just answer me, please."

After a long moment, during which Sean was forced to suffer a low-lidded glare, Dad forced his answer between stiff lips. "I would honor my commitment to the church team—"

Sean slumped back in his chair, shaking his head.

Dad came out of his chair, hands on his desk, to bring his face near Sean's. "Because as a Christian businessman, I lose my credibility if I don't deliver what I've promised. Remember what Paul told Timothy—to be a '*workman* that needeth not to be ashamed.' I can't do that if I dishonor my commitments."

Sean rose to his feet and looked into his father's eyes. "But what about commitment to family, Dad? Doesn't that count for anything?"

Slowly Dad straightened his spine.

Pressing his palms to the desktop, Sean said quietly, "Jesus, on the cross, expressed concern for His mother's care. While He was taking the penalty for the sins of mankind—what greater task was there, ever?—He still thought of His mother. To me, that says family should come first."

Sean faced off with his father over the distance of the desk's width. Neither man spoke for several minutes that felt like an eternity. When it became clear Dad wasn't going to respond, Sean took a step back and released a sad sigh.

"Okay, Dad, you're right." He lowered his gaze to the floor. "You're the boss, and it is your decision who we hire to design the windows for our churches. But would you think about one more thing?" He lifted his head.

Dad was staring out the window, the muscles in his jaw quivering. He didn't turn his head.

Facing his father's stern profile, Sean went on. "McCauley Church Construction has touted itself as a family business determined to bring glory to God. You chose to focus solely on church construction, because, as you've told countless committees over the years, the church is God's family in the flesh. It seems to me that by placing her family's needs above her job, Beth has demonstrated the very dedication you desire. What a sacrifice she made for her mother. Personally, I think that kind of dedication should be honored and trusted."

Dad didn't move.

Sean drew a deep breath and released it slowly, giving his father an opportunity to reply. "Well," he finally concluded, "I've got work to do. I'll touch base with you later about locating a stained-glass window designer."

Sean opened the door and stepped through. As he turned to close it behind him, he glanced once more at his father. Evan McCauley remained standing behind his desk, his gaze aimed out the window, his fists clenched at his sides. Sean shook his head, regret filling him. Then he closed the door and left his father alone.

"You go through Beth's things and pick out some clothes." Andrew ushered Trina to Beth's bedroom while Winky danced around their feet. "I'll take care of the cat."

Two days ago, he and Trina had made a similar visit to Beth's house to retrieve a couple of changes of clothes and her toiletries. Since Beth and Uncle Henry had taken up residence at the hospital, remaining there day and night, they appreciated the fresh clothing, books, puzzles, and snacks delivered by various townspeople.

Although Andrew's parents had driven to Wichita each day of Aunt Marie's hospitalization, Andrew had yet to make the trek. His job, he had decided, was to guard the home front, which included Beth's house, her cat, and the studio.

Trina, watching Winky, giggled. "He likes you, doesn't he?" She crouched down to capture the furry critter, but Winky eluded her, wrapping himself around Andrew's left leg.

"He should," Andrew groused. "I've been the only one feeding him for the past four days. I think he's decided I'm his mother." He plucked the cat from the floor.

Trina tipped her head and puckered her lips into an exaggerated scowl. "You've been really grumpy lately. What's wrong with you?"

"I'm not grumpy." When she raised her eyebrows, he admitted, "Okay, you're right. I am grumpy. But who can blame me?" Winky's tail swished in his face, and he pushed it down. "For the past two months, all we've done is look forward to the day Beth would sign that contract with McCauley so we'd have the funds to really get her studio going. Now, because Beth's spending all her time at the hospital, the window isn't getting done. No window, no contract, no money. . .no studio." Andrew gritted his teeth. "So it's back to the fields for me."

"Why?"

Hadn't she listened to anything he'd said? "Trina, no studio, no job for me. Dad will expect me to work for him if I'm not working for Beth. So everything's ruined."

The girl shrugged. "Not everything. Even if she's not doing those big windows for churches, Beth will still have her studio. So you can still work there."

"Not full-time."

"Stop being so grouchy! Not everybody gets to do what they want to all the time."

Andrew knew Trina spoke from experience. She harbored desires that extended beyond the café, yet she went in with a cheerful attitude every day. A prick of guilt made him squirm.

"Besides that, Beth is very talented. If that McCauley from clear in Kansas City saw it, somebody else will, too. So it didn't happen this time. It doesn't mean it will *never* happen. Have faith, Andrew."

Despite himself, Andrew felt a grin twitching. "When did you get so smart?"

Trina giggled. "Just born that way."

Andrew snorted.

Another giggle rolled before Trina stepped into Beth's bedroom.

Andrew, with Winky squirming under his arm, headed for the basement staircase. "Let's get you fed, huh? Maybe if you're eating, you'll leave people alone."

He fed the cat, then sat on his haunches, idly stroking Winky's back and considering what Trina had said. He wondered if, underneath, he'd thought as Trina did—that the studio would still one day be as big and successful as Beth envisioned it. Because despite his dad's report that Beth had informed McCauley she wouldn't be able to meet his deadline, Andrew had still gone to the studio each day. He'd overseen the completion of the addition and had continued training Livvy and Catherine, just as if nothing had changed.

Trina was right. If McCauley had taken note of Beth's unique talent, someone else would, too. It was only a matter of time. Lowering his head, he offered a silent prayer. *Forgive me, Lord, for my shortsightedness. Beth dedicated the studio to You, and her goal is to glorify You through her artwork. Let me also bring glory to You in whatever tasks I do, whether in the studio or on the farm. Help me to wait patiently for Your plan to unfold.* Perhaps he'd have to do farm work for a while yet, but God hadn't given him an interest in art for nothing. God wouldn't leave him on the farm forever.

"Nope, Winky, not forever." He muttered the thought aloud.

"Not forever what?"

Andrew looked up and found Trina in the doorway between the kitchen and dining room. He straightened. "I won't pet him forever." He looked at the neatly folded clothes in his cousin's arms. "You have everything she'll need for one more night?" His folks had indicated Marie would be released tomorrow, but the twins would remain in the hospital nursery for at least another month, if not longer. Beth, however, intended to return home once her mother's hospitalization was over.

"Yes, but I should have brought a sack."

"I can get you one." Andrew had seen a pile of empty grocery sacks under the sink when he'd come the first time and searched through every cupboard for the cat food. He pulled one out and handed it to Trina.

"You sure know your way around," Trina remarked as she stuffed the clothes into the sack. "But you've pretty much given up on living here, haven't you?"

Andrew jumped as if pricked by a pitchfork. "What do you mean by that?"

Trina blinked in innocence, her dark eyes wide. "Your crush on Beth. You wanted to court her, didn't you?"

Andrew frowned. "Who have you been talking to?"

Shrugging, Trina placed the bag on the counter and then rested her hands on top of it. "Nobody. I could tell by watching you watch her. But you're over it."

It seemed his little cousin had grown up when he wasn't looking. He fought a grin. "Are you so sure?"

Her emphatic nod made her ribbons dance. "Oh, yes. Now you're watching Livvy Ortmann."

Andrew's ears went hot. "Trina. . ." A warning growl.

She giggled and snatched up the bag, swinging it from her hand. "It's okay. I won't tell anyone." She pranced by him, heading for the back door. "And just so you know, she watches you, too."

"Trina!"

The girl laughed and skipped out the door.

Beth's hand trembled as she reached inside the Isolette and ran her finger gingerly down the length of her baby brother's spindly arm. Little Teddy bent his elbow and drew up his knees. Beth murmured, "Yes, it's me, your big sister. Don't worry. I won't hurt you." Slowly she retraced the path upward, then transferred her attention to his leg. She followed the curve of his tiny knee and the inside of his ankle, ending with his impossibly small toes.

The baby blinked and shifted his head on the sheet. Beth laughed, a controlled, whispered laugh. "Are you ticklish?"

Next to her, Mom gave Dorothea the same treatment—a one-fingered, gentle massage. Beth flashed her a grin over the tops of the Isolettes. Although the babies were five days old, they had yet to be held and rocked by their parents or doting big sister. But touching them, Beth decided, was the next best thing. She hoped the powdered latex glove didn't feel rough on the delicate, wrinkled skin. The nurse had explained many preemies were sensory intolerant, so it was important to use the gentlest of touches.

"Are his eyes open?" Mom whispered.

Beth nodded. It was rare to see either of the twins awake. The nurse had assured them sleep was good medicine, and each rest allowed the babies to gain strength. Still, Beth relished the opportunity to peer into Teddy's eyes and pretend he peered back.

"Dorothea's are, too." Mom's voice purred, rising and falling as gently as if wafting on an early morning breeze. "As deep and blue as the sea, but I think they have a brown rim. I'd like it if they turned brown like her daddy's. Pretty girl. Pretty baby. Mama loves you."

Beth marveled at how the babies, even separated, still seemed to be in sync with one another. The few times she'd seen them awake, they were both awake. And when one became agitated, immediately the second showed signs of distress, although Teddy had proven easier to calm than his stormy sister.

Already hints of personality could be read in their reactions and precious facial expressions. Despite the fact her relationship with them was just a few days old, Beth loved them so much there were times her eyes welled with tears just thinking about them. It would be hard for her to leave tomorrow, but now that Mom was up and moving around, it was time for her to go.

Only two family members could enter the nursery at the same time. With her going in, either Mom or Henry had to stay out. As much as she loved visiting the babies, Beth knew it was better for their parents to be with them. So tomorrow morning, she would return to Sommerfeld.

"But I'll be back every weekend," she promised little Teddy, caressing his downy head, "and we'll have lots to catch up on."

A nurse stepped near, clipboard in hand, and recorded the numbers flashing on the monitors. Her recording done, she smiled at each baby in turn. "They seem to be enjoying their massages."

"Oh yes. Attention," Mom singsonged. "They like attention."

"Just remember not to overdo," the nurse cautioned. "Overstimulation can be detrimental."

Mom offered a smile and nod. She spoke to the nurse but kept the same sweet, singsong tone she used with the babies. "I've learned their signs of 'too much,' and I won't overdo. Thank you for the reminder."

Beth enjoyed another few minutes of singing softly to Teddy before she and Mom traded places. Beth continued the whisper-soft strokes and low-toned crooning, this time with Dori. Looking down at the tiny replica of her own baby pictures, Beth couldn't help but envision the future two years, ten years, sixteen years down the road and wonder how Dori's childhood and teen years would differ from her own.

Dori would be raised Old Order Mennonite. Her friendships and relationships would be limited by the restraints of the community. Would this little girl, whose personality already seemed to indicate feistiness, blossom or wither within those restraints? Beth couldn't know for sure what lay ahead for Dori, but she silently vowed to pray every day for Dori's contentment. She also vowed never to be a stumbling block in her little sister's life. Somehow, even though she knew she wouldn't adopt the Old Order lifestyle, she would be supportive of it.

Beth shifted her position slightly to relieve a mild cramp in her wrist, and as she did, she glimpsed her own reflection in the Isolette's Plexiglas top. No makeup, hair slicked away from her face in a tight tail, simple silver studs in her ears—as plain as she'd ever seen herself. Yet in her eyes lay a peace and maturity that took her by surprise.

In the past days in this hospital, filling the role of big sister, attentive daughter, and full-fledged member of the Braun and Koeppler families, Beth had found her niche. She closed her eyes for a moment, sending a silent thank-you heavenward to God for opening her heart to the place He had planned for her to call home.

Mom cleared her throat, capturing Beth's attention. Beth raised her gaze, and Mom gestured with her chin toward the large, plate-glass windows that faced the nursery. Turning her head, Beth located Henry standing outside the glass.

Certain he wanted to trade places with her, she offered him a quick smile and nod and slipped her hand from the Isolette. When she looked again toward the window, Henry was gone. In his place stood a tall man with red-gold hair and a neatly trimmed mustache. She clutched her hand to her chest, her jaw dropping.

Sean?

THIRTY

Beth rounded the corner from the nursery. Henry stood right outside, and he briefly touched her hand as she passed him. She paused long enough to give him a smile and nod, then crossed on quivery legs to stop several feet from Sean. Only then did she see that he held a huge cluster of flowers, daisies in every color of the rainbow tied with an abundance of lavender ribbon.

Her gaze bounced from the bouquet to his eyes.

The blue-green eyes crinkled into a self-conscious smile, and he lifted the bouquet. "These are for your mother when she comes out."

"Oh." To her surprise, she was more touched than disappointed. "That's sweet." Although she'd left the nursery, she still whispered. She took two steps forward, closing half the distance between them. "But how did you know where to find us?"

Sean's boyish shrug made Beth's lips twitch with a grin. "I called the studio. Andrew was there, and he told me which hospital. Then I just went online and did some hunting for directions. And here I am."

Here you are. Beth's heart pounded as if she'd just run a race. She pressed her hand to her chest once more, willing things to settle down.

"I—I brought some things for the babies, too. But your dad told me you weren't allowed to have stuff in the nursery, so they're in the waiting room."

"*Your dad*". . ."*dad*". . ."*dad*". . . The word echoed in Beth's head. She liked the way it sounded.

"Teddy bears."

It took a moment to process the meaning of Sean's simple sentence. "You brought teddy bears?" She tried to picture him in a store, picking up stuffed toys. It was easier to envision him behind a desk or a computer.

"Yes. I figured. . .babies. . .toys. . .something soft." He swallowed, the gulp audible in the quiet hallway. "I brought one for you, too."

Beth's eyes flew wide. "For me?"

"It only seemed fair. Everybody else got something, so. . ." His voice trailed off.

They stood in silence, staring at each other, with Sean clutching the bouquet of flowers against his thigh and Beth clasping her hands against her rib cage. The flowers seemed to tremble, capturing Beth's attention.

"Should we go find some water to put those in?"

"What?" Sean appeared startled; then he jerked the bouquet up as if he'd just noticed it. "Yes. That would be great."

"There's a gift shop on the main floor." Beth pointed toward the elevators. "Shall we?"

Sean followed her, and once inside the elevator, he said, "Beth, after we get the vase, can you take some time and. . .visit. . .with my father and me. . .in the lobby?"

"Your father is here, too?" Beth couldn't believe the two men would travel all the way from Kansas City to deliver flowers and teddy bears to a woman they'd never met and her newborn children.

The doors slid open, and they stepped into a bustling hallway.

"Yes. I'll explain later, okay? Right now, let's take care of these."

It didn't take long to choose a clear, fat vase that would hold the bouquet. After paying for it, Sean said, "Why don't you take it up to the waiting room? I'll stay down here and wait for you. My father"—he pointed—"is over there."

Beth spotted a man sitting with his elbows on his knees and his fingers interlocked, who appeared to be five or six years older than Henry. She could see a resemblance to Sean in the square jaw and unusual eyes, but the older man's hair had faded to a dusty peach. Beth wondered briefly if Sean's hair would do the same given time. Embarrassed by her thoughts, she gave a brusque nod and backed toward the elevator.

"I'll be right back."

To her relief, her parents hadn't returned, so she could slip in and out quickly. She left the flowers on the table in the corner and hurried back to the elevator. Her heart hammered, but she couldn't decide if it was excitement at seeing Sean, nervousness about what his father might say to her since she hadn't finished the project, or uncertainty about what lay ahead.

When she approached the two men, they both stood up.

Sean said, "Beth, I'd like you to meet my father, Evan McCauley. Dad, this is Beth Quinn."

Sean's father held his hand out to her. "Miss Quinn, it's nice to meet you." His grip was firm and warm, his expression serious but not intimidating.

"Likewise, but please call me Beth."

The older man gestured to a chair that he had apparently pulled near to create a triangle of seats in the corner. Beth sat, and the two men followed suit. Mr. McCauley assumed the same position she'd seen earlier—hunched forward, resting his weight on his elbows. It made him seem tired and somehow sad, and Beth felt her heart lurch in a sympathy she didn't quite understand.

"Miss Quinn, as you know, we had planned to meet with you today at your studio and complete our arrangements to utilize your skills for future projects."

Beth's chin jerked into a brief nod. "Yes, sir, I know." She didn't apologize. She had done that on the telephone with him, and she didn't see the need. Another apology would sound like an excuse, and she wouldn't excuse her choice. She knew—as difficult as it had been—her choice had been the right one.

The man fitted his fingers together and stared at his thumbs as he continued. "Before driving to Wichita, we stopped by Sommerfeld. Your employee—tall man, dark hair. . ."

"Andrew," Sean and Beth supplied at the same time. They exchanged a quick glance.

"Andrew," Mr. McCauley repeated, "let us look at the incomplete project. It was. . ."

Beth held her breath.

"Amazingly done."

Her breath whooshed out.

Mr. McCauley sat upright. "Even unfinished, the elements of depth were in place. When the piece is complete, it will be magnificent."

"Thank you, sir." Beth glanced quickly at Sean before facing his father again. "Even though you won't be using it, I plan to finish it. It will go into storage for a while, and then I'd like to use it as the front window for my gallery when I'm finally able to open it."

"No."

The blunt response took Beth by surprise. "Sir?"

He shook his head, his brow low. "No, it won't be available for that purpose. Because we will be purchasing it from you."

Beth hadn't thought her heart could race any faster, but it proved her wrong. It was now a steady hum. "B–but I didn't meet the contingency. So the contract with you is void. You aren't obligated to purchase it."

"Obligated, no. But interested? Yes." His heavy brows hooded his eyes, but Beth could see a slight twinkle in their depths. "And it won't be the last window we purchase from you."

Beth looked back and forth between the men, her mouth open in a silent plea for an explanation. Both men held grins that told of a secret yet to be divulged. She turned toward Sean—the one with whom she felt comfortable—and said, "What are you trying to say?"

Although Sean offered no verbal reply, she was certain she read an answer in his steady gaze. The hum in her chest changed to a booming Sousa march.

"Miss Quinn—Beth." Mr. McCauley's deep voice pulled her attention from the son. "Sean and I had a lengthy conversation about. . . dedication. . .and commitment. It has always been my policy to meet—every—deadline." He slapped the backs of his fingers into his palm to emphasize each word. "I saw it as good business sense, and I haven't changed my stance on that one iota. But. . ."

His eyes shifted to Sean, and his expression softened. In his warm look, Beth read a silent thank-you that raised her curiosity.

"I've also come to realize there is something more important than honoring business commitments, and that is honoring one's commitment to faith and family." He leaned forward, bringing his face closer to hers. "We've seen the evidence of your skill. We know you have the ability to do the job. And your choosing to put the needs of your family above all else tells me you have the dedication we're seeking when adding to the McCauley team.

"So, Beth, if you are still interested in signing a long-term contract and designing windows for churches, starting with the ones in Carlton and Denver, then we are very interested and eager to finalize those plans."

Beth's hand shot out. "I'm interested, sir. And thank you."

He sandwiched her hand between his. "Thank *you*." He rose, his hands slipping away. "I have the paperwork drawn up. We took a room at the hotel across from the hospital. Sean can bring you over later and we'll make it official, hmm? But for now. . ." He looked at his son, and Beth was certain she saw him wink. "I believe I'll go over and lie down for a bit. The long drive has worn me out. Sean, I assume you'll want to stay here and visit with Beth?"

"Yes." But Sean looked at Beth when he answered.

"In about an hour then." The man strode away.

Beth watched until Mr. McCauley's broad back disappeared through the wide double doors leading outside, then she turned to face Sean. "Do you want to—"

"Should we—" he said at the same time.

They both laughed, and he held out his hand, giving her the floor.

"Do you want to go outside? There's a small bench where we could sit and talk."

"Clouds were gathering in the west as we drove over. We could get wet."

"I'm willing to take the chance," Beth said. "I could really use the fresh air."

Sean nodded his agreement. He followed as she led him toward the outside doors. "I would imagine you're tired of being cooped up here."

Beth shrugged. "I'm used to being cooped up in the studio, but you're right that it's different here." She pulled in a deep breath of the crisp, scented air as she seated herself on the bench. Sean gave his pant legs a little tug before sitting on the other end. When he was settled just a few inches from her, Beth continued. "Still, I wouldn't have traded my time here for anything. It has helped me develop a much deeper appreciation for my family and helped me put things into perspective. I guess you could say this has been a growing time."

"For my dad and me, too," Sean said, looking to the side. She sensed there was more he was thinking, but he didn't divulge it.

"It has also," she continued, watching his gaze come back around to meet hers, "convinced me without a doubt that my studio—and I—belong in Sommerfeld." She searched his face for signs of disappointment. Since he'd previously indicated the wisdom of relocating, she hoped he and his father hadn't made that a part of her contract. She wouldn't be able to sign if that stipulation was added.

Sean nodded, seemingly unconcerned. "I assumed that when I saw the addition."

Beth slapped her hands to her face. With her focus on Mom and the babies, she'd completely forgotten about the addition. "You saw it? The men finished it?"

"All but the shingles, from the looks of things." Sean smiled, seeming to find humor in her amazement. "Of course, the wall separating the two halves is still in place, so you could hardly consider it a finished job, but I could see the potential. You'll have quite the work area, plus room for an office, if need be."

Beth nodded in slow motion, picturing it. Although she hadn't originally considered including an office space, the idea held merit. Especially if there were several workers on a daily basis, she might need a quiet spot to get away and think.

"If I were you," Sean went on, his forehead creased thoughtfully, "I would put the office in the southeast corner. That way when you get your showroom up, the office will be close enough for you to be available to customers."

Beth bit down on her lip, but she couldn't stop a smile from growing. "Are you planning my studio for me now?"

A boyish grin made her heart skip a beat. "Just a suggestion. . . from someone who plans buildings for a living."

She assumed a high-chinned, formal posture, her lips still twitching. "I'll take that under advisement, Mr. McCauley." Dropping the playful pose, she said, "So it won't be a problem, having my studio so far away from the main office?"

Sean crossed one leg over the other and grasped his knee with both hands, staring at the horizon. "It won't be a problem at all. My reason for wanting you to consider moving was. . .selfish." He flicked a glance in her direction.

She offered a warm smile, which she hoped would encourage him to continue.

He faced her fully. "I admit from the first time we met I've had a difficult time separating our business relationship from a personal one. I wanted you closer. So I could get to know you. . .better."

Beth swallowed. She stretched out her hand and touched his elbow. "I've had the same thoughts, Sean. But I don't know how it could work. Long-distance relationships are pretty hard to maintain. I. . .I can't leave Sommerfeld. It's where God has planted me, and I won't step outside of His will. But your office is in Kansas City." She stopped, the ramifications of the statement bringing a crush of sorrow to her chest.

So slowly she almost thought she imagined movement, his hand slid across the bench until his fingers found her hand. He didn't squeeze, just held her fingers loosely within his. "You know, Beth, my job—drawing blueprints and planning—can be done wherever I choose."

He paused, his gaze seeming to seek her face for silent messages. "With the Internet and fax machines, I can communicate with anyone, anywhere in the world. I'm not limited to working in Kansas City."

Beth's booming heart nearly stole her breath. She understood what he was saying. But things were moving so rapidly she couldn't form a reply.

His lips tipped into a warm smile, and his hand gave hers a squeeze. "But we can talk about that another time. There will be time, since we'll need to be in communication concerning our business relationship. The other? We'll wait for God's leading."

"Can we pray about it now?" Beth blurted out the question, then felt her cheeks fill with heat at her impatience.

Sean didn't laugh. He nodded and bowed his head, and Beth followed suit. She listened as he thanked God for the opportunity to work together to create houses of worship that would meet the needs of congregations both spiritually and aesthetically. Her breath tripped raggedly as he requested guidance concerning their future together. "Lord, whatever You have planned, we are open to Your will. Lead us on Your pathway, please, and may we always bring glory to You as we journey, whether together or individually. Amen."

A distant rumble sounded, alerting them that Sean's prediction of rain could certainly prove true. But they remained on the bench, fingers linked, enjoying the moment of communion they had shared. Beth's chest filled with gratitude for God's hand bringing her to the point of belonging—with Him, with her family, with the community that she now considered her own, and with Sean. Giving Sean's hand a gentle squeeze, she offered a smile she was certain he understood.

A plop of something wet smacked the top of her head. Two more drops landed on her shoulder and lap.

"Here it comes!" Sean said with a laugh.

And come it did! Raindrops pelted them, warm and redolent and renewing. They jumped to their feet, their hands still clasped, and dashed toward the safety of the building. Beneath the brief overhang, they came to a laughing stop. Beth's back pressed securely to Sean's side with her head on his shoulder, and his arms loosely circled her waist.

Together they watched the rain gently bless the earth with moisture. With each patter, Beth envisioned a new blessing from God. Her lips formed the words without effort. "Thank You, Father, for everything."

And Sean's tender voice echoed, "Amen."

ABOUT THE AUTHOR

Kim Vogel Sawyer is wife to Don, mother to three girls, grandmother to four boys, and a former elementary school teacher. A lifelong writer, Kim travels to women's groups to share her testimony and her love for writing, tying together the skill of writing a good story with the good plan God has for each life. She is active in her church, where she serves as an adult Sunday school teacher, directs the drama team, and participates in the music ministry in both vocal and bell choirs.